WINGS
OF
FIRE

BOOK ONE
THE DRAGONET PROPHECY

BOOK TWO
THE LOST HEIR

BOOK THREE
THE HIDDEN KINGDOM

BOOK FOUR
THE DARK SECRET

BOOK FIVE
THE BRIGHTEST NIGHT

WINGS OF FIRE

THE HIDDEN KINGDOM

by
TUI T. SUTHERLAND

SCHOLASTIC INC.

This book was originally published in hardcover by Scholastic Press in 2013.

ISBN 978-93-5275-087-0

Text copyright © 2013 by Tui T. Sutherland
Map and border design © 2013 by Mike Schley
Dragon illustrations © 2013 by Joy Ang

Book design by Phil Falco
This edition first printing, March 2014
This edition September 2019
Reprinted by Scholastic India Pvt. ltd., 2020, Jan. 2021
Printed in India at Shivam Offset Press, New Delhi

For Elliot, born in a
wonderful Year of the Dragon,
like these books

Queen Glacier's
Palace

Ice Kingdom

Sky Kingdom

Under the Mountain

Burn's
Stronghold

Kingdom of
Sand

Scorpion Den

Jade Mountain

Queen Scarlet's Palace

Diamond Spray River

Kingdom of the Sea

Diamond Spray Delta

Mud Kingdom

Scavenger Den

Scavenger Den

Rainforest Kingdom

Ice Kingdom

Kingdom

A NIGHTWING GUIDE TO TH
DRAGONS

Sand

Scorpion Den

Jade Mountain

SANDWINGS

Description: pale gold or white scales the color of desert sand; poisonous barbed tail; forked black tongues

Abilities: can survive a long time without water, poison enemies with the tips of their tails like scorpions, bury themselves for camouflage in the desert sand, breathe fire

Queen: Since the death of Queen Oasis, the tribe is split between three rivals for the throne: sisters Burn, Blister, and Blaze.

Alliances: Burn fights alongside SkyWings and MudWings; Blister is allied with the SeaWings; and Blaze has the support of most SandWings as well as an alliance with the IceWings.

MUDWINGS

Description: thick, armored brown scales, sometimes with amber and gold underscales; large, flat heads with nostrils on top of the snout

Abilities: can breathe fire (if warm enough), hold their breath for up to an hour, blend into large mud puddles; usually very strong

Queen: Queen Moorhen

Alliances: currently allied with Burn and the SkyWings in the great war

SKYWINGS

Description: red-gold or orange scales; enormous wings

Abilities: powerful fighters and fliers, can breathe fire

Queen: Queen Scarlet

Alliances: currently allied with Burn and the MudWings in the great war

SEAWINGS

Description: blue or green or aquamarine scales; webs between their claws; gills on their necks; glow-in-the-dark stripes on their tails/snouts/underbellies

Abilities: can breathe underwater, see in the dark, create huge waves with one splash of their powerful tails; excellent swimmers

Queen: Queen Coral

Alliances: currently allied with Blister in the great war

ICEWINGS

Description: silvery scales like the moon or pale blue like ice; ridged claws to grip the ice; forked blue tongues; tails narrow to a whip-thin end

Abilities: can withstand subzero temperatures and bright light, exhale a deadly freezing breath

Queen: Queen Glacier
Alliances: currently allied with Blaze and most of the SandWings in the great war

— RAINWINGS —

Description: scales constantly shift colors, usually bright like birds of paradise; prehensile tails

Abilities: can camouflage their scales to blend into their surroundings, use their prehensile tails for climbing; no known natural weapons

Queen: Queen Dazzling

Alliances: not involved in the great war

— NIGHTWINGS —

Description: purplish-black scales and scattered silver scales on the underside of their wings, like a night sky full of stars; forked black tongues

Abilities: can breathe fire, disappear into dark shadows, read minds, foretell the future

Queen: a closely guarded secret

Alliances: too mysterious and powerful to be part of the war

THE DRAGONET PROPHECY

When the war has lasted twenty years . . .
the dragonets will come.
When the land is soaked in blood and tears . . .
the dragonets will come.

Find the SeaWing egg of deepest blue.
Wings of night shall come to you.
The largest egg in mountain high
will give to you the wings of sky.
For wings of earth, search through the mud
for an egg the color of dragon blood.
And hidden alone from the rival queens,
the SandWing egg awaits unseen.

Of three queens who blister and blaze and burn,
two shall die and one shall learn
if she bows to a fate that is stronger and higher,
she'll have the power of wings of fire.

Five eggs to hatch on brightest night,
five dragons born to end the fight.
Darkness will rise to bring the light.
The dragonets are coming. . . .

PROLOGUE

The five dragonets were fighting. Again.

Bright scales in green and red and gold caught the rising sun as the young dragons darted between the rocks, claws and teeth flashing. Five forked tongues hissed with fury. Beyond them, below the cliff, the sea crashed against the sand with a muffled rushing sound, as if it didn't want to compete with the shouts of the dragons.

It was embarrassing, was what it was. Nautilus glanced up uneasily at the massive black dragon beside him. The dragonets were so busy yelling at one another that they hadn't even noticed him yet. Nautilus wished he could read Morrowseer's mind the way Morrowseer was undoubtedly reading his.

He also wished there were more Talons of Peace around, but when word spread that the NightWing was coming, most of them suddenly found urgent missions elsewhere. The peace movement's hideout in the seaside cliffs was virtually deserted this morning. Occasionally a dragon snout would emerge from one of the caves, spot Morrowseer, and instantly vanish again.

The five dragonets were the only ones on top of the cliffs; although there were several other young dragons living with the Talons of Peace, they'd all been whisked out of sight.

But apparently no one had seen fit to warn the objects of Morrowseer's scrutiny that he was coming, or that they were going to be inspected.

"Well," Morrowseer said. "They are . . . energetic."

"They were just a backup plan," Nautilus said defensively. "Nobody thought we'd need them. Especially not all of them; we thought maybe one, or two, if something went wrong with the originals. We haven't spent a lot of time training them."

"I can see that." Morrowseer's dark eyes narrowed as Viper, the SandWing, fell into a crevice and the MudWing promptly tripped and landed on top of her. With a hiss, Viper whipped around and bit Ochre's tail, setting off a yowling whine.

"Excuse me," Nautilus said. He could see where this was going. He stepped forward, cuffed Viper's ears, and snatched Squid, the little green SeaWing, out of the way before the others could set his tail on fire.

"Stop this!" he hissed. "You are being watched!"

Flame, the red SkyWing dragonet, snapped his mouth shut and whipped his head around, scanning the twisted rocks of the sea cliff. Morrowseer stepped into the light of the sunrise and looked down his snout majestically.

"I knew it!" crowed the little NightWing dragonet. Fatespeaker leaped off a stone pillar, flapping her wings proudly. "I knew a NightWing was coming to see us! Didn't I tell you guys this would happen?"

"Did you?" Ochre scratched his large brown head.

"No," said Viper.

"Don't think so," piped up Squid from behind Nautilus's back.

"Even if you did, you also predicted an earthquake, a new Talon of Peace, and that we'd have something besides seagulls for breakfast this week," said Flame. "And since none of those have happened, you can see why we might have stopped listening."

"Well, I knew," Fatespeaker said blithely. "I *saw* it with my *powers*! *And* I foresee that he brought us something *great* for breakfast. Didn't you?" She beamed up at Morrowseer.

He blinked slowly. "Hmmm. Nautilus, a word, please."

"Can I come, too?" the black dragonet asked, bouncing closer to Morrowseer. "I've never met another NightWing before. Although, of course, I feel a very strong psychic connection with our whole tribe."

"Stay. Here." Morrowseer pressed one claw into her chest and moved her back to the other dragonets. She sat down and curled her tail around her talons with a huffing snort.

Morrowseer stepped down the rocks, out of earshot. When he turned, he found Nautilus right behind him. But clinging to his tail was the SeaWing drag-onet. Morrowseer gazed at Squid disapprovingly.

"I can't leave him alone with them," Nautilus said apologetically. "Whenever I'm not watching, one of them bites him."

"Or they *all* do," sniffed the small green dragon.

Morrowseer flicked his tongue out and in, consid-ering. "It is clear to me," said the enormous NightWing after a moment, "that leaving the dragonets of the prophecy in the care of the Talons of Peace was a mis-take. Both the real ones and the false ones."

"Who?" asked the dragonet.

"Hush," said Nautilus, covering the dragonet's snout with one talon. He saw the look on Morrowseer's face and added hastily, "You remember, Squid. We taught you about the prophecy. You know the war that all the dragon tribes are fighting?"

"The one you want to stop," Squid said. "Because we're the good guys! We want peace!"

"Right," said Nautilus. "Basically right. So the prophecy says that five dragonets were hatched about six years ago — a SeaWing, a SkyWing, a MudWing, a SandWing, and a NightWing — who are going to end the war. They get to choose which sister should be the new SandWing queen: Burn, Blister, or Blaze."

"Oh," said Squid. "Hey, I hatched about six years ago."

"Really," said Morrowseer. "You're barely the size of a three-year-old dragonet."

"I have a big personality," Squid informed him, as if he had been told this enough times that he was certain everyone knew it.

"And your friends are about six years old, too," Nautilus said quickly.

"They're not my friends," Squid grumbled. "They're all bullies, except for Fatespeaker, who is plain crazy."

Morrowseer glanced back at Fatespeaker, the NightWing dragonet. She was sitting on top of a twisted stone column, leaning so far toward them that she looked in imminent danger of overbalancing and toppling off.

"Well, Squid," Nautilus said. "What if you were one of the dragonets in the prophecy? What would you think about that?"

The SeaWing gave Morrowseer a canny look. "Would I get treasure?"

"You'd get fame and power," said Morrowseer. "If you did what you were told, that is."

"How about treasure?" Squid insisted.

Morrowseer gave Nautilus an incredulous look. "Is this dragonet bargaining with me?"

"I like treasure," Squid pointed out. "The Talons of Peace are so lame because none of them have any treasure."

"We gave up worldly things to fight for a higher cause," Nautilus said. "Peace is more important than jewels or gold."

"Eh," said Squid. "I'd rather have gold."

"Would you be willing to choose whichever SandWing queen we told you to?" Morrowseer asked. "If so, we could perhaps talk about gold."

"All right," Squid said with a gleam in his eye. "But I don't want Flame to be part of it. He has to stay here."

"Why? What's wrong with your SkyWing?" Morrowseer asked Nautilus.

"Nothing," Nautilus said. "They're just having a fight today."

"And every day!" Squid said. "Because he's mean!"

"The SkyWing is nonnegotiable," said Morrowseer.

"*You're* nonagoshabibble," Squid said.

"Squid, be polite," said Nautilus tiredly.

"I foresee that I am going to regret this," said Morrowseer, frowning down at the SeaWings. "But I will be taking over the training of the prophecy dragonets. They have been mishandled for too long. Obviously they need clearer guidance."

"What does that mean?" Nautilus asked. A sense of dread was starting to creep across his scales. He glanced at Squid. Perhaps they should have chosen a different SeaWing to be the fake dragonet of the prophecy. *If Morrowseer hurts Squid . . . if anything happens to him . . . his mother is going to kill me*, Nautilus thought.

"It means they're coming with me," Morrowseer said with a flick of his tail.

"Where?" Squid demanded.

"You'll find out when we get there," said Morrowseer. "And if you know what's good for you, you'll stop asking nosy questions and do what you're told."

"*I* can do that," Squid said, "but good luck with Flame and Viper." He thought for a moment. "And Fatespeaker, for that matter."

"Wait, no," said Nautilus. He tried to fill his mind with noise so the NightWing couldn't read his thoughts. "You can't *take* them. Except for Fatespeaker, who came from you, all their parents are Talons — that's how we got their eggs in the first place. They won't want them to leave."

"Except Ochre," Squid offered. "His mum won't care. It's a MudWing thing."

"Shut up," said Morrowseer. He studied Nautilus with narrow black eyes.

Don't think it, don't think it, don't think it, Nautilus repeated to himself.

"Three moons," Morrowseer said with disgust. "This dragonet is your son."

Nautilus stared down at his claws. It had seemed like a good idea when the Talons first decided to have backup dragonets. Squid hatched *around* the right time, if not exactly *on* the brightest night. And it meant that everyone in the movement treated the dragonet like the precious creature Nautilus knew he was.

"Of course I am," said Squid. "Isn't that a funny coincidence? Wow. I'm the son of the leader of the Talons of Peace *and* a dragonet of destiny." He puffed out his chest. "I'm even more important than I thought I was." He strutted off toward the other dragonets, having forgotten, as he often did, that none of them liked hearing about how important he was and that he would almost certainly end up with a singed snout before long.

Nautilus watched him go, wondering how everything had gone so wrong. Why had the Talons agreed to work with Morrowseer? Why had they decided to get involved with the prophecy in the first place? And how had they lost the real dragonets? That was the question that drove him crazy.

Kestrel, Dune, and Webs should have been able to keep a handle on five dragonets, especially when they were conveniently trapped in a secret cave. Instead the five had escaped, then possibly killed Queen Scarlet of the SkyWings, thrown the Sky Kingdom into upheaval, turned Queen Coral against her allies, wrecked the SeaWing palace, and disappeared once more into the wilds of Pyrrhia.

Worse yet, there was no one to punish. Kestrel and Dune were dead, while Webs had wriggled away from the Talons and vanished. And who knew where the dragonets were or when they'd turn up again with their spectacular talent for trouble and chaos.

"*Quite* a coincidence," Morrowseer echoed Squid's remark, sounding rather unimpressed.

"Well," said Nautilus. "I thought, why not? Of course, none of these five actually hatched on the brightest night, or else they'd be the real dragonets of the prophecy, wouldn't they? But they're about the right age, and nobody has to know the rest."

"Except anyone who was at their hatching," Morrowseer mused. "It would be tidier if we could kill any witnesses."

Nautilus blanched. *Do their parents count as "witnesses"?* he wondered before he could squelch the thought.

"We'll cross that bridge when we come to it," Morrowseer said briskly. "Since we can't be sure yet which of these we'll use and which we'll discard." He frowned at Fatespeaker, who was eagerly interrogating Squid.

Nautilus felt properly faint now. "Discard?" he echoed.

Morrowseer snorted. "Very well. I'll try to bring yours back in one piece." He wrinkled his snout, looking as close to amused as Nautilus had ever seen him. "But isn't *peace* the most important thing, SeaWing? Don't you tell your Talons all the time that any sacrifice must be made to end this war?"

"Yes, but —"

"The alternate dragonets were your idea in the first place. A good idea, as it turns out, since the real ones have proven to be so unsatisfactory." Morrowseer hissed softly. "So we get rid of the most dangerous ones. I train their replacements myself."

He smiled in a way that made Nautilus feel queasy right down to his claws.

"And then we make sure the prophecy is fulfilled the way it was supposed to be."

PART ONE
RAINFOREST MONSTERS

CHAPTER 1

It had been raining for five days.

Glory officially hated it.

She also was not enjoying the comments from the other dragonets about how, "as a RainWing," she should love this weather.

She most certainly did *not* love this weather. In the caves under the mountain, the dragonets had never, ever been rained on. This downpour felt unnatural and unstoppable and horribly, unpleasantly *wet*.

I don't care if a "real" RainWing is supposed to like this, she thought as droplets rolled off her snout, seeped through her scales, and soaked her wings until they dragged heavily behind her. *If they do, there's something wrong with them. No sensible dragon should enjoy weather that makes it so hard to fly.*

Three moons, please let them be sensible dragons. Let them be nothing like the stories.

Everyone said RainWings were useless and lazy. But the tribe lived off by themselves in the rainforest where no one ever saw them, so everyone might be wrong. Glory was really hoping they were wrong.

She shook her whole body and glared at the fog-shrouded sky. What she wanted was more sun. She'd missed the sun her whole life and hadn't known it until it hit her scales the day they left the caves. More long sunny days would be fine by her.

Instead there was this. Rain. Mud. More rain. More mud.

Plus one moaning, groaning, dripping slowpoke of a wounded SeaWing.

"Can we stop?" Webs gasped. "I need to rest." He floundered through the mud to a slightly drier spot under a tree.

Glory narrowed her eyes at him as the blue-green dragon flopped to the ground. The other dragonets stopped, too, exchanging glances. They were walking today instead of flying because Webs said it was easier on his injury. And yet he still asked to stop nearly every ten steps. Glory was starting to suspect he didn't really *want* them to get to the rainforest.

But why? she wondered. *Is he hiding something? Does it have to do with my parents?*

As the guardian who had stolen her from the RainWing tribe in the first place, Webs should have been a helpful fount of knowledge about where she came from. Instead, he got all mumbly and forgetful whenever they asked about the rainforest dragons.

Clay paced over to Webs and peered down at his wound. They'd wrapped it with seaweed soaked in ocean water for as long as they could, but now they were too far inland to get any more. The poisoned scratch near Webs's tail had become an ugly gash surrounded by blackened scales, and the black seemed to spread a bit more each day. None of them had any idea what to do to combat SandWing poison.

Not to mention we have no idea why Blister wanted Webs dead so badly. I mean, I think he's awful, but she doesn't even know him. Glory glanced at Starflight, the black NightWing who was the smartest dragonet she knew — and probably still would be even if she knew more than four dragons. She wondered if he had any theories about Blister and Webs.

Clay swept his tail through the mud, looking worried. "I hope the RainWings can help him," he said. "This isn't exactly like their venom. But maybe they'll have more ideas than we do."

Glory shook out her wings and looked away. She didn't care. The other dragonets felt some kind of misguided loyalty to their old guardian, as if it was their responsibility to save him.

She was the only one who seemed to remember how he'd been willing to stand by and let someone kill her.

Stealing her egg had been his idea, too. The prophecy called for a SkyWing, but when the Talons lost their SkyWing egg before it hatched, Webs had decided to replace it with a RainWing. It was his fault Glory had been forced to grow up under the mountain, far from her home and family, learning about a prophecy that didn't even have a place for her in it.

It was easy for the others. There was no question about their destiny. But Glory . . . if she was meant to help save the world, then why hadn't the prophecy called for a RainWing? And if she wasn't necessary for this big grand destiny, then what was the point of her life at all?

Maybe it was all one big mistake, but when she thought like that, she ended up having violent dreams about ripping Webs apart. So, better not to think about it. Destiny would have to sort itself out.

Right now she was going home.

The branch above Glory suddenly dipped and dumped a lake's worth of water onto her head. She leaped back with a hiss and glared up into the tree.

"Shhh," Tsunami said from above. She dropped down to the ground and peered around at the gloomy swamp. "There's a pair of MudWings headed this way, but they'll never see us in this weather."

Rolls of thick gray fog hung over the mud, wreathing the stunted trees like smoke around a dragon's horns. It was hard to tell what time of day it was. The sky was gray in every direction and the rain drizzled down unrelentingly. Glory agreed with Tsunami; a dragon could barely see her own wing tips in this, let alone another dragon.

"We should still hide," Starflight said anxiously. "We're only a day's flight from Queen Moorhen's palace right now. If we get caught —"

"More prison," Clay said with a sigh.

Every queen they'd met so far seemed determined to keep the dragonets trapped under her claws. They'd escaped Queen Scarlet's prison in the Sky Kingdom only because of Glory's venom — a secret weapon even she hadn't known about until she'd needed it.

She touched her forked tongue to her fangs and glanced at the sky. They still had no idea if Queen Scarlet had survived Glory's attack. Given their luck, Glory was pretty sure Scarlet was alive and planning some horrible revenge.

After that escape they'd gone looking for safety with Tsunami's mother, Queen Coral of the SeaWings. Of course Coral had decided to lock them up as well. Glory hadn't been surprised. Not even family could be trusted when it came to the prophecy. Everyone had their own plans for how this war should end.

So if Queen Moorhen of the MudWings found them in her territory, she *probably* wasn't going to give them tea and send them on their way.

The MudWing queen held court beside a large lake on the southern edge of the Mud Kingdom. Glory remembered the map of Pyrrhia and a shiver of realization ran down her spine. If Starflight was right and they were only a day's flight from there, then they must be only a day's flight from the rainforest as well. From the rainforest . . . and Glory's tribe.

And then I'll belong somewhere. The RainWings won't care that I'm not in some prophecy.

"Glory," Tsunami scolded. "Bright yellow scales are the one thing they *might* see. Go back to camouflage."

Glory glanced down and saw the starbursts of gold that had appeared all across her scales. Those meant happiness or excitement, as far as she knew, since she'd seen them pretty rarely in her life. It drove her crazy when her scales changed color without her telling them to. They did that way too often. She had to squash every big emotion before it splashed all over her.

She concentrated on the steady *drip-drip* of the swamp around them, staring down at the thick brown mud oozing through her claws. She imagined the fog winding around her wings, slipping into the cracks in her scales, and spreading like gray clouds rolling across the sky.

"Aaaand she's gone," Tsunami said.

"She's still there," Sunny piped up. She edged closer to Glory and bumped into one of her wings. "See? Right there." She stretched out a talon, but Glory moved out of reach. Sunny felt around in the air for a moment and then gave up.

The little SandWing had been unusually quiet for the last few days. Glory guessed Sunny hated the rain, too — the desert dragons were designed for searing heat, blazing sun, and endless clear-sky days. Even an odd-looking SandWing like Sunny still had the instincts of her tribe.

Really, Clay was the only one happy about the weather. Only a MudWing could appreciate the squishing and squashing under their claws as they traveled through the swamp.

Starflight swiveled his head suddenly. "I think I smell someone coming," he whispered. He shuddered from horns to claws.

"Don't panic," Tsunami whispered back. "Clay, you hide me and Sunny. Starflight, find a shadow and do your invisible petrified-NightWing thing. Glory, you can shield Webs."

"No, thanks," Glory said immediately. She wasn't going anywhere near Webs, certainly not to save his life. "I'll take Sunny." She didn't like touching other dragons, but Sunny was better than Webs.

"But —" Tsunami started, stamping her foot.

Glory ignored her. She lifted one wing and tugged the little gold dragon in close to her side. When she lowered her wing again, Sunny was hidden by Glory's gray-brown camouflage.

"Yikes," Clay said. "That was so weird. Like Sunny just got eaten by the fog." His stomach grumbled woefully at the word *eaten*, and the MudWing shuffled his big feet in embarrassment.

Starflight peered at the spot where Sunny had just been, twisting his claws in the mud.

"She's fine," Glory said. "Go follow orders like a good dragonet, or Tsunami might fling you to the eels."

Tsunami frowned in her direction, but Starflight slunk away and found a dark tree hollow where his black scales melted into the shadows.

Now Glory could hear it, too: the *tramp-squelch-tramp-squelch* of enormous claws marching through the swamp toward them. The heat from Sunny's scales was uncomfortably warm against her side.

Webs hadn't moved while they talked. He lay curled against the tree roots, snout resting on his tail, looking miserable.

Clay shepherded Tsunami up next to Webs and spread his mud-colored wings to hide them both. It wasn't a perfect solution — a blue tail stuck out on one side, the edge of blue-green wings on the other. But in this fog, they looked mostly like a blobby mound of mud, which should be good enough.

Tramp. Squelch. Tramp. Squelch.

"I don't like this patrol," a deep voice grumbled. Glory nearly jumped. It sounded like it was coming from two trees away. "Too close to that creepy rainforest, if you ask me."

"It's not really haunted," said a second voice. "You know the only things that live there are birds and lazy RainWings."

Years of learning self-control kept Glory from flinching. She'd heard "lazy RainWings" thrown around often enough by the guardians, under the mountain. But it felt like an extra stab in the eye to hear it from a total stranger.

"If that were true," said the first voice, "then Her Majesty would let us hunt in there. But she knows it's not safe. And you've heard the noises at night. Are you telling me it's the RainWings screaming like that?"

Screaming? Under Glory's wing, Sunny turned her head a little, as if she were trying to hear better.

"Not to mention the dead bodies," the first voice muttered.

"That's not some kind of rainforest monster," said the second guard, but there was a tilt in her tone that sounded unsure. "That's the war. Some kind of guerilla attacks to scare us."

"All the way down here? Why would the SeaWings or the IceWings come all this way to kill one or two MudWings here and there? There are bigger battles going on every-where else."

"Let's go a bit faster," said the second voice uneasily. "They should really let us patrol in threes or fours instead of in pairs."

"Tell me about it." *Tramp-squelch-tramp-squelch.* "So what do you think about the SkyWing situation? Are you for Ruby, or do you think . . ."

Glory strained her ears, but their voices faded into the mist as the two MudWing soldiers sploshed away. She badly wanted to know what "the SkyWing situation" was. Maybe her friends wouldn't notice if she slipped away for a moment.

"Be right back," she whispered to Sunny, lifting her wing and stepping away.

Sunny caught her tail, wide-eyed. "Don't go!" she whispered. "It's not safe! You heard what they said."

"About rainforest monsters?" Glory rolled her eyes. "Can't say I'm terribly worried about that. I won't go far." She shook Sunny off and slipped after the soldiers, carefully step-ping only on the dry patches so her claws wouldn't splash in the mud.

It was weirdly quiet in the swamp, especially with the fog muffling most sounds. She tried to follow the distant rumble of voices and what she thought might be the sound of march-ing MudWing talons. But after a few moments, even those became impossible to hear.

She stopped, listening. The trees dripped. Rain drizzled

moodily through the branches. Small gurgles burbled out of the mud here and there, as if the swamp were hiccupping.

And then a scream tore through the air.

Glory's ruff flared in fear and pale green stripes zigzagged through her scales. She fought back her terror, focusing her colors back to gray and brown.

"Glory!" Sunny yelled, behind her somewhere.

Shut up, Glory thought furiously. *Don't draw attention. Don't let anything know we're here.*

The other dragonets must have had the same thought and stopped her, because Sunny didn't call out again.

Unless it was one of them who screamed. But it couldn't have been. The scream had come from somewhere up ahead.

Glory checked her scales again to make sure she was well hidden and then sped up, hurrying through the trees toward the scream.

The fog was so dense, she nearly missed the two dark lumps that looked like fallen logs. But her claws came down on something that was decidedly a dragon tail, and she leaped back.

Two brown dragons were sprawled in the mud, surrounded by pools of blood that were already being washed away by the rain. Their throats had been ripped out so viciously that their heads were nearly severed from their bodies.

Glory stared into the rolling gray fog, but nothing moved out there except the rain.

The MudWing soldiers were dead, and there was no sign of what had killed them.

CHAPTER 2

"Remind me why we're walking *toward* the place with the monster and the screaming and the something that kills dragons?" Clay asked.

"We could go somewhere else," Starflight said. "Maybe to the IceWings?"

"IceWings! Yes!" Clay said. "That sounds like a great plan. Let's do that. No mysterious dragon-killing things in the Ice Kingdom. Right? What are those animals they have up there? Penguins? I bet I could beat a penguin or two in battle. Couldn't I? How big are they? Maybe just one penguin."

"So we can freeze to death instead," Glory said. A rumor and a couple of dead soldiers were not going to scare her away from her home when she was finally this close. "Fantastic plan, Starflight. Not to mention the Ice Kingdom is half a continent away while the rainforest is right here."

"Besides, Webs will never make it all the way to the Ice Kingdom," Sunny chimed in. She glanced nervously up at the trees, which seemed to be getting taller and taller as they walked.

It was also warmer the farther they went, and up in the vines overhead Glory could see flashes of color. The bright summer yellows and purples and blues might have been birds or flowers, but they were definitely not typical of the brown, brown, brown Mud Kingdom. Glory wasn't sure, but she guessed the dragonets were in the rainforest for real now.

The gnarled claw shapes of the marsh trees were half a day behind them and so were the MudWing bodies. Tsunami had wanted to stop and search the area for clues, but she'd been outvoted by the other dragonets when Starflight pointed out that now they'd *really* be in trouble if they were caught right next to a double murder . . . not to mention whatever had killed the soldiers couldn't have gone far. That was enough to get everyone, even Webs, to fly through the night, and they'd circled down to walk again only once the sun was up and they were looking for food.

"See?" Glory said to Clay and Starflight. "Even Sunny is acting braver than you scaredy-scavengers."

"*Even* Sunny?" the SandWing flared. "What's that supposed to mean? I'm brave! I'm brave all the time!" She lashed her tail and ducked away when Clay reached to pat her on the head.

Warm bursts of sunlight nudged through the leafy canopy, making all their scales glow. Glory let her scales turn whatever color they wanted. A shimmery beetle green spread all over her, touched here and there with curls of amber. She liked the feeling of matching the trees and sunbeams.

We'll be there soon, she thought with a shiver of anticipation. *But I mustn't get my hopes up. Maybe it won't be what I imagined. It just has to be better than life under the mountain, trapped in a cave by guardians who hate me. I'm not setting the bar too high here, I think.*

Something crackled off to their left, but when Glory whipped around, all she saw was a shaggy gray sloth, hanging from a tree and blinking sleepily at her.

"Have I mentioned this place makes me nervous?" Clay asked.

"Only about a thousand times," Glory said.

"I wish we knew what the MudWings were talking about," Sunny said. "How can they live right next to the rainforest and not know why it's dangerous?"

"How can the RainWings live *in* the rainforest if it's all that dangerous?" Glory countered.

Webs sniffed faintly, the first sound he'd made in a while. He muttered, "Because they're RainWings. They probably haven't even noticed."

Glory glared at him. "Maybe you'd like a matching venomous wound on your other side," she snarled.

Tsunami whirled and grabbed Webs's snout. The bigger SeaWing snorted with surprise and tried to jerk back, but she held him firmly so she could glare into his face.

"All right, enough. What do you know about this?" she demanded. "You're the only one who's been to the rainforest. Does it have some kind of monster?" She shook his snout, none too gently. "Stop drooping like a wet fern and tell us what you know."

"Nuffing," Webs mumbled through Tsunami's grip.

"Stamp on his tail," Glory suggested. "Or poke that scratch. That'll get him talking."

"Don't be horrible," Sunny said. She nudged their guardian's shoulder with her snout. "Webs, please warn us if you know something. It's not safe for you either."

Webs sighed, and Tsunami let go of him.

"I swear I don't know anything about a monster," he said. "I didn't see anything dangerous when I snuck in to steal Glory's egg. Honestly it was really easy. It was the night before the brightest night, so you could tell which eggs were about to hatch, and I just took one and flew back to the mountains. I didn't even run into any RainWings, let alone a monster."

"My parents weren't guarding their nest?" Glory asked.

Webs looked down at his talons and shook his head.

That doesn't mean anything, Glory thought, but she remembered the MudWing village and Clay's mother, who had sold one of her eggs to the Talons of Peace for a couple of cows. She hadn't missed Clay at all, and she certainly didn't want him back. Glory hoped her parents wouldn't be like that.

Both Clay and Tsunami had been disappointed. Maybe parent dragons were always disappointing . . . especially when you'd spent years dreaming about what they might be like.

Well, Glory didn't particularly care whether her parents were the most amazing dragons in the world. She just wanted to meet other RainWings and show her friends that they weren't all lazy fruit-eaters, like the other tribes thought. With their camouflage scales and secret venom, surely they had to be tougher and stronger than anyone suspected.

"Maybe it's a new monster," Clay suggested. "Something that's come to the rainforest since you were here six years ago."

"Maybe," Webs said. "The Talons never sent anyone down this way."

"I can't tell you much about this place either," Starflight said, worrying at one of his claws. "There were almost no scrolls about the rainforest or the dragons who live here."

Glory knew that. She'd memorized every reference she could find anywhere to the RainWings, and all put together they told her essentially nothing. There'd been one scroll called *Dangers of the Rainforest*, so she knew a fair amount about quicksand, poisonous snakes, and deadly bugs. But even that one barely mentioned the RainWings themselves, and certainly nothing about creatures big enough to massacre the MudWing soldiers.

Something chattered loudly in the branches overhead and they all jumped.

"It was just a monkey," Glory said fiercely, clamping down on her nerves so her scales wouldn't change color. "Or a . . . a toucan or something."

"Can we eat toucans?" Clay asked hopefully.

"Only if we can catch them," Tsunami said. She flexed her wings and glanced up at the branches and vines overhead.

Glory wasn't hungry anymore, now that the sun had finally come out. Each touch of sunlight felt as if it filled her up better than any cow. With a twinge of guilt, she remembered the SkyWing palace and the sculptured tree Queen Scarlet had set up to display Glory on, like a piece of treasure.

There had been *so much sun* there — nothing like she'd ever had in her whole life under the mountain. Queen Scarlet would roll Glory into the sunlight and let her change colors however she wanted all day long. She didn't try to talk to her. She never touched her or yelled at her or insulted her or compared her to anyone. Scarlet's only wish had been for Glory to sleep and be beautiful.

But I didn't love it, Glory told herself fiercely. *It was just new and different. A new, different way to be a prisoner and have my life chosen for me. I'm more than a lump of treasure.*

I guess Scarlet found that out the hard way.

"CAW! CAW!"

Tsunami leaped into battle pose, her teeth bared, with Clay a step behind her. The others stopped as she glared around, looking for the source of the noise.

"I'm telling you," Glory said. "It's only toucans. There's nothing to be scared of. You're just jumpy."

"Now why would we be jumpy?" Tsunami said. "Oh, right. *The dead bodies.*"

"At least I told you about them," Glory said, her ruff flaring. "You saw a dead body — of someone we *knew* — on day one in the Kingdom of the Sea and decided not to tell us."

"Guys —" Starflight said.

"That was different! That was Kestrel!" Tsunami cried. "I had to find a way to tell you properly."

"Super job you did there," Glory said.

"GUYS!" Starflight yelled. They stopped and looked back at him. He was turning in frantic circles, staring out at the trees. It took Glory a moment, but she realized what he was looking for right before he said, "Where's Sunny?"

They all fell silent.

Sunny had vanished into thin air.

CHAPTER 3

"SUNNY!" Clay bellowed at the top of his lungs.

"She was mad," Starflight fretted. "Maybe she ran off because she was mad at us."

"She was?" Clay asked. "Why was she mad?" Glory couldn't remember either.

"Run off into a strange rainforest on her own?" Tsunami said. "That's not like her."

Glory closed her eyes and ransacked her brain. *Poisonous snakes. Deadly swarms of ants. What were the other "dangers of the rainforest"? Quicksand?* She opened her eyes and peered at the ground around them, but it was all plain dirt, tree debris, and tangled roots. Nothing looked like quicksand.

"SUNNY! SUNNY!" Clay yelled again.

Tsunami growled. "We made it through the Sky Kingdom and the Kingdom of the Sea without losing anyone, and now we're two minutes into the rainforest and one of us is gone?"

"She's not gone," Starflight said, his voice vibrating with panic. "She can't be! She has to be here somewhere. I was looking at her only a few moments ago!"

Glory turned her gaze up to the trees. Another gray sloth hung from a nearby branch, yawning. It looked like perhaps the least threatening creature she'd ever seen. She frowned at it.

"Webs, what do you think happened?" Tsunami demanded, following Glory's gaze.

There was no response. They all turned around.

Webs was gone, too.

"No way," Clay said, flaring his wings. "He was *just* here. I saw his face when we realized Sunny was gone. Maybe ten seconds ago. He couldn't have disappeared in *ten seconds*."

"But he did," Starflight cried. "He did, and Sunny did, into thin air."

"Ouch!" Tsunami said, clapping a talon to her neck. "Something just stung me."

Clay jumped and clawed at his neck as well. Starflight's eyes went wide, and then he threw himself to the ground and rolled under the nearest low-hanging bush with his wings over his head.

"What in the world are you —" Glory started, ducking to look at him. She heard a soft buzz as something whizzed by her ear, followed by a tiny *thunk* as it hit the tree behind her.

She spun around and saw Clay literally disappear right in front of her. It was as if the forest reached out leafy arms, quietly wrapped him up, and bundled him away. One moment he was there, blinking dizzily, and then he was gone. A heartbeat later, so was Tsunami.

Aha, Glory thought.

She planted herself next to Starflight's hiding spot and flared her ruff. She could sense the waves of pale orange and dark red rippling across her scales, but she didn't try to hide them. She didn't care if her audience knew she was angry.

"That's enough!" she called. "Come out here right now."

There was a pause, and then the air seemed to shimmer for a moment, and suddenly a dragon the color of raspberries stood in front of her, grinning.

Glory had never seen anyone else use camouflage scales like hers. It was startling and unsettling and kind of the coolest thing she'd ever seen. *Holy moons*, she thought. *That is awesome. We do that. RainWings, like me.*

Another dragon, dark blue dappled with gold, appeared beside the first. She was grinning, too.

Rustling overhead made Glory look up.

Suddenly the trees were full of dragons.

RainWings curled around the trunks or hung from the branches by their tails. Several of them were colors she'd never even imagined. She saw deep shades of violet, iridescent peach, pale jade, and a yellow so bright it was like being stabbed in the eyes with the sun.

We are beautiful.

"Aw, look!" said the raspberry dragon. "She's happy to see us!" He beamed at her, and Glory realized that small bubbles of rose pink were rising up from her talons to her wings.

"Poor little dragonet," murmured the dark blue RainWing. "Why are her scales so dull?"

Glory blinked. *Is she talking about me?*

"Shhh, don't be rude," said the first RainWing. "Hello, tiny one. I'm Jambu, and this is Liana. What's your name, and why don't we know you already?"

"Glory, and the easily terrified black one is Starflight," she said. She glanced behind her and saw Starflight peering out from under the bush. "Where are my friends?"

The dark blue dragon — Liana — tilted one of her wings up at the trees. Amid the dragons clustered overhead were four hanging nets woven of vines. Sunny, Webs, Clay, and Tsunami were inside; they all had their eyes closed and hung limply like sacks of fish.

"Are they OK?" Starflight cried.

"Sleeping darts," said the raspberry dragon, producing a tiny blowgun from a pouch around his neck. "Let's just say we have some tree frogs around here you wouldn't want to lick. Your friends will wake up fine in a few hours."

"It's easier to meet new dragons this way," said Liana. "We've had a couple of grumpy brown ones stumble in here, and for some reason they start biting us before we can even say hello. This way we get to chat first, while they're still a bit groggy."

"Plus it's more fun," said Jambu. "Practicing dart-shooting on ourselves isn't the same."

"They probably won't think it's so fun," Glory said. "Especially the blue one. She can be a little cranky. Just to warn you."

"So . . . are we your prisoners now?" Starflight asked glumly.

The dark blue dragon burst into gales of laughter, and amused noises swept through all the dragons in the trees.

"RainWings don't take prisoners, funny little black dragon," Liana said when she could speak again. "Whatever would we do with them?"

"Interrogate them for information," Glory suggested. "Trade them for hostages or weaponry. Contain them to minimize any threats."

The RainWings blinked at her as if she'd suddenly started speaking toucan.

"Just a few ideas," she said with a shrug.

"If we're not prisoners," Starflight said, "then what are you going to do with us?"

"Well," said the raspberry dragon, glancing up at the position of the sun over the canopy. "Is anyone hungry?"

And then the trees began to scream.

──── CHAPTER 4 ────

Starflight nearly leaped out of his scales. Glory felt her talons dig into the leafy dirt as she tried not to bolt into the jungle.

The screams faded, and she realized that all the RainWings were staring at her quizzically.

"Are you all right?" Jambu asked. "Wow, that's a spooked color. You weren't freaked like that by us! We clearly need to work on our scariness."

"I'm not *spooked*," Glory said, gritting her teeth and regaining control of her scales.

"I am," Starflight stammered. "What — what was that noise?"

"Oh!" Liana said. "The screamer monkeys." She pointed up, and Glory spotted a pair of large brown monkeys lounging on a branch overhead. "They started doing that a few years ago."

"It startled us at first, too," Jambu said sympathetically. "They used to make these deeper grunt-y noises, but now it's all shrieking and gibbering like dragons being murdered. You get used to it."

"*Do* you?" Glory asked. On the one talon, that explained what the MudWing patrols were hearing from the rainforest. On the other, it definitely did not explain the dead soldiers. And on the third talon, why would monkeys suddenly start making different noises than they had before? And on the fourth, why didn't the RainWings think that was weird?

"Come on back to our village," Jambu said. "We could knock you out for the flight there, if you want. You might be more comfortable. There are a lot of branches in the way."

"No, thank you," Starflight said.

"Absolutely not," Glory said at the same time.

Jambu shrugged. "All right. Then follow us." He leaped gracefully into the air and spiraled up toward the treetops. The rest of the dragons did the same. It looked a bit like a rainbow exploding and spattering color all over the trees.

Glory and Starflight followed them into the canopy, high above the forest floor, where they were surrounded by sunlit emerald green and the whirring whisper of tiny wings. Birds darted and hopped all around them, as brightly colored as the RainWings. Whenever Glory paused for more than a moment, purple and gold butterflies landed on her talons or head. Perhaps they thought she was a flower; they stayed away from Starflight's darker scales.

The RainWings moved through the treetops with a weird grace, using their tails or spreading their wings to glide between the trees. It looked more like swimming in the air than flying. Glory wasn't sure she'd ever get the hang of it.

But it made sense, since straight flying between the densely packed trees would be difficult for creatures the size of dragons. Starflight kept smacking into vines as he tried to keep up with them. Glory wondered if he was wishing he'd accepted the offer to be knocked out in a net like the others. She saw Sunny's net soar past them, handed smoothly from talon to talon, from RainWing to RainWing.

With a quick glance to make sure no one was watching her, Glory tried wrapping her tail around a branch and swinging in a full circle, like the other RainWings did.

"Almost there," Jambu said, landing beside her. His weight on the branch threw off her swing, and she ended up hanging upside down by her tail for an awkward moment. With a grin, he reached down and helped haul her back upright. Her back talons gripped the rough bark of the branch; it felt like ancient dragon scales under her claws.

"You really aren't from around here," he said.

"No," Glory said as Starflight thudded down clumsily on the branch as well. "My egg was stolen from the RainWings six years ago."

"Well, I can take you out tree gliding anytime you want to practice," he said. "I bet you'll figure it out pretty quickly." He spread his wings and leaped off again.

Glory frowned at his departing pink tail.

"Yeah, that was weird," Starflight said, answering her unspoken thought.

"Wasn't it? As if he didn't care at all," Glory said. "He didn't ask who stole me or where I was raised or even act like he remembered an egg getting stolen. As if eggs just vanish all the time, no big deal." She scratched her ruff thoughtfully. "Well, whatever. Maybe they do. Maybe there is a rainforest monster, and the dragons are used to losing eggs to it."

"That is really, really not comforting," Starflight said. He wrapped his black wings closer to himself, peering down at the forest floor as if he expected something toothy to pop up and try to grab him.

Comforting. Glory couldn't think of *any* particularly comforting explanations for Jambu's lack of interest in her abduction. *Perhaps he's just a weird dragon who doesn't pay attention to dragonets or eggs. Surely the rest of my tribe will care.*

"Come on, let's keep up," she said to Starflight.

A few swings and glides later, suddenly all the RainWings around them veered up, spiraling even higher into the treetops. Starflight made an anxious noise as the nets whooshed by with their unconscious friends in them.

And then the dragons started to land, and Glory began to see the home of the RainWings.

"Oh," she breathed. She stopped to hover in the air so she could look at everything.

The iridescent colors of the dragons brought the hidden world forward; otherwise the village was camouflaged as well as any RainWing.

Wide vine walkways, shimmering with talon-sized orange orchids, hung between leafy platforms. A few of the treehouses had low walls or woven ceilings; others were open to the sky and carpeted with soft white flowers like fallen clouds. Glory spotted a few of the sleepy gray sloths ambling or swinging between the walkways. She wondered if they weren't smart enough to know they were surrounded by dragons who could eat them at any moment.

This is the coolest place I've ever seen, Glory thought triumphantly. *And it's my place.*

"Visitors!" Liana called. She had one corner of Clay's net in her claws; carefully she and the other RainWings lowered him onto a platform wide enough for twenty dragons. Glory swept up to land beside him and watched her tribe gently set down her other friends.

Dragon heads popped up all around the village. Glory realized that most of them were in hanging contraptions like hammocks. She studied the closest one. It was strung between two trees, sturdily woven of vines and lined with violet feathers and blue petals. The dragon inside was impossible to see until he poked his head out; his scales matched the green and purple around him perfectly.

"Clever," Starflight said, tilting his head at the hammock. He glanced at the ground miles below them and shivered. "I certainly wouldn't want to sleep up this high without something like that. Look at that hammock design — you can't fall out, and with RainWing camouflage, enemies aren't likely to spot you either."

Glory glanced down at her scales and saw a color rolling through them that she had never seen on herself before — a vibrant blue-purple she guessed meant pride. She was *proud* of her tribe. She'd barely met them, and already they were as impressive as she'd hoped. *So there, guardians,* she thought. *All those years of making me sleep on uncomfortable rock ledges in the dark! And who are the backward dragons, exactly?*

"I know, isn't it pretty? We quite like our village, too," Liana said, practically in Glory's ear. Glory jumped back, flicking her tail. All right, there was one thing that made her uncomfortable: the way the other RainWings looked at her as if they expected to understand every thought she had, just by reading her scales. She clamped down on her emotions, turning her scales back to a treetop green that matched the background.

Liana didn't seem ruffled by Glory's reaction. The RainWing scanned the leaves overhead, then smiled as five small dragons in shades of sky blue and copper dropped through the canopy toward them.

"Hope you're hungry," Liana said as the dragons opened their talons. Strange shapes bounced and rolled across the platform, bumping against Glory's sleeping friends. Glory picked up the one closest to her: lime-green and star-shaped, it smelled like pineapple and basil. She poked it with one claw, wondering if she had to peel it.

Under the mountain, the dragonets had almost never eaten fruit. She knew more from reading about it in scrolls than from the few berries Webs had sometimes brought back. Queen Scarlet was the one who'd given her pineapple.

Don't think about Queen Scarlet.

Starflight scanned the platform with a disappointed expression. "Is all of this fruit?" he asked. "Isn't there any meat?"

Liana wrinkled her nose. "You can hunt if you want," she said, "but really, it's a waste of energy." She glanced up at the sky again. "And it's almost our sun time, so if you must, then do it quietly."

"Sun time?" Glory asked.

"Oh, sweetheart." Liana shook her head. "Is that what's wrong with you?"

"I was not aware that anything was wrong with me," Glory said, firmly keeping her scales from changing color. "Not from a RainWing point of view, anyway."

"It's just your scales," Liana said. "They're so . . . mousy."

Glory stared at her. *Mousy?*

"You know," Liana said apologetically. "A little dull. Not like ours." She stretched out one wing and let a waterfall of rainbows ripple through it.

Is she saying I'm not as beautiful as other RainWings? Certainly they were all very bright and shiny. Maybe her own scales weren't quite as vibrant.

Glory wasn't sure what to think of that. In fact, she was pretty sure she didn't care. She'd always been "the pretty one" and it had never gotten her anywhere, other than chained to a decorative tree in the SkyWing Palace.

"So tell me about sun time," she said with a shrug.

A few streaks of orange and emerald flashed through Liana's scales and then vanished into dark blue again. Orange and emerald . . . if their scales worked the same way, then that meant Liana was feeling a little surprised and a little irritated. As if she'd hoped to prod more of a reaction out of Glory.

This scale-reading business can go both ways, my new friends.

"Sun time," Liana said smoothly, as if her scales hadn't changed at all. "It's the hours when the sun is highest, so we climb up as close to it as we can and sleep."

"Oh," Starflight interjected in his figuring-things-out voice. "Glory! It's like those naps you always take after lunch. I *knew* that must be a RainWing thing. But I could never figure out the point. Why sleep in the middle of the day? Don't you all have anything more important to do?"

Glory flicked her tail and narrowed her eyes at him, but Liana didn't seem offended.

"The sun recharges our scales while we sleep," she explained. "It makes us prettier, better at camouflage, smarter, and happier. What could be more important than that?"

"Oh," Starflight said again. He studied Glory like a scroll that finally made sense. "*Oh.* Happier? Like . . . less grouchy?"

"Shut up," Glory said, giving him a shove. She'd already put some of these pieces together in her own mind. She knew that what the guardians had done — keeping her trapped underground, away from the sun her whole life — had probably made her into a grumpier, less powerful dragon than she could have been. But she didn't need the others figuring that out because she didn't need their pity.

And who knew what she would have been like otherwise? Being prickly was kind of an essential part of being Glory, if you asked her.

The truth was, in the Sky Kingdom, where Queen Scarlet left her in the sun all day, Glory had never felt happier or more at peace . . . or less like herself. She knew it was the effect of the sun and nothing else. She knew that what she'd experienced was like finally getting to eat as much as she needed after a lifetime of starvation. She knew that Queen Scarlet was evil and that Glory was only another sparkly piece of treasure to her.

Part of her had hated it — hated the weird sleepiness and the unmotivated contentment that made her feel like a puddle of slugs.

And yet there was a part of her that could have stayed that way forever.

She shook herself fiercely. "So go sleep," she said to Liana. "We're not going anywhere." The other RainWings who'd carried the nets had already flown off to higher platforms in the treetops. Some were sprawled out in open patches of sun, while others were stretched inside the clever hammocks, snoring.

"True," said Liana. "We'll wake up before your friends do."

"Don't you want to ask all your questions first?" Starflight said to Glory. "Don't you want to find your family and —"

"There's no rush," Glory said, cutting him off. "They're asleep now anyway. The answers will be the same in a few hours." She knew she was good at looking like she didn't care. She particularly wanted Liana to think she didn't care.

It was lucky that questions couldn't parade across her scales like her emotions, or she'd have been covered in them. But she wasn't about to look desperate in her first moments with her new tribe. They certainly didn't seem to have a million questions for her. So fine, she could act like this reunion was no big deal to her either.

Maybe acting cool and unconcerned was a natural RainWing thing.

Starflight scratched his head. "Can we at least ask about the monster?"

"Monster?" Liana laughed. "There's no such thing as monsters."

"Really?" Starflight asked. "Then what's killing MudWing soldiers on your borders?"

"Oh," Liana said. "*That* monster."

Starflight's wings flared, and his eyes went wide as the moons. Liana burst out laughing. "Your face!" she cried. "That was so worth it. I'm just kidding, little black dragon. I don't know anything about any dead MudWings, but I do know we don't have any monsters here."

"Just relax, Starflight," Glory said. "Think about libraries or something."

"Little dragon," Jambu called from a perch high above Glory's head. She squinted up at him, dazzled by the bright light reflecting off his magenta scales. "Are you joining us for sun time? Want a hammock?" he offered. "Or a platform?"

Glory blinked at her friends. Clay was snoring louder than all the RainWings combined. Tsunami frowned even in her sleep, her claws twitching as if she dreamed about fighting. Sunny was curled up in a peaceful ball like a snoozing chinchilla, and Webs, with his shallow breathing, looked and sounded halfway dead.

If they weren't going to wake up soon anyway . . .

"Go ahead," Starflight said. "It's OK. I'll watch them." He shook his wings and puffed out his chest imposingly, which came across a bit like a tree frog trying to look menacing.

"Wake me if you need to," Glory said. "If I hear someone shrieking like a tiny scavenger, I'll assume it's you."

Starflight huffed in outrage as Glory scooped up a couple of mysterious fruits and flew to Jambu's branch.

"I'll take a platform," she said, landing beside the pink RainWing.

"You sure?" he asked. "Usually dragonets stick to the hammocks, in case they roll off in their sleep. You'd wake up before hitting the ground, but you'd probably hit a few other things first. So, you know, we're not talking death or anything, but some serious ouch."

"I'll be fine," Glory said. She'd never fallen off the ghastly rock ledge where she'd been forced to sleep for six years. And even in her Sky Kingdom sun-overdose almost-coma, she'd always stayed perfectly balanced on the marble tree.

"A calm sleeper, huh?" said Jambu. "Clear conscience, peaceful dreams?"

"Sure," Glory said. *As if I would tell my dreams to a dragon I just met. Or my crimes, for that matter.*

"Then you can join ours," he said, hopping from the branch to a platform covered in overlapping leaves, laid out to look like one gigantic leaf. The other two dragons on it nodded sleepily at her. Glory turned in a circle and lay down with her wings spread wide to catch as much sunshine as possible.

Warmth flooded through her, as if she were rolling in molten gold. *This*, she thought as her eyes closed and all her muscles relaxed. *I could have slept in the sun like this every day of my life.*

Forget the stupid prophecy. This is the destiny I was supposed to have.

—— CHAPTER 5 ——

Glory woke up refreshed and relaxed, but as she lay there with her eyes closed, she felt a wave of strange anger at herself.

All right, sure, I'm not in the Great Magnificent Wondrous Dragonet Prophecy. Maybe no one would ever write a prophecy about a RainWing. Maybe no dragon in Pyrrhia expects any of us to have an important destiny or do anything worthwhile.

But this? Sleeping all day in a patch of sun? Is that all I'm good for — all any RainWing is good for?

There must be more to us than this.

There must be more to me.

She wanted to kick herself. Falling asleep almost the moment she found her home . . . this was exactly what she didn't want her friends to think about her or her tribe. She'd have to show them that there was a good reason for RainWings to have sun time. It must make them smarter and fiercer, or something.

She shifted her wings and froze.

Something was curled in the gap between her shoulder and her wing. Some part of it was also draped across her neck. It was warm, warmer than the sunbeams, and it was breathing deeply and evenly.

She inched her head around and peered sideways at it.

There was a *sloth* sleeping on her.

It had crept into the curve of her shoulder and fitted itself there perfectly, slipping one arm over her neck to pillow its head. Long silvery gray fur draped over her green scales. Its eyes were shut, and it had a peaceful smile on its sleeping face.

What ridiculous creatures. Fearless? Or stupid?

Or maybe this is a diabolically clever plan. After all, she couldn't eat it now. She couldn't possibly eat something that smiled like that. It reminded her a bit of Sunny, who probably would also have no trouble falling asleep on something big enough to eat her.

She twisted her head up, moving as little as possible so she wouldn't disturb the sloth. The other RainWings on her platform were still asleep. The sun had drifted down the sky, but she guessed there were several hours yet until nightfall. A soft breeze tossed homeless leaves across the canopy, and two fat blue frogs on a nearby branch were having a drowsy, ribbety conversation.

"Brrrp?" the sloth chirruped. It opened its enormous dark eyes, looked into hers, and yawned a wide, oddly elegant yawn. "Brrrrrrrple."

"I'm awake," Glory said. "So you should probably flee in terror now."

"Rrrrrmble rrrrrmp rrrrrllp," the sloth said agreeably. It snuggled closer to her scales and yawned again.

"I'm not like these other dragons. I have things to do," Glory told it. "You can't keep sleeping there."

"Mmmm-hrrmble," the sloth concurred, closing its eyes.

The platform vibrated underneath her as Jambu chuckled. He rolled over and nodded at the sloth. "You've been chosen," he said. "That happened fast."

"No, thank you," Glory said. "I don't want to be chosen. Especially by a sloth." She pushed herself up to sitting, but the sloth somehow got both arms around her neck and hung on, nestling against her wing.

"She likes you," Jambu said. "Now you have to pick a name for her. The queen calls hers Shaggy."

"First of all, what, and no; it is seriously undignified for a dragon queen to have a sloth. Also, this sloth is much too pretty for a dopey name like Shaggy," Glory said, then caught herself. "And I'm not naming her, because I'm not keeping her. She'll wander away if I ignore her long enough."

Jambu snorted with amusement.

"Or maybe I'll eat her," Glory said. "Why don't you eat them?" She shot a glance at the sloth, who looked serenely unconcerned.

He shrugged. "Because they're cute. And too hairy; they're all fur. You'd have indigestion for days."

Glory reached up and poked the sloth with her claw. It did seem to be mostly fur.

"Rrrrrrble." The sloth wriggled as if it was being tickled.

"I'm not playing with you," Glory said. "You have to go away. I have important things to do, like finding my parents."

Jambu tilted his head at her. His raspberry-pink scales had drifts of light pink whorls in them. Glory was pretty sure she'd never been that color, and she had no idea if it meant anything. Sometimes pink popped into her scales when she was happy, but Jambu was pink from head to toe. Nobody could be *that* happy.

"Finding your parents?" he echoed. "How?"

"You tell me," Glory said. "I can tell you when I was stolen, and one of those SeaWings down there can tell you from where. Isn't that enough?"

"Ha!" Jambu laughed as if he genuinely thought she was joking, then smothered his giggles when he realized she wasn't. "What are you talking about? RainWings don't *do* 'parents.'"

Glory tried to ignore the twist of disappointment in her stomach. *You knew that might happen. Remember the MudWings. Maybe the RainWings are the same, raised by their siblings instead.*

"So —" she started.

"Why would you want to find them anyway?" Jambu asked.

Glory stamped down her temper so it wouldn't show up in her scales. "Two reasons," she said. "One, I want to know where I came from and what I've missed. And two, I want my family to know I'm all right. They must have worried a lot when my egg went missing." She studied him for a reaction.

Jambu pulled on his snout and looked confused. "But they wouldn't know," he said. "I guess you don't — I mean —" He stopped and glanced around at the sleeping dragons everywhere. A few were up and moving through the village already, but most were still snoozing.

"I'll just show you," he said, spreading his wings.

Glory spread hers as well. "Time to get off, sloth," she said. "Unless you're prepared for some flying."

"Brrrrrp." The sloth wrapped its arms more firmly around her neck.

"Do they understand us?" Glory asked.

"Doubtful," Jambu said. "They're just reading our body language and responding." He shook off a winding vine and dove off the platform.

Glory checked the sloth again. She was pretty sure it was smiling at her. Maybe her sloth *could* understand her; maybe it was smarter than all the other sloths in the rainforest.

She followed Jambu, gliding carefully between the trees and hanging vines. She tried not to care about the furry creature clinging to her, but she found herself flying more slowly than usual and avoiding things that might knock it off.

You ridiculous dragon. It's only prey, no matter how cute.

Wherever Jambu was leading her, it was some distance from the center of the village. They passed more platforms, covered with sleeping dragons, and something like a trampoline of enormous interwoven leaves stretched between four trees, where a few little dragonets were bouncing and flapping their wings furiously as they learned to fly.

Everyone looked happy. There were none of the horrible war wounds and scars Glory had seen in the other kingdoms.

Nobody seemed tense or terrified. Nobody was being forced to fight to the death or punished for failing at guard duty.

No fighting, no worrying about the war, no starving or bowing to an insane queen — well, as far as I know, anyway.

Who needs a prophecy when they could have a home like this?

Jambu angled down toward a structure shaped like a gigantic green egg. Holes all over the roof allowed sunlight through the overlapping leaves, but the bottom was reinforced with tightly woven vines and branches, so it looked sturdier than anything else Glory had seen so far. She wondered for a moment if this was the palace, but surely it wasn't big enough for that. She hadn't seen anything large or regal enough to be the RainWing queen's palace yet.

They landed on a branch next to one of the window holes, and Jambu gestured for her to look inside.

Pale eggs lined the entire floor, packed closely together. In the sunlight from above, shimmering colors glowed under the thin shells as the unhatched dragonets wriggled and squirmed. Glory guessed that the eggs around the outer edges were the closest to hatching, since she could see more movement inside them. A few even had tiny cracks along the top already.

"So?" she said. "So you have a hatchery. All the queens do. I mean, sure, this is a lot of eggs for one queen, but . . . wait, are you saying this is the hatchery I was stolen from?" *Am I the daughter of a queen, too?* Not that it made much difference to her, but it would be pretty funny to see the look on Tsunami's face if that was true.

"I have no idea," Jambu said. "There are three hatcheries, so it could have been any of them. But you're missing the point. These eggs aren't all from one queen, or any one dragon. We keep *all* our eggs together like this."

Glory blinked at the array of smooth white shapes in front of her. "So these are a third of the eggs in the village right now. All . . . stuffed in together."

"Exactly," said Jambu. "They keep each other warm and hatch whenever they need to. We stop by every couple of days to check for newly hatched dragonets. Otherwise, we don't have to worry about our eggs. They're all safe in here."

"Except for mine," Glory pointed out. "Which was stolen." She paused, realization dawning. It felt as though the wind had just been sucked out from under her and she was falling with useless wings.

"And nobody noticed," she said slowly. "That's what you're telling me. You had no idea my egg was missing at all."

Jambu shrugged. He didn't even look embarrassed. "Why would we?" he said. "As you can see, we have plenty of eggs. New ones roll in every week, so why go to the trouble of counting them?"

"Because I wasn't just an egg 'rolling in' and out of your hatchery," Glory said, flaring her ruff. "There was a real live dragon in there. A dragonet who had to grow up for six years with no family, no rainforest, and no sun."

"Rrrrrrrrrrrrrrp," the sloth said sympathetically, hugging her neck. Glory had forgotten it was there.

A cloudy blue-gray began to march up Jambu's scales from his talons. He made an almost comically sad face at her. "No sun?" he said.

"Hey, I survived just fine," Glory said. She stepped away from Jambu's wing as he reached for her. "This isn't a tragic pity-me situation. I'm just saying maybe you should care a little more about your eggs and the dragons inside them."

"We do care," he said, dark green distress flickering in his ruff. "We take very good care of our dragonets! We just don't worry about the eggs because we've never lost any before."

"How do you know?" she cried. "If I was stolen so easily, you might have lost others, too."

He opened and closed his mouth a few times, looking so stupid that she wanted to punch him in his snout. This went beyond parents who didn't love their eggs. *Nobody* had missed her. She had no family wondering what had happened to her. Nobody had cared that she was gone.

Webs must have known the RainWings were like this. That's why he came to the rainforest to steal an egg. That was what he hadn't wanted to admit to her on the way here.

The RainWings weren't a secretly wonderful, perfect tribe. It was worse than she'd feared. Her tribe was too lazy to even count their own eggs.

"Oh, now you're mad," Jambu said woefully. Glory couldn't stop the dark red streaks appearing along her wings. She scowled at him.

"So how do you know which dragonets belong to which parents?" she asked.

"We don't," he said. "We raise them all together, the whole village. Everybody helps. I teach tree gliding," he said proudly. The blue-gray of his scales was already fading back into pink again.

"But then," Glory said slowly, "doesn't that mean you don't even know who you're related to?"

"Oh, I know what you're thinking," Jambu said. "Don't worry, we have a way to tell. Before two dragons decide to have eggs together, they do the venom test." He pivoted in a circle and plucked a floppy oval leaf from one of the trees, then laid it on the branch between them. "Watch."

He opened his mouth wide, nearly unhinging his lower jaw, and spat a small amount of black venom on the leaf. Glory had imagined herself looking cool and menacing when she shot her venom, but the other RainWing mostly looked creepy, like a mentally unbalanced snake.

The leaf immediately began to sizzle and melt.

"Now you shoot your venom at it," he said. "Just a little. Try to hit the same spot."

Glory hadn't exactly ever practiced aiming her venom, or controlling how much she shot out. She bared her fangs at the leaf and ended up nearly drenching it in black poison. The branch below and around the leaf started smoking and fizzing as well.

But, strangely, where Glory's venom hit Jambu's, those spots stopped melting instantly.

"Whoa!" Jambu said. He sprayed a little more of his venom, carefully, on the rest of the leaf and the branch where Glory's had splashed. All of the smoking and sizzling stopped. The leaf sat peacefully in a puddle of what appeared to be harmless black goop.

Glory blinked at it. "Hmmm," she said. "Unexpected."

Jambu thwacked one of her wings with his, radiating delight in every pink scale. "Don't you see what just happened? Your venom counteracted mine. Isn't that awesome? That's so awesome!"

"Is it?" Glory asked.

"That means we're related!" Jambu cried. "You're my little sister!"

Glory flexed her claws and thought about that. She'd come to the rainforest looking for some family, after all. But it figured that she'd find out Jambu was her brother right after deciding he was the dizziest, most useless dragon she'd ever met. And what good was a family who'd never been there for you — who'd never known or cared you were alive, and lost, and in danger?

"Oh," she said. "Wow. Related." She reached up and scratched the sloth's chin. It snuggled in closer to her with another burbling sound.

"That's how we know," Jambu said, waving a talon at the half-melted leaf. "If your venom made it melt faster, then we'd know we're not related, so we could have eggs together. But when your venom cancels out the other dragon's, you come from the same family. Can you believe we're brother and sister? Well, OK, we're probably only half brother and sister. But still, it's pretty cool."

"You're definitely not my dad, though," Glory said. "Right?"

Jambu let out a shout of laughter. "I'm only nine years old," he said. "I promise I haven't fathered any eggs yet, and I especially didn't have any when I was three."

Well, that's a relief, Glory thought. "That must be how the tribe cures dragons who've been hit by venom, too, right?" she said. "Find a family member to stop the spread of the poison?"

Her newfound brother looked horrified. "We don't use our venom on *other dragons*," he said, bright green flaring across his ruff. "Who would *do* that?"

"Um. No one," Glory said. *Maybe not in your perfect world. But talk to me again when you're held prisoner by a queen who's forcing your friends to fight to the death.* "I meant if someone hit someone else by accident. That's not impossible. Right?"

"Our venom trainers would never let that happen," Jambu protested. He glanced down at the mess she'd made on the branch. "I bet you could get a few sessions with one of them if you want. We only ever use it for this kind of test and, very rarely, for prey if we need it, or, you know, things that attack us, hypothetically."

"Things that attack you?" Glory asked, perking up her ears. *Liiiiike . . . mysterious rainforest monsters?* she wondered.

"We should get back to your friends," he said. "They'll be waking up any minute. And we can tell them our good news about being related! So awesome!"

"All right," she said. "I've seen enough here." *And I'm pretty sure I've gotten all the answers about my family that I'm ever going to get.*

"A long-lost sister!" Jambu yammered, curling his tail around the branch. "So cool! I can teach you tree gliding and show you all the different fruits in the rainforest and how to take care of your sloth and —"

He swung around the branch and glided off, still talking. Glory took one more look at the village hatchery and followed him. She couldn't help but notice that he had no questions for her. He didn't care where she'd been or who'd stolen her or why. He didn't ask about the world beyond the rainforest. He had lots of ideas for what he could show her, but didn't seem interested in what she might be able to teach him.

She shook her head and navigated around a mossy tree trunk.

Who cares, anyway? Even if it's all true, everything the guardians said about RainWings . . . even if they are all useless and don't care about the right things . . . I'm still me. And I am not going to be like them. Not ever. No way.

— CHAPTER 6 —

Glory was not surprised to find Tsunami twitching violently in her sleep when she and Jambu landed. The SeaWing would probably be ready to fight someone the moment her eyes opened.

What was surprising, though, was discovering what Starflight got up to when he was bored.

"Hey, Glory," he called the moment he spotted her. "Watch this!"

The NightWing rolled one of the larger pieces of fruit — a round, light pinkish melon-looking thing — in front of Clay's nose and jumped back.

Although he was still knocked out, Clay's nose started twitching. His snout trembled and sniffed and inched closer and closer to the melon. His stomach growled loudly. His tongue flicked in and out.

Starflight took the melon away again, and Clay stopped moving with a long, tragic sigh.

"Isn't that hilarious?" Starflight asked Glory.

She gave him an amused look. "I've always figured torturing our sleeping friends would be funny."

He sat back and flung his tail over his talons, frowning. "I didn't have anything else to do. It's been unbearably quiet with everyone sleeping." His eyes flicked to Jambu. "Have you asked him about your —"

"Yup," Glory interjected. "Dead end."

"We're brother and sister!" Jambu announced gleefully.

Starflight tilted his head slowly to one side and gave Glory an "is he joking?" look. "You don't seem . . . much alike," he politely understated.

She shrugged, and the sloth on her back said, "Squerble!"

Starflight's eyes nearly popped out of his head. "Glory!" he said. "There's a sloth on you! You've got sloth — a sloth — it's sitting right on your neck!"

"I know," Glory said. "Apparently they're like pets to the RainWings. This one likes me. Even though I've explained to it that I'm pretty disagreeable."

"Oh, fascinating," Starflight said. His talons twitched as if he were dying for a scroll to check or somewhere to write notes. "If I remember right, pets don't tend to do well in dragon communities. They usually get eaten by forgetful relatives or sometimes by the owner herself. Scavengers, on the other talon, apparently keep all kinds of odd prey animals as pets, like cows and goats and fish. That's according to *A Longitudinal Study of Peculiar Scavenger Behavior*, anyway."

Glory remembered that scroll, but she hadn't taken it very seriously. Some of the things scavengers supposedly did were too absurd to be real.

"We would never eat our pets," Jambu interjected. "Why bother? There's enough fruit in the rainforest to be sure no RainWing will ever go hungry, and the sun gives us more than half the energy we need to survive anyway."

"So you really don't eat meat?" Starflight asked, giving Glory a sideways glance. "You're all vegetarians? Vegetarian dragons?"

Jambu waved his front talons airily. "We're not strict about it. We eat what we feel like eating. Bananas are easier to catch and peel than monkeys are, that's all."

Lazy fruit-eaters, Glory thought. *Just like everyone says they are.*

But they also have tranquilizer blowguns and a cleverly designed hidden village, she reminded herself.

It didn't help. *They didn't even notice my egg was gone.*

"Ouch!" said a small voice behind them. "I think something . . . bit me . . . what — where are we?"

Starflight bounded over to Sunny's side. "Are you all right?" he asked, helping her stand up.

The little SandWing blinked several times and stared around at the RainWing village. "How did we get here?" She shook out her wings and peeked over the edge. "Oh my gosh, that's a long way down. Glory, you have a cute furry thing! Can I hold it, please please?"

"Why not," Glory said, disentangling the sloth from around her neck. "Just don't eat it." She passed it over to Sunny, who cradled it gently between her front talons. The sloth poked Sunny's snout in a curious, exploratory way, then climbed up it onto her head and sat down with a yawn.

"It's not afraid of dragons at all," Starflight mused. "Fascinating."

"Ooooooorgh," Webs moaned. He clutched his head with his eyes still closed. "Everything hurts."

Sunny crawled over to him and checked his wound. Even from where she was, Glory could tell that it looked worse. The blackness was spreading and the scratch looked angrily twisted and raw.

"Nothing's going to get me!" Tsunami yelled, leaping to her feet. "I'll fight off any poisonous bugs! *ACK WHERE ARE WE?*" She wobbled on her talons and tipped over with a thud.

"Don't move too fast," Jambu suggested helpfully. "The tranquilizer takes a little while to completely wear off."

"TRANQUILIZER?" Tsunami shouted. "How dare you —"

"Tsunami, stop yelling," Glory said. "Or I'll ask him to knock you out again."

"I'd like to see him try!" Tsunami cried.

"Please do," Glory said to Jambu. "Do you have any darts that last for, say, days?"

"We don't do multiple darts in one day," Jambu explained, taking Glory seriously. "Just to be safe."

Tsunami flared her wings and glowered fiercely at Jambu and the other RainWings who were beginning to gather on the platform around them. Suddenly Glory thought the bright purples, deep oranges, turquoise blues, and lemon yellows looked somehow *too* shiny and *too* vivid now. She'd guess that they were showing off for her friends, except she got the feeling all RainWings woke up every day and spent hours trying to look more colorful than everyone else.

"Clay?" Sunny said. She nudged the slumbering MudWing. "Clay, wake up. Are you all right? Is he all right?"

"He should be fine," said Liana, swooping up behind Jambu. "His dose wasn't any different than the rest of yours."

"I'm awake," Clay muttered. He buried his head under his talons. "I'm just waiting until Glory and Tsunami stop fighting. I was dreaming about sheep and buffalo and bears. They were all on the table in front of me and I had to decide which to eat first. Oh, and they all smelled like melons. That part was kind of weird."

"Sunny!" Tsunami cried, making the SandWing jump. "Stay very still. There's a sloth on your head. If I hit it just right, we can share it for dinner." She stepped forward, flexing her talons. There was a murmur of disapproval from the watching RainWings.

"Oh, no you don't," Glory said. She brushed past Tsunami and snatched the sloth away from Sunny. It cheerfully wrapped its arms around her neck and reburied its nose in her ruff. "It's mine," Glory said to Tsunami.

"Yours?" Tsunami echoed. "Yours as in you're saving it for a midnight snack?"

"Mine as in don't touch," Glory answered. "And don't make snide comments either."

"*Me?*" Tsunami said. "*You're* telling *me* not to make snide comments?"

"Clay, come on," Sunny said, tugging on his ears. "Make them stop so somebody will help Webs."

Glory had more or less forgotten they'd come to find a cure for the poisoned SandWing scratch near Webs's tail. She glanced around at the watching RainWings. Their eyes were wide as full moons and their scales glowed with pink and blue bubbles of curiosity and enthrallment. They looked as entertained by Glory's spat with Tsunami as the SkyWings were by actual gladiator arena battles.

Maybe they resolve all their arguments by taking naps, she thought grouchily.

Clay heaved himself upright and stretched, his muscles rippling. A few of the younger RainWings went "ooooo" and tried to change their scales to match his — muddy brown with undertones of glowing amber in the sunlight.

"That's right," Starflight said to Sunny. "We should focus on Webs. Of course you're right. I'll take care of this." He turned to Jambu and Liana. "We urgently request an audience with Queen Dazzling."

The two RainWings wrinkled their snouts thoughtfully. "Queen Dazzling?" Liana said. "You don't mean that."

"I do," Starflight insisted. "It's of the utmost importance. We must see her at once."

"Dazzling," Jambu said to Liana. "It's not her month, is it?"

"I don't think so," Liana agreed. "I guess they could see her anyway."

"We must!" Starflight said firmly. "Take us to her at once!"

"Wait," Glory jumped in. "What do you mean, 'not her month'?"

"Well," Jambu said, "wouldn't you rather see the current queen? If it's so important?"

Starflight's pompous attitude fizzled out like someone had dumped a pile of snow on it. "But," he said, "but the *NightWing Guide to the Tribes* said — I'm *sure* it said Queen Dazzling —"

"It also said we have no natural weapons," Glory pointed out. "So perhaps it's not the most reliable source, at least about RainWings. Who's the current queen?" she asked Liana.

"I'm pretty sure it's Magnificent right now," Liana said. "Unless she handed it over to Grandeur a bit early."

Oh, no, Glory thought. *Don't say it. Don't say it.*

"You *take turns* being queen?" Tsunami burst out. "Are you *serious*?"

"Only the ones who want to," Liana said. "Most of us find it way too much work, you know?"

"Yeah, *SO* boring. Dragons bother you all day long," Jambu agreed. "Makes me glad *I* can't be queen."

"So who can?" Glory asked. "Anyone? Or only the royal family?"

"Royal family!" Jambu echoed with great amusement.

"Oh, right," Glory said. "RainWings don't *do* families," she informed her friends. Sunny tilted her head, but luckily the RainWings kept talking before she could say anything sympathetic.

"Pretty much any female in the tribe can be queen if she wants to," said Liana.

"Really?" Tsunami said curiously. "How about me? Can I be queen? I'm originally a princess, you know. And I'm really good at telling dragons what to do."

Liana and Jambu looked at her dubiously. Tsunami shifted her sea-blue wings, raised her snout in a queenly way, and flashed the royal glowing patterns in her scales.

"Well," Jambu said, "I guess you could ask."

"Absolutely not," Glory said. "Have a little tribe dignity, for moons' sake. You cannot have a SeaWing as queen of the RainWings. Tsunami, quit that."

"When you say it like that, it does sound weird," Liana agreed, scratching her ruff with one talon.

Glory didn't want to know what Tsunami was thinking right then. Something about what a useless, ridiculous tribe this was, probably. "So, fine, take us to Queen Magnificent," she said. "How far is the palace?"

Most of the RainWings politely tried to muffle their laughter.

"We don't really *do* palaces," Liana said. "Come on, follow me."

Jambu and the other RainWings stayed behind, waving, like a bowlful of butterflies, as Glory settled the sloth on her shoulder again and she and her friends followed Liana up into the treetops.

The treehouse she led them to was not much different from all the others, although it was a bit higher and closer to the sun, with an open roof and five giant open windows in the curved outside walls. A short hanging walkway, glowing with fuchsia flowers shaped like dragon tongues, led from the doorway to another large platform. Seven dragons were standing in a line on the platform. Most of them looked bored or sleepy, although one or two had angry red flickers sparking through their scales.

"Here you are," Liana said, landing and nodding at the end of the line. "Magnificent will get to you eventually." She squinted up at the sky. "Probably before dark. Depending on what these others are here to complain about."

"We have to *WAIT*?" Tsunami barked. "In a *LINE*? Shouldn't visitors to the rainforest automatically go to the front?"

The waiting RainWings all shimmered green with displeasure and shot Tsunami unfriendly looks.

"We can wait," Glory said. "No big deal." The sloth flopped out on her back and made a snoozy sound.

"It's a big deal to Webs," Sunny pointed out. "Look how much pain he's in."

Webs contrived to look even more pathetic than he had a moment earlier. He flopped down on the platform and groaned softly.

"Sorry," Liana said. "This is how we do it, to be fair. Nobody gets to go ahead of anyone else."

Tsunami drew herself up as tall as she could and glared at her. "Didn't I mention that I'm the royal daughter of the queen of the SeaWings?"

"That sounds lovely for you," Liana said. "I'm on a gathering patrol now, but I'll come back to check on you all afterward." She took a step back, made a cheeky little bow to Tsunami, and flew away.

"Well, I never," Tsunami sputtered. "Maybe we should tell them who we really are."

"Shhh," Glory hissed at her. "We agreed to stop doing that."

"You don't think Queen Magnificent would lock us up, do you?" said Sunny.

"Doubtful," Starflight agreed. "I bet these dragons haven't even heard of our prophecy. I'm not sure they'd particularly care."

"True," said Glory. "They don't care about much."

"Better safe than sorry, don't you think?" Clay said. "I vote we keep it quiet. I mean, you never know how dragons will react, right? Sorry, Tsunami."

"No, you're right," she grumbled. She stretched her wings and neck. "I just can't believe they knocked us out and now they're making us wait around to see the queen."

"Yeah," Glory said. "It would make so much more sense if they'd chain you all up in a cave and starve you and ignore you for a day or two and then throw you in prison after you save one of their princesses. Oh, no, wait, that's what *your* mom did."

"At least there's food here," Clay said over Tsunami's sputtering. He had scooped up a pile of the fruit from the first platform and brought it with him. Looking pleased with himself, he started arranging the choices in front of him.

"What do you think these are?" He poked a branch covered in what looked like bright yellow sundrops.

The dragonets shared the fruit; even Webs perked up enough to eat. But Glory wasn't hungry. She passed a small orange fruit up to the sloth, but didn't eat anything herself. Like Jambu had said, the sun had filled her up more than any food ever had. Which was weird, and she didn't want to think about it or about what it meant that she'd been kept away from something so important for practically all her dragonet years.

Instead, she wandered toward the walkway and back, trying to peek across to the queen's treehouse. Through the windows she could see rainbow scales, bright blue and shimmering yellow and emerald green. She also spotted garlands of white flowers with petals like dragonfly wings. The RainWings seemed to use flowers for decoration the way the other tribes used jewels and precious stones.

Glory glanced at Tsunami. The SeaWing was still wearing the strands of pearls her mother had given her in the Kingdom of the Sea. She acted like she'd forgotten they were there, but occasionally Glory saw her running them through her claws.

But her mother was a little bit crazy and a smidgen evil, Glory thought to herself. *Wouldn't I rather have no mother than one like Queen Coral? Even if she did come with pearls?*

"What are you seeing the queen about?" she asked the first dragon in line. He jumped, startled to be spoken to.

"Oh, uh," he said slowly. "I'm just wondering if I can get my assignment changed. Like, right now I teach dragonets about fruit gathering, but I really think I'd be better at, like, advanced napping techniques."

Glory only barely managed not to laugh out loud. He was clearly not joking. Was "advanced napping techniques" an actual subject? She decided it would be rude to ask.

"What about you?" she asked, turning to the next dragon in line. This one was tall and pale orange, and a small gray-blue dragonet sat in the curl of her tail, frowning grumpily.

"I'm bringing this dragonet in for punishment," said the tall dragon. "He seems to think it's funny to stuff berries up the noses of sleeping dragons during sun time."

The little gray-blue dragon huffed a noise that was somewhere between amused and outraged and made a gruesome face at Glory. She made one right back, and he gaped in surprise.

"I'll tell you why I'm here," snarled the third dragon in line. He was one of the two with the furious red flickers along his ruff; the other was at the back of the line. Glory thought they might be the only angry RainWings she'd seen so far.

"Uh-oh," said the "napping techniques" dragon with a sleepy smile. "Mangrove is complaining about something again." The tall orange dragon chuckled appreciatively.

"Complaining about *something*!" Mangrove yelped. "I'll say! Something we should all be complaining about! My Orchid isn't the only one who's missing, you know!"

Glory tilted her head. "Your orchid?" she asked. Was this another weird RainWing thing, where it would turn out they were bizarrely attached to their flowers?

"My partner," Mangrove growled. "Orchid. She's been missing for three weeks. I've asked the queen every day since then to send out a search party."

"Sometimes dragons need a break," said the first dragon with a shrug.

"Maybe she's taking a really long nap somewhere," agreed the tall orange dragon.

"*Three. Weeks*," Mangrove hissed.

"And other dragons are missing, too?" Glory asked Mangrove.

"At least twelve in the last year, including Orchid," he said grimly.

A chill crawled down Glory's spine. So the MudWing soldiers weren't the only ones encountering something malevolent in the rainforest.

There *was* something out there, lurking behind the colorful birds and exuberant flowers and tall whispering trees. Something that could take out two MudWings at once . . . and also make twelve RainWings disappear without a trace.

CHAPTER 7

"NEXT!" boomed a voice from the queen's treehouse.

The first dragon ambled across the bridge, yawning, and slid through the curtain of silvery yellow flowers that hung in the doorway.

"Can I come in for your audience?" Glory asked Mangrove. She wanted to know how Queen Magnificent would handle the problem of missing RainWings.

"Why?" Mangrove asked suspiciously. "I'm not letting you have my turn."

"I'll just listen," Glory promised.

"Hmmm," he said. "All right, I suppose."

She turned to the last RainWing in the line and took a guess. "Are you here about a missing dragon, too?"

"A dragonet," the RainWing answered. The scarlet flickers in her ruff were reflected in the dark burgundy of her scales. "Everyone thinks I lost her while we were venom training, but I know it wasn't my fault." She stamped her talons on the wood platform and hissed at the skeptical look on the nearest dragon's face.

"So what happened to her?" Glory asked.

The burgundy dragon flung her wings up. "I don't know. Maybe she ran off. She's a terrible student and a pain in the tail. I just want to be cleared so I can have my assignment back."

"Poor Bromeliad. If you have no assignment, that means last choice of sun-time spots and only leftovers at feeding time," the pale orange dragon explained to Glory. "It's not a lot of fun."

"You must also want to find her," Glory said to Bromeliad. "Aren't you worried?"

"She'll show up eventually," said Bromeliad, flipping her burgundy tail back and forth.

Assuming she's still alive, Glory thought. "If you're both here about missing dragons," she said, "wouldn't it make sense to see the queen together?"

Bromeliad and Mangrove blinked at each other, considering.

"NEXT!" called the voice again. The first dragon emerged and flew away, and the orange dragon hauled her dragonet across the bridge into the treehouse.

"There could be totally different explanations," Mangrove said. "I'm sure something terrible happened to Orchid."

"And I'm pretty sure Kinkajou ran off to spite me," said Bromeliad.

"Still," Glory said. "I mean, it makes no difference to me. But maybe she'd listen to two dragons more than she'd listen to one."

Bromeliad glanced at the three dragons in the line between her and Mangrove. One was fast asleep, and the other two seemed to be half listening, half watching butterflies.

"NEXT!"

"Come on," Mangrove said, reaching back and hauling Bromeliad up with him. "And you, too," he said to Glory.

"Wait here," Glory called to her friends. Clay looked up with melons stuffed in each cheek. As she hurried over the walkway after the RainWings, Glory heard Tsunami starting to protest and then the voices of Starflight and Sunny hushing her.

The hanging vines of yellow flowers smelled like honey and vanilla. They swished against Glory's snout as she pushed through into the sunlit room beyond.

To her surprise, there were no guards — no soldiers protecting the queen, no heralds announcing each arrival. The only dragon in the room was Queen Magnificent herself, curled on a sort of nest made from lacy scarlet flowers and scraps of russet monkey fur. The queen was as large as Coral, but personally Glory thought she was a lot more impressive. Instead of gaudy ropes of pearls, Magnificent wore only a few garlands of the white dragonfly-wing flowers, which set off the iridescent brightness of her shifting scales.

Settled under one of her wings was a silvery gray sloth much like the one on Glory's back. It made a welcoming "yerp!" noise, and Glory's sloth burbled in response.

The queen flicked the point of her tail and leaned forward

to sniff at Glory. Her green eyes were friendly and a little sleepy-looking.

"You're new," she said cheerfully. "Aren't you? How exciting. I like new things."

"It's my turn," Mangrove insisted. "This dragonet just wanted to watch."

"All right," said Queen Magnificent, as if she wasn't that curious anyway. She turned to Mangrove and Bromeliad and wrinkled her snout to look like she was listening. "Go ahead."

"You know why I'm here," said Mangrove. "Orchid is still missing! It's been three weeks! We have to go looking for her!"

"Orchid," said the queen, tapping her chin thoughtfully. "Of course. Still missing. *Orc*hid."

"I come to you about this every day," Mangrove said. "Remember? We were fruit gathering and she disappeared?"

"Mmmm-hmmm," said the queen. "What about you?"

Bromeliad shook out her wings. "My student Kinkajou ran off during a venom training session and hasn't come back. I want the blame lifted from me so I can go back to my regular life."

"How long ago was this?" the queen asked.

"About eighteen days," said Bromeliad. "She's no one's favorite dragonet, I might add."

"All right, then," said the queen. "You may start training again."

"Thank you," said Bromeliad with a bow, backing toward the door.

"Hang on," Glory said. "Not that it means anything to me, but isn't anyone worried that two dragons disappeared within a few days of each other?"

"Did they?" said the queen. She curled her front talons around her sloth and stroked its head. "They'll probably turn up. Dragons usually do."

"Not lately," Mangrove said. "We have twelve dragons missing from our village right now, including Orchid and Kinkajou."

"Twelve," murmured the queen. "Someone's been counting? Who has that kind of energy?" She yawned and looked at her claws.

There was an awkward pause. Bromeliad shuffled a few steps closer to the door. Mangrove coiled his tail tightly around his talons and glared at the queen.

"Um," Glory said. "Look. Again, this is none of my business, but maybe someone should investigate. Like, find out if they all disappeared from the same general area. Or if they have anything in common. Or if they left any clues behind."

"All right," the queen said genially. "Sounds tiring. Who wants to do that?"

Glory looked at Mangrove, but he was already pointing at her. "She should do it," he said. "She seems like she has useful questions."

"Splendid," said the queen. "Let's do that. Problem solved. NEXT!"

"Wait," Glory said. "I don't do stuff like this. And I'm

kind of busy with other things." *Well, I guess that depends. Saving the world and stopping the war is what the dragonets in the prophecy are supposed to do, and I'm not actually in the prophecy. But I guess if I accept my regular RainWing destiny, then there's absolutely nothing I have to do.*

Tag along on someone else's destiny, or settle for a future as a snoozing dingbat. Fantastic choices you've left me with, Talons of Peace.

Mangrove and Bromeliad had already swept out the door. Glory started to follow them and then jumped back as Tsunami burst in, followed by the other dragonets. Clay and Starflight had their shoulders under Webs's wings and their guardian was staggering like his tail was about to fall off.

"Ooooo!" said the queen, perking up. "You're *all* new!"

"What about —" Glory glanced out at the waiting platform and saw that the other three dragons were gone.

"We convinced them that our situation was an emergency," Starflight said. "Well, Sunny did."

Sunny beamed.

"Greetings, Queen of the RainWings!" Starflight said grandly. He swept his wings out and bowed low.

"Ooooo," the queen said again.

"We have come to you despite great peril, in a time of crisis, to throw ourselves upon your merciful —"

"We need your help," Tsunami said.

Magnificent's wings drooped a little. "Oh dear," she said. "Do I have to do something?"

"This is Webs," Sunny said, tugging on his talon to lead him forward. She pointed to the venomous gash near his tail, and Queen Magnificent made a disapproving "tsk" noise.

"That is very ugly," the queen observed.

"It sure is," said Glory. "Also, it's killing him. Minor detail."

"Your dragons know about poison," Tsunami said. "We need someone who can help us cure him."

"That doesn't look like something one of us did," said the queen. "We never use our venom on other dragons!"

All of the dragonets shot sideways looks at Glory. She narrowed her eyes back at them. *I dare you to tell her what I've done to save your stupid scales.*

"It's not RainWing venom," Starflight said hastily. "He was scratched by a SandWing's tail barb."

"Oh," said the queen. "I don't know anything about those." She took a deep breath to yell "NEXT!," but Sunny interrupted before she could.

"Oh, please, you must have healers," she pleaded. "Someone who could look at it? Please? We don't want him to die."

"Well, some of us don't," Glory muttered.

Queen Magnificent tapped her claws on the treehouse floor. Her sloth seized one of her talons and tried to gnaw on it.

"We do have healers," said the queen, rolling her sloth playfully onto its back. "I guess you could talk to them. They're about twelve tree lodges down from here, in the one with the red berries growing on the balcony." She pointed out one of the windows. "They might not be able to do anything, but you may ask."

"Thank you," Sunny said, backing toward the door.

"And don't forget to report back to me on that investigation," Magnificent said to Glory. "It'll be nice to have something to make Mangrove go away. What's your name, anyhow?"

"Glory," she answered. "I was stolen from the RainWings by this dragon six years ago, when I was still an egg." Glory pointed at Webs.

"Oh, my," said the queen. "That is rude. Well, I'm glad he finally brought you back, dear."

"He did nothing of the sort!" Glory flared. "I brought myself back! He was going to let me die!"

"Glory," Tsunami interrupted with a frown. "What are you doing?"

I don't know, Glory thought. *Maybe I just want someone to be punished for everything I've been through . . . and the fact that nobody here even noticed I was gone.*

She took a deep breath and forced all the dark rolling red and billowing orange out of her scales until she was a calm white, like the blossoms around the queen's neck.

"Nothing," she said to Tsunami. "Whatever. I just figured Magnificent would want to know what happened to me. But she doesn't, and who really cares, anyway." Glory bowed to the queen and stepped over to the door. "You all go see the healers. I'm going to start looking for the missing dragons." She pushed through the yellow flower curtain.

Because someone should care when a dragon disappears.

CHAPTER 8

Halfway across the bridge, Glory heard Clay's voice behind her.

"Wait," he called. His heavy talons thumped on the walkway, making it shake and jump underneath her. "What missing dragons?"

"Some big scary thing is prowling the rainforest," Glory said. She resettled her wings. "Or, at least, something is making RainWings disappear. Probably the same something that killed those MudWings. I'll figure out what. No big deal. I'll catch up with you all afterward."

"We don't all have to escort Webs everywhere," Clay said with a smile. "I'll come with you. And we'll bring Starflight, too. Maybe we can help. Starflight!" he called. The NightWing poked his nose out through the hanging flowers. "Let Tsunami and Sunny take Webs. You come with us."

Glory shrugged, but her wing tips turned rose pink against her will. At least there were a couple of dragons who cared if she existed. After all, the only reason she was still alive was because Clay had been willing to risk his life in the underground river to save her.

The golden sunlight was slanting sideways through the tall green trees. As Glory, Clay, and Starflight glided between the branches, small whirlwinds of orange and blue butterflies lifted off and landed again behind them. Funny-faced little monkeys with long tails chattered indignantly when the dragons swooped by.

They found Mangrove on a small platform by himself, sorting fruit. Glory landed lightly in the middle, while Clay perched on the edge and tried to keep his feet and tail from squashing any of the berries. Starflight found a nearby branch and studied the fruit as if he were trying to match it with pictures from the scrolls he'd memorized.

The red streaks in Mangrove's ruff had been replaced by whorls of dark purple. He looked up and nodded brusquely at Glory.

"You got me into this," Glory said. "So I'm starting with you, since you might be the only dragon who even knows about all the missing RainWings. Who was the first to disappear?"

Mangrove put down a banana and looked up at the sky, thinking. "It must have been Splendor," he said. "She'd just finished her turn as queen and passed it to Dazzling."

"Whoa," Clay said. "There's a queen missing?"

"Well, she wasn't queen that month," Mangrove pointed out. "And when she didn't come back, they just started skipping her turn. If she wanted it, they figured she'd show up for it."

"Was anyone with her when she went missing?" Glory asked. She felt the sloth circle and settle around her neck again. She kept forgetting it was there; it felt like a warm floppy necklace when it wasn't moving.

Mangrove shook his head. "Not as far as I know. I noticed she was gone only when her turn came back around and she wasn't there. But I can guess when she went missing because her sloth found someone else to live with right around then."

Glory tapped her claws on the platform and thought about the SeaWing court, where politics and intrigue and betrayal all simmered below the surface. Not to mention the SandWings, where three sisters were tearing apart the entire dragon world in their fight for power.

"Maybe one of the other queens took her out," she suggested. "Maybe Dazzling or someone wanted a longer turn or less competition." Starflight nodded as if he'd had the same thought.

Mangrove's ears popped faintly yellow and then back to purple again. "Nothing like that changed," he said. "The turns are the same length, one month each. And there were only six dragons in the tribe willing to be queen in any case — now five — so none of them have to wait very long in between. Besides, nobody enjoys being queen."

"Can I eat this?" Clay asked, poking a rubbery red sphere near his claws.

"If you must," said Mangrove. Clay scooped it into his mouth and started chewing with a startled expression.

"Who disappeared after Splendor?" Glory asked.

"Two dragons who were out venom training," said Mangrove. "One of them was having trouble aiming his venom properly, so the other took him away from the village to practice, and neither of them came back."

"Kinkajou was working on her venom, too," Glory said. "Is there a particular spot where RainWings go to do that?"

Mangrove shook his head. "Wherever the venom trainers choose."

"Mshish vemmy shmewy," Clay mumbled around the fruit in his jaws.

"Yes, those fruits are," said Mangrove. "It'll probably take you an hour to swallow it and then several days to pick the bits out of your teeth."

"Ha," Starflight said. "Let's take a few back for Tsunami."

Glory hid her smile, trying to look responsible and investigative. "What else can you tell me about the missing dragons?" she asked Mangrove. "How many females, how many dragonets, stuff like that?"

Mangrove counted on his claws. "Seven females, five males. Four dragonets under the age of seven. Kinkajou is three, so she'd be the youngest, and Tapir is the oldest; he's around a hundred and ten."

"Do any of them have any enemies in the tribe?" Glory asked. "Anyone who'd wish them harm?"

Mangrove drew himself up, and bolts of orange flashed along the underside of his wings. "RainWings don't ever fight each other," he said. "There's no such thing as enemies within the tribe. Haven't you noticed how peaceful and harmonious everyone is?"

"Well, sure," Glory said. "Everyone but you. *You* seem a little grumpy. So apparently it's at least *possible* to be a grumpy RainWing."

He stared at her for a moment with his mouth open. *Whoops*, Glory thought. *I hope I didn't just lose my best source of information.*

"I mean," she added, "there's nothing wrong with that. *I'm* pretty grumpy most of the time."

"*Most* of the time?" said Starflight.

"Mmmm-hmmph," Clay mumble-agreed.

"Some things just deserve being grumpy at," Glory said, frowning at her friends.

Mangrove let out a bark of laughter. "All right. You're right. I guess I've been neglecting my sun time since Orchid went missing," he said. "I used to be as cheerful as everyone else, but I'm worried about her." He rubbed one talon over his ruff and ears. "Trust me, Orchid was perfection in every scale. No one could possibly want to hurt her."

That's what I was afraid of, Glory thought. If another RainWing wasn't behind the abductions, then it had to be something more mysterious — and more dangerous. She couldn't help thinking of the dead MudWing soldiers.

But what was dangerous and strong enough to kill dragons, and why didn't anyone know it was out there?

She glanced at Starflight, but he looked as puzzled as she was.

"I don't really want to talk about this anymore right now," said Mangrove, hunching his shoulders.

"Then do something else for us," Glory said. "Take me to the last place you saw Orchid."

Mangrove bowed his head, shuffled the unsorted fruit into a lopsided pile, and spread his wings. Glory and the others followed him over the edge and rapidly down in giant loops toward the rainforest floor.

It grew darker the farther down they went, with the sunlight caught in the treetops far above their heads. Glory watched the forest for signs they could use to follow the trail back — a toppled banana tree here, a spiderweb as large as one of her wings there. She caught glimpses of other creatures in the undergrowth. A large furry anteater had its nose buried in a hole, rummaging around. A pair of long-legged lavender-colored birds paused in their stroll through the forest to shoot suspicious looks at the dragons whisking by.

Glory was surprised at how far they flew from the village.

"Isn't there fruit to gather closer to home?" she called.

Mangrove nodded and twisted his head around to glance back at her. "Orchid and I like to search farther out in case we find something new. The rainforest is full of surprises — we find a new kind of fruit at least once a year."

He landed beside a giant fallen tree, overgrown with moss and vines. The undergrowth around his talons erupted as lizards and insects scurried busily away. Several bug-eyed sky-blue frogs peeked out from the branches of the fallen tree, flicking their tongues in and out just like dragons.

"Don't eat any of those," Mangrove warned Clay, seeing the MudWing's gaze following the frogs.

"Stmmph chmmphing," Clay mumbled, pointing to his jaws, where the red fruit appeared to be stuck.

"Are they poisonous?" Starflight asked. He poked the branches, but the frogs stared at him like "Oh, yeah? Bring it, you big lizard."

"No," Mangrove said, "but they will give you the weirdest hallucinations about insects for about a week. Really not worth it."

"So Orchid disappeared around here?" Glory asked. "Do you know if Kinkajou was in this area as well?"

Mangrove shrugged. "Possibly. Bromeliad likes as much privacy as possible for training her more difficult pupils, so no one else will see her yelling at them."

Glory turned slowly, studying the forest around them. She could hear monkeys and birds chittering in the trees overhead. Wings flapped, twigs snapped, and claws rustled in the bushes. The air smelled like mangoes and wet leaves, as if there were a pond or waterfall nearby. And there was another scent, too, a horrible one, underneath the others.

"Starflight," she said. "What do you smell?" She'd noticed that his nose seemed stronger than the other dragonets' — he'd been the first to smell fire when the SkyWings attacked the SeaWing Summer Palace. Maybe it was a NightWing skill.

The black dragon inhaled slowly, then wrinkled his snout. "Something decaying," he said. "Like a dying animal."

Mangrove blanched from horns to tail, turning a pale sickly green.

"Don't panic," Glory said quickly. "I'm sure it's not her. It's not a dragon, right, Starflight?"

"I'm not sure," he said, lifting his snout and sniffing again. She stamped on his foot and he jumped with a yowl of pain. "WHAT? I can't tell!"

"We'll go find it," Glory said to Mangrove. "You stay here."

The RainWing leaned against the fallen tree with a stricken expression.

"Couldn't you be a *little* reassuring?" Glory hissed at Starflight once they were out of earshot. "Didn't you see his scales?"

"Since when do you care how other dragons feel?" he asked.

"I care better than you do," she countered. "Maybe if you had actual NightWing powers and could read minds you'd notice what's going on around you."

"*HMMP. QUMP FFMPHING,*" Clay ordered from behind them.

Starflight folded his wings close to his body and glared at her.

"Well?" Glory demanded. "Can you follow the smell or not?"

He turned and stamped off through the trees.

"Nnnmph vmmy nnnmph," Clay said to Glory sternly.

"Aw, your lectures are even cuter when I can't understand a word of them," she teased.

He gave her shoulder a playful shove that nearly sent her through the nearest tree.

When they caught up to Starflight, the NightWing was standing next to a small waterfall, as high as Clay's shoulder, that splashed into a tiny pond. A stream no wider than a dragon tail burbled at the top of the waterfall and away from the pond at the bottom. Thick brownish weeds choked the slimy surface of the pond, and a dead fish floated in the shallows.

The top of the waterfall was flanked by a pair of tall dark trees, as fat around as the columns where SkyWing prisoners were kept. Their trunks were so brown that they were nearly black, and their branches began far overhead, so they looked more like black pillars than trees.

The closest one had a boulder leaning up against it that was twice the size of Morrowseer. On the same side of the waterfall, at the base, halfway into the pond, lay a furry, wheezing sloth, although it took Glory a moment to figure out what it was through the cloud of flies around it. The terrible smell was thick in the air.

"Rrrrrrp?" said Glory's sloth, leaning around her neck to peer at the one on the ground. Glory lifted her wing to block the gruesome sight from her new pet.

"What's wrong with it?" Glory asked. She inched toward the gasping sloth and realized that it had a serious bite on one leg. The wound was black and crawling with insects; it looked even worse than Webs's injury.

"I'm not entirely sure," said Starflight. "I mean, that bite shouldn't have been enough to kill it, but it's clearly dying."

"Could it be RainWing venom?" Glory asked. "It looks about the size of a dragon bite." Her sloth started chirruping in a tragic, distressed way. She slid it off her neck and held it to her chest, facing away from the sloth on the ground. It was comforting to feel its silky fur under her talons.

"Maybe," Starflight said doubtfully. "But it looks like something slower-acting to me. I'd guess it's been dying for several days."

"It does smell awful," Glory said. "Poor thing."

Clay crouched beside the sloth and lifted its leg carefully in his talons, inspecting it as if he were hoping to find a way to fix it. The flies zipped angrily around his snout with loud buzzes of outrage. The dying sloth whimpered softly.

Glory stepped around them and ventured up the slope to the pillar tree. Something about the boulder looked weird to her. It leaned almost too casually against the tree, as if it had been set there on purpose.

She circled around to the other side and stopped, staring.

There was a hole in the boulder.

More than a hole — a doorway.

CHAPTER 9

Glory wasn't quite sure how she knew this was not an ordinary hole in a rock. It *looked* like a hole — dark, with smooth stone edges, and just big enough for a full-grown dragon to pass through. A moss curtain partly covered it in a way that didn't look quite accidental enough.

But looking into it made her head spin, as if she were standing on the edge of a cliff in high winds. A faint sound whistled out of the hole, like a storm howling on the far side of the world.

She could sense that this hole opened into a tunnel, and that tunnel *went* somewhere. It was impossible; she could walk all the way around the boulder, and there was nowhere for a tunnel to go. But she was sure of it.

"Starflight," she said as calmly as she could. "What do you think of this?"

The NightWing climbed up beside her, peered around the boulder, and jumped back when he saw the hole. A tremor shivered through his wings.

"I think it's horrible," he said. "Can't you feel it? There's something horribly wrong with it. Like someone ripped a hole where there shouldn't be one. Don't go near it."

"I think I have to go into it," Glory said.

"You say that like you're not terrified," Starflight said, "but I can see your scales turning the same pale green that Mangrove's just were. That means frightened, doesn't it?"

"Don't try to read my scales," Glory snapped. She deliberately turned herself as black as he was. "It's not a coincidence that this hole is here, close to where at least one dragon disappeared. Maybe Orchid went through — or maybe something came out and got her."

"Um, exactly," Starflight said. "And she was never seen again. I'm pretty sure you just made my point for me."

"I promised I'd figure this out," Glory insisted. "Not run and hide the moment we found a clue."

Clay joined them, his wings drooping. His jaws were finally free of the rubbery red fruit. "There was nothing I could do for the sloth," he said. "It was too far gone."

"Wrrrrrrb," said Glory's sloth mournfully. Glory looked over Clay's shoulder at the still, silvery gray figure flopped on the ground.

"Is it dead?" she whispered.

He nodded. "I didn't want to leave it in pain like that."

"But you're not going to eat it?" She tilted her head at him.

"Seems a little heartless, you know?" he said.

"And from the smell of it, it would probably make you sick," Starflight pointed out. "I wonder what bit it, and whether it has any connection to this hole."

Clay noticed the hole for the first time and flared his wings in surprise. "Creepy!" he yelped. "Why is it so creepy?"

"Glory wants to go in there," Starflight said, rolling his eyes.

Clay stalked up to the hole, sniffed it, and nodded thoughtfully. "Yeah, we probably have to."

"No, we don't!" Starflight cried. He curled his wings in toward his body. "That's insane! There could be anything lurking in there!"

"Including the answer to what is attacking the RainWings," Glory said. "I'm going in. You two wait here."

Clay pounced on her tail and sat on it.

"OW," Glory yelped, trying to wriggle free. "Get off, you giant lump."

"We might be doing this, but we're doing it sensibly," Clay said. "As in tomorrow morning, when it's not almost dark, with backup and a rope and a plan."

"Tomorrow morning?" Glory shoved him as hard as she could, but he didn't budge. "I want answers now!"

"Sounds like something Tsunami would say," Starflight said with a smug face that meant he knew she wouldn't like that comparison.

"You are so asking to get bitten," Glory growled. She stared at the boulder for a moment, thinking. Rushing in *was* the Tsunami thing to do. Glory could be sensible and patient instead. "All right, we can wait until morning, but I'm staying right here to watch this hole."

"I don't think it's going anywhere," Starflight said patronizingly.

"Yeah, but maybe I'll see something go into it," Glory said. "Or come out."

Starflight backed away from the hole in a hurry, his wings twitching nervously.

"I'll stay with you," Clay said. "Starflight, bring the others back here in the morning, along with the longest, strongest vines you can find."

"And tell Mangrove we'll be here all night, so he can go home," Glory said. "Try to be a little sympathetic, if you can muster that. Like, please point out that we haven't found Orchid's dead body or anything."

"All right," Starflight said, taking several more steps back. "Don't do anything stupid while I'm gone."

"We'll try to contain ourselves," said Glory.

He flew off into the trees, and as the shadows quickly swallowed him up, she noticed how dark it was already. Especially down at the bottom of the forest; there was probably still a bit of sunshine up in the treetops. But night was coming on fast. She realized she was a bit relieved that Clay had stopped her from going into the hole. She needed to be able to see in the dark like Tsunami or breathe fire like the others if she wanted to explore with no light.

"You can get off my tail now," she said to Clay.

"Let's find a place to hide," he suggested, standing up. "Ooooo, and maybe something to eat. Are you hungry? I'm hungry."

"Shocking," Glory said with a laugh. "You know there's

still enough of that fruit left stuck to your teeth to make a whole other meal."

"I know," Clay said ruefully. He ran his tongue across the gummy red bits stuck between his white teeth. "But I kind of wish I had a sheep or a cow instead."

"Sorry," Glory said. "You probably won't find any of those here." She spread her wings and leaped into the low branches of a fat gray tree. Vines covered in purple blossoms hung in long loops all over the tree, and another, skinnier tree seemed to be growing up around the fat one, winding its trunk around and around it like a monkey's tail.

They found a spot where the branches wove together thickly enough that they could both lie down without worrying about falling off. Through the vines, Glory could watch the hole in the boulder, although it, too, was rapidly disappearing into the growing shadows.

Clay curled up close to her but not touching her, which she appreciated. She wondered if other RainWings preferred not to be touched, or if that was a special thing of her own, picked up from living with three guardians who hit her almost as often as they looked at her.

Let's be fair, she thought to herself. *Webs never hurt me himself. He just let the other two do whatever they wanted.*

So whenever Kestrel or Dune felt frustrated — whenever the war was going badly, or someone screwed up in battle training, or there wasn't enough dinner for everyone, or they just remembered they had a RainWing instead of the SkyWing who was supposed to be in the prophecy — Glory was an easy target for an angry claw swipe or vicious tail thump.

Well, whatever, she thought. *I'm free now, and Kestrel and Dune are both dead.* She reached up and stroked the sloth curled around her neck. It snuggled into her talon with a soft warble.

"How does it feel to be home?" Clay whispered after a while. His shape was just a blacker outline in the dark beside her.

Glory coiled her tail around the branch. She'd been avoiding thinking about this ever since visiting the hatchery. *I did exactly what I told myself not to — got my hopes up so they could be smacked down.*

"It doesn't really feel like I *am* home," she said slowly. "The sun time was great, and I like all the fruit, but the other dragons . . . I don't know, it's weird. I thought they'd be more like me, but they're nothing like me at all."

Clay's wings rustled. "I thought the same thing," he said. "I thought the guardians and the scrolls must be wrong about RainWings, because you're never lazy or boring. But I guess you're just different from the others."

"Maybe I'm not really," Glory said. "Maybe more sun time would make me as lazy as they are." She remembered the Sky Kingdom again, and the warm, hypnotizing feeling of sleeping in the sun all day long.

"I doubt that," Clay said. "Not all RainWings are the same. You'd be different no matter where you grew up."

I wonder, Glory thought. *And even if I am, what good does that do me?* "Not different enough to be part of the prophecy," she said. "I'm still not a SkyWing."

"We don't want a SkyWing," Clay said firmly. "Have you thought about what to do next? Like if we all go look for Blaze . . . you don't want to stay here, do you? With your tribe?"

I have no idea.

"Shhh," Glory said suddenly. "Listen."

They both fell silent.

The rainforest was full of strange noises at night. Hidden birds hooted and squawked; the branches shook and rustled as if animals made of wind were rushing through them. A chorus of burps and gurgles came from the stream, which Glory guessed was a gathering of frogs.

But now there was something else — something stamping slowly on enormous feet.

Stamp. Slither. Stamp. Slither.

The sloth had a stranglehold on Glory's neck. She could feel it shaking. She was sure her own scales were turning green with fear, and she had to force all her energy into staying black.

The something made a sniffing, snorting sound.

Slither. Slither.

It was near the pond now. It stopped moving for a long moment. Glory wasn't sure whether she was imagining the great hulking shape she thought she could see, like shadows within shadows.

Crunch crunch slurp sluuuuuuurrrp crunch.

Gulping and smacking sounds followed and then abruptly stopped again.

Stamp. Slither. Stamp. Slither.

And as suddenly as it had arrived, the creature vanished again. Glory strained her ears, but she couldn't hear any footsteps retreating into the forest, or the crackling of branches underfoot. Whatever it was had disappeared very close by.

As if it had gone back into its hole.

Neither she nor Clay said anything for a long time. She wasn't sure enough that the slithering thing was gone to risk making any noise. She held as still as she could, even when her legs started to cramp.

After what seemed like hours, she heard soft snoring coming from Clay's perch. She adjusted her wings and tried to sleep, too. But every noise made her heart thump fiercely, and all she could do was swim in and out of a drowsy haze for the rest of the night.

It was a relief when the sun finally started to drift down through the leaves again. She sat up, rubbed her tired eyes, and glanced toward the pond and the boulder.

The dead sloth was gone. All that remained were a few tufts of gray fur and some blood-spattered leaves, soaking into the wet, wet ground.

— CHAPTER 10 —

By the time the other dragonets arrived, Glory had wiped out any trace of green fear from her scales. She waited by the boulder, her wings speckled gray like the stone, as they swooped down to join her. Sunny jumped up to hug Clay's neck as soon as she saw him.

"How's Webs?" Clay asked.

Tsunami snorted. "I don't think these 'healers' have seen anything worse than a sprained wing or a stubbed claw before," she said. "They're doing a lot of peering at the scratch and muttering."

"But I'm sure he'll be fine," Sunny said. "The RainWings are trying their best." She turned and caught Tsunami rolling her eyes behind her back. Sunny frowned. "They are."

"Sunny, you think everyone's always trying their best," Tsunami pointed out.

The little SandWing huffed a small snort of flame. "So? Everyone is! Why wouldn't they be?"

"Yes, dear," Tsunami said, not unkindly.

"Halloooooo!" a voice interrupted. A pink comet streaked through the trees and thudded down beside the dragonets.

Glory jumped back and flared her ruff at Jambu as he bowed to all of them, grinning.

"What are *you* doing here?" she asked.

"I heard what you were up to, and it sounded like fun," he said brightly. "So I took the day off to see if I could help. Brother and sister, working as a team! Awesome, right?" He craned his neck to see the hole in the boulder behind her. "Oh, *freaky* thing! No wonder it feels so weird in this part of the forest! Most of the RainWings avoid coming anywhere near this pond. But no one's ever reported a mystery hole before, I don't think. So what's the plan?"

"The plan is I go in," Glory said. "And everyone else waits here."

Well, nobody liked that plan. Tsunami wanted to go first; Clay wanted to go together; Starflight was still in favor of not going in at all. Even Jambu started whining about not wanting to be left behind.

Glory folded her tail over her talons and waited for them to shut up.

Sunny sidled up to her. "Maybe we could compromise," Sunny suggested quietly. "Maybe you could take someone with you. Someone with fire, maybe, who could help you with the darkness in there."

Unfortunately, that was a good point. Glory didn't love the idea of blundering into total darkness alone, and if she was right, and it was a tunnel, there was no way to know how long it was or how lost she could get.

"Like, maybe —" Sunny started to say.

"All right!" Glory shouted, silencing the others. "All right, fine, different plan. Clay and I go in first and see what's in there."

Sunny looked disappointed. Glory wasn't sure why; she was doing exactly what the SandWing had suggested.

"What about me?" Tsunami said, bristling.

"You hold the other end of the vines," Clay said. "If we yank on them three times, it means we're in trouble, so either pull us out or, if you can't, come in and get us."

Glory didn't love the idea of having a vine tied around her shoulders, but she was outvoted. As Starflight tightened the knots, she untangled her sloth and passed it to Sunny.

"Here," she said. "Watch Silver for me while I'm gone?"

"Aww," Sunny said, brightening. "Pretty name."

Glory hadn't meant to say it out loud. She didn't want the others to notice that she was starting to like the weird little mammal. "Well, you can call it whatever you want," she said.

"Hrrrrgle," the sloth disagreed, but it flopped across Sunny's back with a blissful expression. *It must like the SandWing warmth of her scales*, Glory realized. *What if it doesn't want to come back to me?* She shook out her wings. *Then it'll be Sunny's problem, I guess.*

"Let's go catch a monster," she said to Clay.

"Remember, three tugs," Clay said to Tsunami. He squared his shoulders and marched up to the boulder alongside Glory. She knew he must be remembering the awful noises and dark creature from the night before, too. She was glad he'd followed her lead of not telling the others about it. Starflight didn't need another reason to try to stop her from going into the hole.

"Let me go in first," Clay whispered. "So I can light the way."

Glory nodded reluctantly, and he stepped forward into the darkness. She followed right away, nearly stepping on his tail.

He breathed out a plume of flame, and they saw a stone tunnel stretching ahead of them, then turning abruptly to the right.

"That's impossible," Clay whispered. "This tunnel is much longer than the boulder. And it's not going down into the ground . . ."

"Some kind of magic?" Glory guessed. "Maybe animus magic?" Glory couldn't think of anything else that could have made a tunnel like this. Unless there were mystery creatures with powers similar to animus dragons.

When she was four years old, she'd gone through a phase of reading all the animus dragon stories and hoping she was one, so that she could enchant Dune's dinner to eat *him*. Of course, no powers had ever manifested, and it was probably lucky they hadn't, given what they'd learned about that kind of magic from Tsunami's sister Anemone in the Kingdom of the Sea.

On the one talon, the ability to manipulate and enchant any physical object, Glory thought. *On the other, say good-bye to your soul.*

She squeezed past Clay and set off down the tunnel. He stayed close enough to brush her wings with his snout.

"I thought the scrolls said there hasn't been an animus dragon in generations," Clay said, scratching his head. "But between Queen Coral's daughters and this being here, I guess I remembered wrong."

"No, that is what the scrolls said — but remember, that was in the histories written by NightWings," Glory said. "NightWings can't stand animus dragons because animus power is much cooler than what they can do, and NightWings would rather be the only magically powerful dragons out there. So maybe they lied."

"Or they didn't know that it runs in the SeaWing royal family," Clay said. "Or perhaps any dragons who do have animus power make sure to keep it hidden so they won't be forced to use it, like, for the war or something." He breathed out another spurt of fire, and they saw the turn a few steps ahead of them.

"This tunnel might not be an animus thing either," Glory said. "Maybe there's some other kind of creature who can do this type of magic."

Clay didn't answer, but she felt the shiver that ran through his wings.

At the turn, Glory leaned forward to glance around the corner. Even before Clay could use his fire, she saw light — enough light to realize the tunnel turned again to the left, and that was where the light was coming from.

They crept to the next corner and peered around it.

Another long tunnel stretched ahead of them, and at the end of it waited an outline of bright sunlight — much too bright for the floor of the rainforest.

Clay and Glory exchanged glances.

"Did we miss something?" she whispered. "I thought this tunnel would be much longer. Also that it would have, you know, a monster in it."

"It must have come from out there," Clay said, nodding at the circle of sunshine.

They slid along the tunnel, keeping an eye out for hidden entrances, but as far as Glory could tell, there were none. There were only the long, smooth stone walls leading to that brightness, which got more and more blinding the closer they came.

She paused at the doorway, blinking, and realized that sand was piled up outside as high as her shoulders, nearly blocking the exit. She dug into it, shoving sand aside until there was a hole big enough to crawl through, then poked her head out.

The sun beat down on her scales, but not in the same way that it did in the rainforest treetops or in the Claws of the Clouds Mountains. Here the heat was dry as ancient bones, sucking all the moisture out of her scales, and there was no breeze that she could feel.

Grains of sand trickled between her talons. As her eyes adjusted, she realized that the sand stretched, endless and pale, to the horizon ahead of her. There were no trees. The sky was aggressively blue and cloudless. A sickly stench of death hung faintly in the air. There was nothing but desert as far as the eye could see.

Clay squished himself up beside her and stuck his nose out into the blazing heat.

"Yowch," he said.

Glory's ears twitched. Out in the sky, a pair of tiny dark shapes appeared, approaching fast.

"Hide," Glory ordered, shoving Clay back into the tunnel. Throwing off the vine rope, she wriggled out of the hole. She stretched her talons across the sand and focused on her scales, watching them blur quickly into the pale brown-gold-white colors. Camouflaged, she stared up at the approaching dragons.

They were two SandWings, swooping lower as they got closer. For an uneasy moment, Glory thought they must have seen her. But they whooshed past without even glancing down, and she realized they were aiming at something beyond and behind her.

Moving cautiously, Glory crept out another few steps and turned around.

On this side, the hole was hidden in a dune surrounded by a semicircle of dull green cacti. Each cactus was half as tall as a full-grown dragon, with tiny thorns as sharp as fangs. A few dusty white flowers bloomed between the prickles.

Beyond the cactus sentries, the dunes slanted down to an enormous structure in the distance. The two SandWings spiraled into it, vanishing behind the thick sandstone walls.

There were no windows that Glory could see. There was only the solid block shape, like a monstrous brick dropped on the sand.

Wait, she thought. There was *something* dotting the top of the walls — small dark shapes at regular intervals, fluttering now and then in the very slight breaths of wind.

She squinted, trying to process what she could see. It looked like . . . but it couldn't be . . .

She closed her eyes abruptly and clutched her stomach. It was. She remembered the scroll now where she'd read a description of this place.

The dark shapes were dragon heads. The heads of dragons who had been executed and mounted where everyone could see them, to remind others of the dangers of disobedience. According to the scroll, you could smell them for miles in all directions.

Glory knew where she was now.

She was standing in the Kingdom of Sand, within sight of Burn's stronghold.

PART TWO
SAND, ICE, AND SMOKE

── CHAPTER 11 ──

Burn's stronghold had once been the original SandWing palace. That was where all the trouble had started. Glory flattened herself against the sand and stared at it, remembering the history Webs had taught them.

Eighteen years ago, Queen Oasis had ruled the SandWings from here. Her three daughters, Burn, Blister, and Blaze, had been minor dragons, footnotes in the scrolls of the time. Oasis was old, fierce, and canny, with a vast and impressive treasury. No one expected her to be challenged for many years yet.

And certainly no one would ever have expected a puny treasure-hunting scavenger to kill her, but that was exactly what had happened.

Now the treasure was gone, and the three sisters had drawn all the other tribes into their struggle for power. Eighteen years of bloodshed. Glory flicked her tail, concentrating on keeping her scales the color of the sand.

Burn had driven out the other two and kept the palace for herself — or, depending on which scrolls you read, Blister and Blaze had escaped before she could kill either of them.

They'd gone in search of allies, knowing that neither one could beat Burn on her own.

This wasn't how the palace had looked during the reign of Queen Oasis. Burn had added the thick walls . . . and, of course, the dragon heads on top of them.

Glory wondered if Burn was down there in her stronghold right now. Or was she in the Sky Kingdom, trying to hold on to her alliance after what Glory had done to Queen Scarlet?

The real questions were: Did she know about this passageway? And did she have anything to do with the missing RainWings?

"Glory," Clay hissed from the dark hole in the dune. "What's going on?"

Glory slid back down the hill to face him. "We're in the Kingdom of Sand," she said. "I have no idea how or why."

"What's that over there?" Clay asked, pointing north.

Glory turned and saw a wing of dragons flying high up in the sky. Their scales sparkled in the sunlight so that even from here she could guess that they were IceWings, white and pale blue as diamonds. From their angle of flight, they seemed to be returning from the Sky Kingdom to their own home on the frozen peninsula to the north.

"IceWings," Glory said. "We're not too far from the Ice Kingdom here." That was hard to imagine in this blistering heat, but she remembered it from the map on the wall of their underground cave.

"Oh," Clay said brightly, "so we could go find Blaze."

"Hooray," said Glory. She knew the others were hoping that Blaze would be a good candidate for queen, so they could choose her instead of Burn or Blister. But Glory's hopes weren't very high, based on what she'd read about Blaze.

Could Blaze or the IceWings have anything to do with this passageway to the rainforest?

But what had they heard in the middle of the night — and where had it gone?

"All right. Let's go tell the others," she said.

"But that is completely impossible," Starflight said for the millionth time. "The Kingdom of Sand is literally half a world away, on the other side of the *mountains*, for moons' sake. You couldn't have *walked* there down a tunnel in the rainforest."

"Go look for yourself," Glory snapped. "It's for real. Someone built a secret passage between here and SandWing territory." She dipped her tail in the stream, glad to be back in the coolness of the rainforest. Her scales felt as if she'd run through a fire. Silver sat on one of Glory's talons, dipped her paw in the water, and patted it against Glory's leg.

"But why?" Tsunami said. "What is the point?"

That, Glory couldn't answer. So they could sneak through and eat a sloth here or there? That made no sense. And what made even less sense was kidnapping RainWings.

"Do you think SandWings are coming through here to attack the MudWings?" Sunny asked hesitantly. "Maybe it was a SandWing who killed those soldiers."

"Seems like a roundabout way of doing things," Tsunami said. "If the SandWings have an animus, they could create a passage straight into MudWing territory or something more useful."

"I still think this passage has something to do with the missing RainWings," Glory said, "but I don't understand what. If they wandered into it by accident, they'd just come back, the way we did. If they were taken . . . what would SandWings or IceWings want with a few RainWings?"

"Burn likes collecting things," Starflight remembered.

"But you saw her face when Queen Scarlet was showing me off in the Sky Kingdom," Glory said. "Burn looked like she'd never seen a RainWing before. And she doesn't like pretty things; she likes horribly weird things. You're all so lucky you didn't see the creepy gift Queen Scarlet got for her when she came to visit. It was this dead stuffed crocodile with bat wings sewn on its back so it looked sort of like a dragon." She shuddered. "Totally hideous. But Burn loved it."

"And you don't know anything about this passage," Tsunami said to Jambu.

Glory's brother lifted his brightly colored wings, looking baffled. "I know the RainWings didn't put it there," he said. "Why would we want a way out of the rainforest? Life is perfect here."

"Unless you make the mistake of going missing, and then good luck, because no one's going to look for you," Glory pointed out.

"Well, maybe," Jambu said as if that were a perfectly normal problem for a dragon tribe to have. "But it's great for the rest of us."

Glory wondered what color his scales would turn if she bit him.

"Do you even have an animus dragon?" Starflight asked.

"What's that?" Jambu answered.

"Never mind," Glory said. "Do SandWings ever visit you? Or have you ever seen one in the forest?"

Jambu shook his head. "Don't think so. I don't even know what a SandWing looks like," he said.

"Me," Sunny said. "Sort of."

"But you've seen them in scrolls, right?" Starflight said.

"Scrolls," Jambu said. "Um. Those are . . . ?"

Starflight looked as if someone had just asked him whether breathing was really necessary. "You don't have any *scrolls*?" he gasped. "Don't you read? Do you really not read? Not anything?"

Jambu shrugged apologetically. "I'm not sure what you're talking about," he said.

Starflight had to sit down and fold his wings over his head for a minute.

Glory coiled her tail as Clay described SandWings for Jambu. Every new thing she learned about RainWings made them sound worse. A tribe without scrolls, who didn't care what was beyond their own borders? Why weren't they at least curious about the rest of the world? It made her want to shake all of them.

"Nope, doesn't sound familiar," Jambu said. "I'm pretty sure the only other-tribe visitors we've ever had looked like him." He pointed at Clay. "And they're usually lost and want to get out of the rainforest as fast as possible."

"Maybe we should destroy it," Sunny said unexpectedly.

They all turned to look at her. She shuffled her talons on the damp forest floor. "The passageway, I mean. It can't be here for anything good, right? I know I don't like the idea that Burn could pop out of there any minute. And if it's making RainWings disappear . . . well, who cares why? Let's just smash the boulder or stuff the tunnel full of trees and set them on fire or something."

Glory blinked.

It did sort of make sense. There was definitely something not right about this hole someone had ripped through normal space. Maybe destroying it would solve the problem — but Glory wanted to know the answer, too. There had to be a *why*.

Tsunami spoke first.

"I don't think that'll work. If there's someone, or some-*thing*, behind this, then wrecking their secret passage won't stop them. At least this way we have an advantage because we know about it."

"And what if the missing RainWings are alive on the other side?" Clay said. "What if there's a chance to save them?"

"Oh," Sunny said. "That's true."

"*I'm* not going into Burn's palace," Starflight said immediately. "No way." A monkey in the trees overhead dropped a nut, and Starflight jumped nervously aside as it tumbled down beside him.

"I will if I have to," Glory said. She should have been the one to think about saving the missing RainWings. If they were still alive, of course she had to help bring them home, even if she did think the whole tribe was empty-headed.

"But we don't know for sure that Burn is involved," Starflight pointed out. "It could certainly be the IceWings instead. We need to spend a lot more time gathering information — maybe spying on the stronghold and on the Ice Kingdom, charting their movements, studying the tunnel —"

Suddenly something much larger than a nut thudded out of the tree behind Starflight. The NightWing yelped and leaped out of the way as a bright green dragon galloped past him and dashed into the hole in the boulder.

"Hey!" Glory shouted.

"That was Mangrove," Jambu cried. "What is he doing?"

"He's going to look for Orchid." Glory tucked Silver into the nearest tree. "Wait here," she ordered the sloth. She folded her wings and ran into the tunnel after Mangrove.

"Mangrove!" she called as his tail whisked around the corner. "Come back! We're making a plan! Dopey freaking dragon," she added under her breath. Even the one RainWing she liked was a nimrod.

She shot around the last corner just in time to see him disappear out into the bright desert sunshine. By the time she burst out behind him and her eyes adjusted to the light, he was a green claw mark in the sky, flying away as fast as he could. A moment later, his scales shifted color, and he vanished against the blue.

Glory flapped her wings in frustration and sat down with a sigh.

One by one, her friends emerged from the tunnel.

"Oh, three *moons*," Tsunami said as the heat hit her scales. "It's *horrible* here."

Sunny stretched her wings wide and tilted her face up to the sun. "Wow," she whispered.

Starflight blinked and gazed around. "You're right," he said to Glory. "I can't believe it. This is really the Kingdom of Sand."

Jambu tumbled out behind them. "Where's Mangrove?" he asked.

"Did he head for Burn's stronghold?" Starflight guessed, shading his eyes to look in the direction of the faraway palace.

Glory shook her head and pointed north. "Nope," she said. "I don't think he even noticed it. Looks like we're off to the Ice Kingdom."

— CHAPTER 12 —

"This isn't safe at all!" Starflight called. "This is the opposite of safe. We might as well just hand ourselves over to Queen Glacier."

"I'm right next to you," Glory said, and grinned when Starflight lost a beat and had to flap harder to keep up. Not only was it funny, but it was also nice to know that her camouflage was working so well.

Her brother certainly seemed to have no problem. She glanced around at the endless empty blue that surrounded them as they flew north.

"Jambu?" she said.

"Still here," answered a patch of sky from off to her left.

"You really don't have to come with us," she said again. The semicircle of cacti was now half a day's flight behind them, but Jambu could still make it back before dark.

"Nah," he said. "This is better than sun time! I feel like I've been rolled in sunlight and stuffed with bananas. I bet the rest of the tribe would love to come through that tunnel and have their sun time here on the sand."

Glory pictured a hundred RainWings suddenly sprawled in the desert, snoring away, only a few miles from Burn's stronghold. She shuddered.

"That would be a really, really terrible plan," she said. "It's not safe here for basically any dragon."

"That's what I'm trying to say!" Starflight yelped from her other side.

"Even RainWings?" said Jambu cheerfully. "Nobody cares what we do."

"The world is still at war," Glory said. "And some of the queens are really not to be trusted. I don't know what they'd do with you, but it wouldn't be friendly."

"Why not?" asked Jambu.

Because you're so dopey you're just asking for it. "Because most dragons are naturally unfriendly," she said. "Biting and fighting is what we're built for."

"Really?" said Jambu. "*We're* not." There was a ripple in the air as he flicked his tail.

"Well, you should be," said Glory. "One day some other tribe might come to you and you'll have to be able to defend yourselves. Promise me you'll be careful when we get to the IceWings. Don't let them know what you are."

"All right, all right," he said. "I think it's pretty cute, my little sister getting all worried about me over nothing."

Glory rolled her eyes. Why *did* she care? If her tribe wanted to do idiotic things, did it really affect her?

Well, it did if she planned to stay in the rainforest.

But was that her plan? The RainWings were far from the family she'd hoped for.

But if she didn't stay with the RainWings, where would she go? With the other dragonets, to fulfill a prophecy she wasn't supposed to be in? What about after the prophecy was fulfilled? Clay had brothers and sisters in the MudWings. Tsunami had loved the Kingdom of the Sea, apart from her crazy mother — maybe she'd still go back and challenge her for the throne one day. The NightWings, of course, would welcome Starflight with open wings anytime.

Glory glanced over at Sunny. The little SandWing flew in a tired, flappy way, but her jaw was set and determined. Would *she* ever fit in somewhere? She was such an odd-looking SandWing, without the poison-tipped tail all the rest of her tribe had. Would anyone want her, if the dragonets did fulfill the prophecy and end the war?

Well, presumably whichever queen they chose for the SandWings would be pretty grateful. Surely she'd take Sunny in . . . and besides, everyone liked Sunny.

Glory shook her head and stretched her talons. She was getting way ahead of herself. *First we find Mangrove and get him home. Then I find the missing RainWings and whoever or whatever is taking — or killing — them. Then the great dragonets of destiny figure out how to stop the war, and maybe I tag along for that. And then we'll see what happens.*

"I wouldn't mind stopping for a nap, though," Jambu's voice said out of the blue.

"We won't have time for that," Glory said. Then again, Mangrove was a RainWing, so maybe he *would* stop mid-idiotically-foolish-rescue for a nap — but they couldn't count on it. "Also, Jambu, it's not going to be like this the whole way. It's going to get really cold by tonight, and tomorrow we'll be in the Ice Kingdom. Where it will be seriously freezing."

"I'm sure it'll be fine," Jambu said breezily.

It was already colder than it had been back at the tunnel entrance, and the desert sand below had changed to rocky, treeless hills, gradually sloping up as they flew farther north. Glory saw Sunny casting a wistful glance back at the desert behind them.

Starflight was right; this wasn't particularly safe. Glory and Jambu were camouflaged, but there wasn't much of a way to explain a MudWing, a SeaWing, a NightWing, and a SandWing all flying together — especially right into IceWing territory. They'd agreed to stop telling everyone they were the dragonets of the prophecy, but arriving like this, they might as well be carrying HERE WE ARE! PLEASE IMPRISON US! banners. Glory wished again that her friends had just let her come on her own. She was sure she could retrieve Mangrove by herself.

They were lucky to avoid any IceWing patrols — Sunny heard one coming, which gave them time to hide down in the rocky landscape — and they landed some time after dark on ground that crunched ominously under Glory's claws.

"Is this snow?" Clay asked, poking the dirt.

"No," Starflight said in his know-it-all voice. "It's just frozen dirt. We're going to be really cold tonight." They'd chosen a spot at the base of a short cliff, which would help block the wind, but Glory could already feel the cold seeping up from the ground through her claws and underscales.

"And we shouldn't use fire," Tsunami said bossily. "We can't risk being seen."

"Dibs I get to sleep next to Sunny," said Clay. He grinned at her, and she beamed back. Her warm scales would be the only source of heat they had. Even Glory would have to put up with close contact if she wanted to get through the night without freezing.

Glory knew Clay was joking — he was more likely to use his own body as a shield to keep the wind away from the rest of them — but she glanced over at Starflight and caught the crestfallen look on his face.

Oh, Starflight. Maybe you should actually do something about that crush of yours. He'd never admitted it out loud, but Glory was pretty sure he'd been hopelessly in love with Sunny his whole life. She was also pretty sure Sunny had no idea, and that she might never find out at this rate.

Not my problem, Glory reminded herself. But as they huddled up to sleep, she edged around so Starflight ended up curled next to Sunny's wings, with Clay behind both of them. She coiled herself as tightly as she could and found a spot along Clay's tail. Jambu immediately lay down practically on top of her.

"Ooof," Glory whispered. "A little more personal space, please."

"I don't know what that is," Jambu whispered back. "But I'm *really freaking cold*, aren't you?"

Glory sighed. She was. And Jambu was warm. And he *was* her brother.

She curled up for a second night in a row of uncomfortable sleep.

Glory woke up shortly before dawn. The sun was a thin pale line of light on the horizon, and the dark purple sky still glittered with stars. She could see her breath in the air, trails of smoke as if she could breathe fire like the others.

She wriggled out from under Jambu, who slept with his mouth open and his wings flopped wide. At least he wasn't pink today. She found it a little easier to take him seriously when he was the gray and brown colors of the rocks below them.

She glanced down at her scales to make sure they matched the landscape as well. She liked how there was even a subtle sparkle to them, just like the frost that covered the ground.

Tsunami shifted in her sleep, growling softly. Glory realized that Starflight was already awake; he blinked at her over Sunny's back, looking exhausted. She flicked her tail and signaled that he should go back to sleep; then she spread her wings and hopped up to the top of the small cliff to see what the land ahead looked like.

A lot like the land they'd left behind and the land they were on, apparently. Except — was that snow in the distance? Glory gave her scales a moment to shift, and then she lifted into the sky.

They hadn't been able to see it in the dark the night before, but there was definitely snow on the taller hills ahead of them, and more snow beyond that. Glory shivered. It would get colder from here, and it was already close to unbearable. This had to be tough on Sunny and Clay as well. Maybe the others could stay here while she went on ahead. In fact, maybe she should go ahead right now, without them, so no one else would be at risk.

Except she knew perfectly well that her idiot friends would follow her and just get in worse trouble without her there to help. If she wanted to go on without them, she'd have to convince them to be smart, listen to her, and stay behind.

There was something large up ahead in the snow-covered hills — some kind of building. It couldn't be Glacier's palace, though; Glory knew that was far to the north, on the coldest tip of the peninsula, where no other dragons would ever want to go. This building was almost too far south for IceWings.

Glory flew a bit closer and saw smoke rising from a few of its chimneys.

Smoke means fire, she thought, *which means not IceWings.* She circled in the air and studied it a bit more.

It had to be Blaze and her SandWings. Glory had been wondering how they survived in the Ice Kingdom. Apparently the answer was "by not going very far into it."

Suddenly a movement below caught her eye. She froze, hovering in the air and hoping her camouflage was perfect.

There was a dragon among the rocks, not far from where her friends were sleeping, but not close enough to see them either. He was stamping his feet and slapping his wings together as if he was trying to warm up.

Mangrove? Glory thought hopefully, gliding a bit closer. He wasn't camouflaged, exactly, but he was black like a NightWing . . . maybe he thought that would hide him well enough. . . .

And then the dragon below let out a small plume of fire, heating the ground below him before curling up on it.

So it wasn't a RainWing. It was an actual NightWing, on his own in IceWing territory.

Well, that *can't be good news.*

CHAPTER 13

Why was there a NightWing here, of all places? Glory glided quietly away and landed softly out of his sight. Her curiosity was too strong to resist, so she needed a disguise. The only logical dragons that should be wandering around here were IceWings and maybe some of their SandWing allies.

She closed her eyes and remembered the IceWing who had fought Clay in the arena. Fjord. The first dragon she'd killed with her venom. She'd had no choice; he'd been moments away from killing Clay. Plus she'd had no idea what her venom would do. She'd just known instinctively that she could do something, that she had to do something — that she had a weapon she'd never known about.

Starflight thought that perhaps she couldn't have used her venom under the mountain anyway. He said it might have been activated by finally exposing her scales to full sunlight, the way Clay's fireproof abilities had come to full strength once he'd encountered mud for the first time.

Glory couldn't help but wonder how different life might have been if she could have threatened the guardians the way they threatened her.

Focus. Fjord.

His pale blue scales, the color of sky-filled snow. His darker blue eyes. She felt the changes shimmer across her scales. The hardest part was the extra horns IceWings had around their heads. She concentrated on making her ruff look like it was made of icicles and hoped that would do. She also couldn't make her claws ridged like IceWing claws, and her tail wasn't as whip-thin at the end as an IceWing's would be.

Maybe this is a bad idea. Maybe there's no way I'll get away with it.

But it was still pretty dark out . . . and she really, really wanted to know what a NightWing was doing out here.

Well, she thought ruefully, *if he figures me out, I guess I'll just kill him.*

Somehow it didn't sound as funny as she'd hoped.

She leaped into the air and flew back to the spot where she'd seen the strange dragon. For a moment she was afraid she'd lost him, before she realized that he was lying down, his black scales half-hidden in the long shadows.

Confidence, she told herself. *It's all about attitude.*

"Hey!" she barked, landing with a thump beside him. "Who are you, and what are you doing in our territory?"

The NightWing leaped up in surprise and stared at her. He was a lot younger and smaller than Morrowseer, wiry and graceful in his movements even when he was startled. The silver scales sparkling under his wings caught the morning light like trapped stars.

"Great moons. Where did you come from?" he asked. He looked up at the sky with a puzzled expression.

"Where do you think?" she said. "And I'm asking the questions here. What are you doing in the Ice Kingdom?"

"Technically this isn't the Ice Kingdom yet," he said. "Or didn't you know that?"

It isn't? she thought. The map she'd memorized didn't exactly have borders drawn on it, not that those would have helped her out here anyway.

"You're close enough," she growled. "Explain yourself." She wished she had a spear or something she could poke at him.

"It *will* be Ice Kingdom territory one day," said the NightWing. "If Blaze wins the war, that is. She's promised Queen Glacier all the land you can see from here to the southern horizon — basically where the desert starts." He pointed, but Glory stopped herself from looking and kept her eyes on him.

The NightWing smiled. "I suppose you know all that," he said. "But it's interesting, isn't it? That's a lot of land Blaze is willing to hand over. But not exactly useful land to either tribe, so what would Queen Glacier want with it? Do you think there's treasure under these rocks? That would be my guess. A diamond mine, perhaps. Maybe you know. Maybe all the IceWings know and are wisely keeping it a secret from Blaze and her SandWings." He gave her a wry, clever look as if he'd just opened up her mind and spread it out on the rocks for them to admire together.

A horrible sinking feeling shot through Glory. She'd forgotten that NightWings could read minds. *Some* NightWings, she reminded herself. Certainly not Starflight. And she thought not Morrowseer, judging from his lack of reaction to all the thoughts she'd had about him. Maybe this dragon was one who could see the future instead.

Still, she forced every thought out of her mind except *What are you doing here?*

"Answer my questions, NightWing," she said. "Or I'll take you to Queen Glacier and you can explain yourself to her."

"That wouldn't be a good idea," he said. "You really don't want the rest of my tribe to come looking for me."

"And *you* really don't want to sit in a dungeon made of ice until they show up, which would most likely be sometime *after* you froze to death," she pointed out. "So tell me what you're doing here, and perhaps I'll let you go. Win-win."

He tilted his head, looking amused.

"All right," he said after a moment. "I'm waiting for someone. Well, a few someones."

"Who?" she asked.

"I can't tell you that," he said. "NightWing business, I'm afraid. I'm on an assignment."

"I didn't know NightWings had 'business,'" Glory said. "I thought you just skulked around in your secret location congratulating one another on knowing everything and doing nothing."

The NightWing started laughing. "Nobody talks to us like that!" he said. "Where's your sense of awe? Your terror of our powers?" He spread his wings majestically, but his eyes were teasing.

"If your powers were that impressive, you'd do something to stop this war," she said. "Also, I'm the one with the — uh, the freezing death breath here." She'd nearly slipped and said venom . . . but either way, it was true; NightWing powers weren't that spectacular when it came to an actual battle. Starflight's were downright pathetic.

"Maybe we'll help stop the war someday," he said. "Maybe we haven't picked a side yet — like the dragonets of the prophecy."

Glory kept her face calm and bored. "That old thing," she said. "I don't believe in prophecies. Sorry, I know they're a NightWing specialty, but seriously? If you can actually see the future, why be all cryptic and vague about it? Why not give us a prophecy that's like, 'Oh, by the way, Blaze is going to win the war, so give her the crown now and don't even bother fighting about it.' Skip all the death and bloodshed. And leave a bunch of poor dragonets out of it."

The NightWing laughed again. "You feel sorry for the dragonets," he said. "That's interesting. I've seen a lot of that around Pyrrhia, actually. Everyone expects so much of them, but they also think it's a heavy burden for five young dragons. I wonder if the dragonets would be surprised by all the sympathy for them." He looked thoughtful for a moment, then yawned. "You haven't seen any sign of them here, have you? Rumor has it they were headed for the Ice Kingdom next."

"Really?" Glory said impassively. "Why?"

"To meet Blaze, I suppose," he said. "So . . . are they here? In Queen Glacier's dungeon already, perhaps?"

"Nope," Glory said. "No sign of them. None at all." She thought of snowstorms and sheets of ice, blocking the way to all her other thoughts.

He studied her for a moment. "Right," he said. "Well. They couldn't have gotten here that fast anyway. It's a long way from the Kingdom of the Sea."

"How do you know they were there?" Glory asked. "Oh, wait, I forgot. NightWings are all-knowing, all-seeing, and all-brilliant, right?"

"Don't forget all-wonderful and all-handsome," he said.

She snorted to cover her laugh. "How would anyone know that, when you all stay hidden away like turtles?" she said. "Seriously, come hang out with dragons in the real world sometime."

"Is that an invitation?" he asked. "I probably have a day or two before the — before my work can begin. I wouldn't mind seeing the inside of an IceWing tavern, if you'll be there."

Glory felt a shiver of danger slip along her spine.

"So let me get this straight," she said. "You're telling me nothing about why you're here, but you expect me to bring you into our kingdom and buy you a drink. NightWings really do think highly of themselves, don't they?"

"What if I bought *you* that drink?" he offered.

"Oh, then I'm sure Queen Glacier would understand, no problem," Glory said. "She loves strange dragons in her territory. It's her very favorite thing."

The NightWing smiled a little wistfully. "All right," he said. "Never mind. But maybe you could come back and see me sometime. I'll be here for a few more days at least, probably, and it's pretty boring just sitting here."

"Waiting for your mysterious someones," Glory said. "Which you're not going to tell me anything more about."

He spread his wings. "Sorry. I wish I could. I bet my job would impress you."

"I'm not easily impressed," Glory said, and was surprised when he laughed again. "Well . . . good luck with your assignment, I suppose."

"What's your name?" he asked as she took a step back.

"Sorry, I can't tell you that," she said mockingly. "IceWing business."

"Who knew sarcasm could grow in a place this cold?" he said with a smile. "Will you tell me your name if I tell you mine?"

"Nope," she said. "Frankly, I'm not that interested." She turned her back and spread her wings.

"I'll tell you anyway," he said as she lifted into the sky. "If you'll come see me again! Will you?"

"Maybe," she called back. "I'm pretty busy."

"My name," he called. She slowed down to listen, but didn't look back.

"My name is Deathbringer."

CHAPTER 14

Deathbringer.

Waiting for someone. A few someones.

You haven't seen any sign of the dragonets, have you?

Glory's head was spinning as she flew away. Was the NightWing here waiting for *them*?

Deathbringer. Seriously?

The only dragon she knew of who the NightWings wanted dead was her. As soon as Morrowseer had laid eyes on her, back under the mountain, he'd decided she was going to mess up the prophecy. So he'd ordered the guardians to kill her, which was why she and the others had escaped. Had he sent Deathbringer to finish the job? Why waste all that energy hunting her down?

But Deathbringer had sounded as if he was waiting for more than just her. She wondered if that meant the other dragonets were in danger, too. Surely the NightWings wouldn't kill off any of them. *That* had to mess up the prophecy much more dramatically than Glory could.

She landed next to her friends and nearly gave Starflight a heart attack.

"IceWing!" he yelped, flailing over backward. Tsunami leaped to her feet, teeth bared. "Look out! It's — oh." Starflight took a deep breath as Glory's scales shifted back to brown and gray. "Glory! Why would you *do* that to me?"

"Because it's hilarious," she said. "And shhh." She thought they were far enough away from Deathbringer, but she wasn't completely sure how far sound would carry in the cold, crisp air.

"You looked very sparkly," Sunny said sleepily.

"I nearly clobbered you with my tail," Tsunami said in a severe voice.

"And I nearly bit your snout when you were snoring last night," Glory said. "So I guess we're both models of self-restraint. Jambu, wake up." She poked her brother, who was the only one who'd slept through Starflight's alarm.

"Too cold," he mumbled, flopping one wing over his head.

"Too bad," she said and poked him again. "Besides, if you get up and move you'll feel warmer."

"More sleeping," he insisted, folding the other wing over his head as well.

Glory sighed and left him alone. "Starflight," she asked, "do you have any idea how literal a NightWing's name is? Like, does it always signal something about what they do?"

The other dragonets started getting up and stretching. Starflight scratched his head. "Well, there's Morrowseer," he said. "He can see the future and deliver prophecies, so that's what 'seeing' the 'morrow' is about."

"Yes, thank you," Glory said. "I figured that one out."

"But did they know he'd be a prophet when they named him?" Sunny asked curiously. "Not all NightWings are. So how would they know that?"

"Maybe another prophet foresaw it," Tsunami joked.

Starflight poked at the frozen ground with one claw. "I don't know any more than that," he said. "Morrowseer hasn't told me any NightWing tribe secrets. And you've read all the same scrolls I have."

"True," Glory said. "Lots of epic nonsense about wonderful NightWings. They all have these awkward mouthful names. I think in the stories their names do usually match their skills, if I remember right."

"Why are you asking?" Starflight tilted his head at her.

"Because I just met one," Glory said, "and I thiiiiiiink he's here to kill us. Well, me, at least."

That got their attention in a hurry. She told them about Deathbringer and everything he'd said. Almost everything, anyhow. She didn't want them to figure out that she'd thought he was kind of cute. That is, before she realized he was there to kill her.

"Let's get out of here," Starflight said when she finished. "Let's fly south right now and get back to the rainforest as fast as possible."

Jambu poked his nose out hopefully. "I like that plan," he offered.

"It does sound like the warmest plan. But what about Mangrove?" Clay asked with a shiver.

"I saw something else," Glory said. "I think it's where

Blaze and her army must be camping out." She described the building she'd seen. Starflight and Tsunami both nodded.

"Makes sense to me," said Tsunami. "Blaze would need a place of her own. She couldn't survive a day in Glacier's palace."

"Right. It's built mostly of ice, so she wouldn't even be able to use her fire there," Starflight mused.

"So here's what I'm thinking," Glory said. "I'm sure Mangrove saw this place, too. He'll head right for it, probably camouflage himself and sneak in looking for Orchid. So I'll go after him and bring him back, while you guys hide somewhere Deathbringer won't find you, and then we all fly south as fast as possible."

"Wait, by yourself?" Clay said. "Can't one of us go with you?"

"Who?" Glory said. "Who else can disguise herself as an IceWing?"

Her friends all looked at Jambu, who blinked sleepily.

"*And* be helpful," Glory added.

"I can be helpful," Jambu said with a yawn. "I bet I'm better at spotting camouflaged RainWings than you are."

Glory hesitated. That actually did sound useful. She wasn't really sure how she intended to find Mangrove on her own.

"You can do that?" she said.

"It's a game we play starting when we're dragonets," Jambu said. "One dragonet camouflages herself, and whoever sees her first, wins. So no guarantees, but it's probably more practice than you've had."

She thought for a moment and shook her head. "It's too dangerous. I can take care of myself, and I don't need any help."

"Glory," Clay said in a sort of amiably threatening voice. "You take him, or we're all coming with you."

Glory could tell by the looks on their faces that this was true. Stupid heroic we're-a-team idiots. "All right, fine. We'll go in camouflaged, but I want to make sure you can look like an IceWing, too. Try matching what I'm doing." She let her scales shimmer back into her IceWing disguise.

Clay winced, and she guessed he'd recognized which dragon she'd used as a model. Watching Fjord die in front of him couldn't have been any easier for him than for her.

"Now make your scales a bit whiter," Glory said to Jambu, "so we're not exactly the same. And shift around the fake icicle horns." She stepped back and studied him. "I think that'll do. Can you remember that if we need to become IceWings?"

"Sure," he said. He held out his wings and looked at them. "This is a pretty cool color. I'll have to remember it once we're home."

"We also need IceWing names. You be Penguin; I'll be Storm. That should be easy to remember."

"I still think one of us should go with you," Tsunami interjected.

"MudWings and SeaWings are the enemy here," Glory pointed out. "And no offense, guys, but it's not like Starflight or Sunny would be much help."

"No *offense*?" Sunny squeaked. "How am I not supposed to be offended by that?" She lashed her tail and scowled.

"We'll get in and out faster if we just keep our scales hidden," Glory said. "Don't worry. We'll be back by tonight."

"What if you find the missing RainWings in there?" Clay asked.

Glory flicked her tail, letting her scales shift back into the color of the rocks. "We'll free them and come storming out in a big invisible herd. All right?"

Clay and Tsunami nodded reluctantly.

"Come on, Jambu," Glory said. "The rest of you stay hidden. I mean it." She sprang into the air with her brother beside her and let her scales adjust to the sky around them. As they beat their way north, she glanced back once and saw Sunny staring after them while Tsunami waved her talons bossily.

"It's still cold," Jambu moaned. "Even with my wings beating. I think it's even *colder*."

"Well, we're up in the air," Glory pointed out. "And the wind probably isn't helping. But this will be over soon, don't worry." She pointed to the building ahead of them. "Just to warn you, there will be snow. But hopefully the SandWings keep the inside warm with their fires."

"Snow!" Jambu said. "And fire! You know, I've never seen either of those."

"I've never seen snow up close either," Glory admitted.

"It looks fluffy," said Jambu.

*   *   *

It wasn't fluffy. It was wet and piercingly freezing against their talons as they landed outside the walls. Jambu let out a yelp of pain, and Glory nearly tackled him to shut him up.

"Who's there?" called a voice from above.

They both froze, their scales the color of the white ground below them.

A SandWing head poked out a window. "Did you hear that?" he asked.

Another SandWing head wriggled out beside his. "No. And I don't see anything. You're imagining things again."

"When Burn's army shows up to crush us —" growled the first dragon.

"We'll see them coming from miles away," said the second. "And they'll be frozen and weak from the cold, and we'll have IceWing backup by the time they get here. Stop interrupting our game." The second guard withdrew into the room. The first glanced around suspiciously, his gaze trailing across the snow where Glory and Jambu crouched. Finally he huffed out a snort and retreated back inside.

Glory flipped her tail into her brother's talons and led the way, slipping around the thick stone walls until she found a dragon-size door. Locked, of course. She glanced up, but she'd already seen from above that there was no inner courtyard or openings anywhere on the roof, other than the chimneys, which were too small. The windows were all too narrow for a dragon to squeeze through as well. This was a proper fortress. She wondered if it had been built early in the war, when Blaze first came to Queen Glacier for protection and an alliance.

This was a pretty generous gift for Glacier to give to her ally — a whole fortress right in IceWing territory. Deathbringer's words came back to her . . . Blaze had promised Glacier all this land if she won the war.

Glory thought of the other two SandWing sisters. She wondered what Burn had promised the SkyWings and MudWings. And whether Blister had promised the SeaWings anything, or if she'd just manipulated Queen Coral into supporting her.

"I'm not seeing a way to sneak in here," Glory whispered. "Do you have any ideas?"

She felt Jambu shrug. "Sorry," he said. "I've never done anything like this."

They tried circling the walls one more time, but there was only the one door. Glory couldn't see any gaps in the fortress's defenses anywhere. Their only choice was to wait for that door to open and hope they could slip inside . . . but who knew how long that would take?

The sun was finally drifting up the pale blue sky, reflecting off the glittering snow. Glory did not want to stand out here all day. For one thing, Jambu would probably freeze to death. She didn't like the cold either, but he'd never been out of a tropical environment before.

Same goes for Mangrove, she realized. In fact, how would *he* have gotten inside the fortress? Maybe he wasn't there at all. Maybe he was lying in a snowbank somewhere, slowly disappearing into the ice.

Glory shook her head. Mangrove wasn't the type to give up, if she read him right. And neither was she.

"We'll have to go in as IceWings," she said. "Just follow my lead."

Jambu's head appeared, nodding agreeably, as his scales shifted color. Glory let her scales change as well, then turned in a circle to check herself as best she could. It wasn't a perfect disguise by any means. But hopefully these SandWings wouldn't look too closely. And between her camouflage scales and venom, she felt like she had a pretty good chance of escaping even if they did catch her.

She marched up to the door and rapped smartly.

"Try to look like a soldier," she hissed at Jambu, who was slouching and rubbing his neck behind her.

"I don't know what that looks like," he whispered back just before the door swung open.

A heavyset SandWing with broken claws on one talon peered out at them. "Eh?" he muttered.

"We have an important message for Queen Blaze," Glory announced. "Take us somewhere we can wait until she returns." Surely, like her sisters, Blaze would be off leading a battle somewhere. Once they were shown into a waiting room, they could change back to camouflage and search the fortress for Mangrove without being seen.

"Eh? Until she returns?" The SandWing looked at her as if she were mad. "Blaze is here. She's always here. I can take you right to her."

— CHAPTER 15 —

Uh-oh, Glory thought.

"But it better be good news," said the SandWing, stomping around and heading into the fortress. "She doesn't like hearing bad news, and we don't like her hearing it either. Queen Glacier needs to figure that out and stop sending all these gloomy reports."

Glory and Jambu exchanged glances and hurried after him. The door thudded shut behind them and another SandWing guard followed close on their tails. Slipping away was not going to be easy.

Blaze's fortress was not much like the glorious, extravagant palaces of Queen Scarlet or Queen Coral. The halls here were narrow and nothing was open to the sky. A fireplace held a roaring fire in every room they passed, so the heat was almost stifling, and yet cold winds still rattled through the small windows. There was no treasure adorning the walls, no gold or pearls embedded in the floor.

Instead, the stone walls were hung with thick woven tapestries. Each tapestry had a bright yellow sun blazing at the center of it, surrounded by patterns of images from the desert — sinuous lizards, prickly cacti, palm trees, camels. White and green and blue covered the dull gray walls almost from corner to corner.

They miss their home, Glory realized, and was shocked to find herself feeling sorry for these SandWings. They'd come here to support Blaze — probably they'd fled alongside her when Burn tried to claim the throne — and now they were trapped in this icy world that was nothing like their own.

Kind of like growing up in a cave instead of a rainforest.

"Cool," Jambu said. He pointed at a tapestry covered in rioting green lizards. "That one's really wild. I like it."

The SandWing soldiers stared at him. "Really?" said the one in the lead. "Our IceWing visitors usually make it pretty clear that they think our hangings are — how do they put it? — garish and gaudy."

"Well, they're not our style," Glory said, stamping on Jambu's foot. "But we can still appreciate the artistry."

"Huh," said the first SandWing. "Never heard that from an IceWing before." He turned and kept walking. Glory shot Jambu a glare and he wrinkled his snout at her.

They reached the center of the fortress — or so Glory guessed, since there were no windows here — and stopped in a small antechamber outside a pair of giant wooden doors. One of the SandWings knocked twice and they all waited.

As the silence stretched out, Glory realized that there was something huddled in a corner of the little room. It looked like a dirty pile of prey fur at first, but when she peered closer, she realized there were two scavengers in there. They leaned against the wall with their arms around each other, shivering.

"What are those?" Jambu whispered to her, spotting them at the same time.

"You're one of those IceWings who's never left the queen's palace, aren't you?" guessed the second soldier, overhearing him. "I hear they rarely see scavengers that far north." He prodded the furs with one sharp claw, and the two scavengers let out tragic little whimpers. "We found one of their hidden dens near the mountains and gathered up whatever we could catch. They're faster than they look — we got only six of them, when there must have been at least twenty." He shook his head. "These two are what's left."

"You're going to eat them?" Jambu said. *Don't sound so shocked*, Glory thought, lashing her tail. But she could understand what he was feeling. With their big eyes and strange arms wound around each other, the two scavengers looked like overgrown, less cute sloths. She couldn't imagine eating them either. The thought made her feel weirdly queasy.

It didn't help that one of them was staring at her in the same plaintive way Silver did when she didn't want Glory to leave her behind.

"Of course," said the guard. "We wreck any scavenger dens we can find and eat as many of them as we can. Glacier's orders. She thinks one day we'll find where they buried our treasure."

"If it still exists. Who knows what scavengers do with treasure," muttered the other guard. He knocked again, and this time the door swung open under his talon.

The room on the other side was larger than any they'd seen so far. The smooth stone floor was covered in sand, and the tapestries on the walls here were more intricate, with images of dragons and crowns and jewels surrounding the yellow suns.

Giant wine-red pillows and camel-hair carpets were piled in a loose nest in the middle of the room, and sprawled across this was a strikingly beautiful SandWing.

She had her chin propped on one talon and was gazing listlessly into a mirror on the sand in front of her. Her tail coiled gracefully across the pillows, with the poisonous barb touching the floor. Her wings were folded, and her scales shimmered like white gold against the red backdrop.

Blaze lifted her dark eyes and saw Glory and Jambu in the doorway. She forced a smile and reached her front talons toward them in a welcoming gesture.

"Oh, wonderful," she said. "We haven't had visitors in so long. I was hoping Queen Glacier would send us news."

Glory bowed and Jambu imitated her. "If this is a bad time, Your Majesty, we can wait until later . . ."

"No, no, please come in," Blaze cried. "Ocotillo, please bring us some tea. Oh, and some of those dried lizards if we have any left."

"Of course, Your Majesty," said the first guard with a respectful bow. Both SandWing soldiers backed out of the room, leaving Glory and Jambu alone with Blaze.

I'm guessing it wouldn't be this easy to get a private audience with Burn or Blister, Glory thought. Blaze was not as cautious or suspicious as her sisters. But then, she had no reason to suspect a pair of IceWings.

"Is it about Queen Scarlet?" Blaze asked, leaning forward. "Did we find out if she's dead? Are the SkyWings still following Burn? You know, if Glacier would let me go to the Sky Kingdom, I bet I could convince the SkyWings to switch alliances to us. I can be really convincing. Everyone likes me."

Or they could throw you in prison, Glory thought. *Or hand you over to Burn.*

"I know what you'll say," Blaze said restlessly. "What Glacier always says. Stay put and let her handle things. I know all that military stuff is too confusing for me. But I think I could be useful with the talking part. Other dragons like hearing me talk."

"I'm sure that is true, Your Majesty," said Glory politely.

"So?" Blaze said. Her pitch-dark eyes were too eerily similar to Burn's and Blister's; they gave Glory the creeps, even though she knew a very different brain was behind them. "What's your important message?"

Option one: Make up a lie.

Option two: Run for it.

Option three . . . tell a version of the truth.

Glory took a deep breath. "The dragonets of the prophecy want to meet you."

Blaze sat up fast. "*The* dragonets?" she cried. "Glacier found them?"

"They're looking for you," Glory hedged.

"Well, bring them here, bring them here!" Blaze said. "We can have a feast! Or a party! We haven't had one of those in *forever*, because, you know, Queen Glacier disapproves of that kind of thing, but for something like this I'm sure we could! Oh, we'll definitely need more dried lizards. We even have a pair of scavengers we could share! Maybe we should roast a camel — one of them's a MudWing, right? He'd probably like that. We don't have anything for SeaWings . . . maybe Queen Glacier can send us some fish, or a penguin, or do you think she'd like a walrus?"

"Wait," Glory said. As tempting as a feast sounded — and she knew Clay would collapse with joy if he were offered a roasted camel — she wasn't about to walk her friends back into another queen's clutches. "There's a catch. They're not willing to risk coming inside. They need you to go meet with them."

Blaze flung herself down on the carpets again, looking petulant. "But what about my *party*?" she said. "And I don't *like* going outside. It's too *cold* and it makes my scales all dry and ugly."

"You won't have to go far," Glory said. Jambu was twitching in a weird, distracting way. She poked him with her tail. "And isn't it worth it if the dragonets end up choosing you to be the next SandWing queen?"

Blaze worried one of her claws between her teeth, thinking.

Jambu poked Glory back and cut his eyes toward the far

corner of the room. Glory squinted, but all she could see was sand and stone walls and tapestry.

Except . . . then the sand moved, and for the briefest moment, a pair of eyes blinked out of the wall, then vanished again.

Mangrove is *here*.

"I should wait for Queen Glacier," Blaze said. "She wouldn't like my going off alone. I'm sure she wants to meet the dragonets, too."

Glory already did not like the sound of the IceWing queen. She'd bet that Glacier was exactly the kind of dragon who would love to lock up five dragonets.

"Actually," Glory said, "she sent us to tell you that it's a good idea. You should go ahead and meet with them, and you can tell her all about it afterward. There's nothing to fear from the dragonets, and besides, um, Penguin and I will be there to protect you."

"Oh," said Blaze. "That is reassuring." She gave Jambu a concerned look, and he managed to stop twitching for a moment.

"Do you think they'll really choose me?" Blaze asked hopefully, turning back to Glory. "Oh, who am I kidding. I'm sure they will if they meet me! All right, I'll do it."

"Great!" Jambu burst out. "Let's go!"

"Right *now*?" Blaze said. "Already?"

Glory wasn't sure if that was a good idea either. Her friends weren't exactly expecting Blaze to show up, and it would be hard to stay hidden from Deathbringer with the SandWing parading along beside them.

Still, this was what they wanted . . . a chance to meet the third queen candidate without risking imprisonment.

"Yup. Right now," Glory said. She shot a significant look at Mangrove's corner, hoping he'd be smart enough to follow them out.

Blaze picked up the mirror and checked her scales from several angles. Finally she swept one of the camel-hair blankets off the floor and flung it around her shoulders like a cape, then led the way to the door.

Jambu darted to the corner, grabbed a patch of sand, which turned out to be Mangrove's elbow, and tugged him along after them.

Blaze started to turn around, but Glory was there to distract her. "Tell me about this tapestry," she said, pointing to one with two large SandWing dragons flying across a blue background. "I don't remember seeing it before."

"Oh, that one was my idea," Blaze said. "It's the tragic, romantic story of how my brother fell in love with a dragon he knew our mother would never approve of, so he kept her hidden from us, but then she ran off and broke his heart, although we were all thinking, *Or did she*, of course, because it is so likely that Mother just found out and had her killed, which was something she would totally do. . . ." Blaze chattered on about the tapestry as she swept through the antechamber.

Glory glanced sideways at the two scavengers. The one with Silver's eyes had fallen asleep and looked even more pathetic now.

Blaze was several steps ahead and not paying attention to anything but the sound of her own voice. Glory scooped up the sleeping scavenger and slid it onto her back. It did not smell very pleasant at all. No wonder the RainWings preferred fruit; bananas never smelled this bad. She folded her wings back over it, hiding it as well as she could.

Jambu saw what she was doing and grabbed the other scavenger. Even though it was awake, it barely struggled as Jambu tucked it under one wing.

They hurried after Blaze, following her back through the hallways to the main door. They went by a few SandWing guards; Blaze addressed them by name and they saluted, but she didn't tell them where she was going and none of them looked suspicious or even curious. None of them paid any attention to Glory and Jambu, or to their poorly hidden stolen goods.

Almost every SandWing they passed was injured in some way. Blaze was unscathed, but all of her soldiers had scars slicing across their scales or missing talons or wounded tails. Glory thought of Dune, their SandWing guardian who had been so maimed by the war that he could never fly again. It had never occurred to her to ask him which side he had fought on before he joined the Talons of Peace.

A blast of cold air smacked them in their snouts as they stepped outside. Blaze wrapped her blanket around herself more tightly, lifted her claws gingerly out of the snow, and whined, "Are you *sure* the dragonets won't come inside?"

Glory glanced back at Jambu. A shimmer in the air beside him was all she could see of Mangrove, but she was relieved to know he was there.

"That way, Your Majesty," she said, nodding south.

Blaze heaved a sigh, spread her wings, and leaped into the air.

Quickly Glory twisted around and dragged the scavenger off her back. She dumped it on the snowy ground and it woke up with a yelp. Jambu dropped the other one next to it.

"Go on, run for your scrawny lives," Glory said, poking her scavenger with her snout. The scavenger scrambled backward, then grabbed the other one's arm and took off running through the snow.

"Do you think they'll be all right?" Jambu asked as he and Glory flew after Blaze. "It's so cold out here."

"I bet that's what all those furs are for," Glory said. "Anyway, I'd rather freeze to death than be eaten by a SandWing."

"Blech," Jambu said. "Meat-eaters. I don't get it."

They caught up to Blaze and steered her toward the spot where their friends were waiting. As they flew, Glory scanned the ground below them for any sign of Deathbringer. The sun was high in the sky, although it felt like it was far away, behind a ceiling of ice. The frost glinted on the ground and now Glory could see scrubby patches of brown grass and twisted shrubs. A gray wolf trotted across the rocks, but he was the only sign of life she saw. Wherever Deathbringer was for the day, he'd hidden himself well.

Her friends had done their best, too; several large boulders had been shoved together below the cliff to look like a fallen rock pile, and Glory nearly flew right over it. She circled back down to land with Jambu and Blaze behind her.

Sunny was the first one out. "You did it!" she cried. "You found . . . him . . . wait." She squinted at Blaze. "Uh, Glory? That's an actual SandWing."

"I know. Don't worry, Mangrove is here, too," Glory said, flicking her tail. "It's all right to show yourself now."

The RainWing slowly materialized in a dull green, unhappy color. He ducked his head and wouldn't meet her gaze.

"Yikes!" Blaze yelped, leaping away from him. "How did that happen? Where did he come from?" She looked around wildly as if she expected more dragons to suddenly poof out of the landscape.

"What do you know about RainWings, Your Majesty?" Glory asked. She watched Blaze's face intently, wondering if the SandWing knew anything about the missing RainWings, and if it would show in her expression.

But the potential queen looked as mystified as before. "I've heard they're pretty," she said, tossing her head. "But I've never seen one."

"You have now," Glory said. She held out her wings and let them shift to a light, nonthreatening purple. At the same time, Jambu's scales shivered back to pink, although a paler, chillier pink than usual.

"Ooooo," Blaze said enviously. She reached out and took one of Jambu's wings in her talons, inspecting the scales as if he were an inanimate tapestry instead of a living dragon. Jambu blinked at Glory but didn't pull away.

"Wow, I wish I could do that," Blaze said. "I'd be a different color every minute!" She turned over the wing so Jambu had to contort himself into an odd position.

She didn't seem alarmed or angry to have been tricked by their IceWing disguises. Glory wasn't sure whether to admire her bravery or roll her eyes at Blaze's lack of caution.

"Do you think the changing camouflage would still work if I had someone make, like, a coat of RainWing scales for me?" Blaze asked. "That could be pretty." She eyed Jambu's scales like she was trying to figure out how to take them off him. Mangrove finally looked up and met Glory's eyes with a worried expression.

By now Clay, Tsunami, and Starflight had all emerged from the rock pile as well. Starflight pointed at Blaze, his eyes wide.

"Glory!" he cried. "This — this is — you found —"

"I know," Glory said. "Everyone, this is Blaze. Blaze, these are —" She hated the phrase, but it was what everyone called them. "These are the dragonets of destiny."

——— CHAPTER 16 ———

"Oh, wow, it is so, so, *so* exciting to meet you," Blaze said brightly. "Where's the SkyWing?"

Glory managed to keep her face and scales from showing any reaction. *The SkyWing is dead*, she wanted to yell. *You're stuck with me instead. Deal with it.*

"Glory is our fifth dragonet," Clay said. He nodded toward her.

"Oh," Blaze said, regarding Glory with skepticism. "But . . . she's a RainWing, and the prophecy calls for a SkyWing. Doesn't it?"

"What prophecy?" Jambu asked. "What's a dragonet of destiny?"

"Are you serious?" Glory said to him. "Do you know *anything* about what's going on out here?"

"It's far too complicated to explain," Starflight said with a flick of his tail.

"There's a war going on," Clay said kindly, "and a prophecy that says five dragonets will stop it, and that's us."

"Oh," Jambu said. "Neat."

"Yes, far too complicated," Tsunami said to Starflight. The black dragonet frowned at her.

"It's a little more specific than that," Blaze pointed out. "It says two of the SandWing sisters will die — hopefully not me! And it says the five dragonets are a MudWing, a SeaWing, a NightWing, a SandWing, and a SkyWing."

"We've got a RainWing instead," said Tsunami. "And we're fine with that."

"There's also me," Sunny piped up. "I'm the SandWing even though I'm weird-looking."

Blaze peered down at Sunny. "Oh my gosh. You *are* weird-looking! What's wrong with your tail? Why are your scales the wrong color?"

"I don't know," Sunny said, spreading her wings. "But I'm still the SandWing in the prophecy."

"Are you sure?" Blaze asked. She circled around Sunny, inspecting her. "Wow. You all are not what I expected. For one thing, you're smaller. And I thought you'd be, I don't know, prettier." She stopped at Glory. "Explain the RainWing again? Also the other two RainWings — why are they here?"

"You should go," Glory said to Jambu. She glanced at Mangrove, who was shivering and tugging his wings around himself. "Take him home. You're both going to freeze if you stay out here any longer."

"I'm sorry," Mangrove said to her. "I thought —"

"I know. We'll find her, but not here." Glory pointed south. "Both of you go. We'll catch up soon."

Jambu didn't argue. He was also shivering from wing tip to wing tip, and he looked especially glad to have an excuse to get away from Blaze.

"Where are they going?" Blaze asked as the two RainWings lifted off. "Isn't the rainforest kind of far from here?"

"You know, we actually have some questions for *you*," Starflight interjected. "Like, can you tell us why you should be queen instead of your sisters?"

"Because I'm prettier and nicer and friendlier than they are?" Blaze said. "Obviously?" She smiled and whirled in a circle, holding the blanket out so it flapped like a flag. "I mean, haven't you met them? Aren't they both awful?"

"Yeah," Clay said ruefully.

"Well —" Starflight said, then caught the look on Tsunami's face. "I guess they are."

"But could you survive a challenge?" Tsunami asked. "If you did become queen, how long would you last before someone tried to take the throne from you?"

"Ouch," Blaze said. "That's kind of rude, isn't it? I'm a much older dragon than you. I've been in a battle — more or less." She flicked her poisonous tail back and forth. "And I do have this deadly tail."

"So do all SandWings," Tsunami said, unimpressed.

"Hey, how do you cure someone who's been scratched by a SandWing tail?" Sunny asked. "I mean, say, by accident." She did a good job of sounding like she was just curious, but Glory knew she was thinking of Webs.

"There's this cactus juice that heals our poison," Blaze said with a dismissive wave. "Grows all over the desert."

Once again, Glory thought, *she's not suspicious at all. Or worried about keeping SandWing secrets, apparently.*

"Anyway," Blaze insisted to Tsunami, "I'll have Queen Glacier to help me if anything goes wrong."

Tsunami snorted.

"Glacier can't fight for you in a challenge for the throne," Starflight said.

"She can't?" Blaze said as if this was surprising news. "Huh. Well, she can still come down and kill whoever's challenging me. She wouldn't mind."

"But that wouldn't be fair!" Sunny said. "That would violate all the challenge rules! Right, Starflight?"

He nodded, but Blaze was already talking over them. "Who cares?" she said. "Don't even worry about it. I'll be such a great queen that no one will *want* to challenge me. There, that's an excellent plan. So how does this prophecy thing work? Are you guys going to kill my sisters? That would make my life much easier."

Glory lashed her tail. She hadn't thought of that. Killing off Burn and Blister — it was certainly one way to fulfill the prophecy. *If* they could do it, which seemed unlikely, considering armies of dragons had been trying to kill all of the sisters for eighteen years already.

Sunny looked taken aback as well. "We're not hired killers," she said. "We were thinking we'd tell everyone who we choose, and they'll all listen to us and stop fighting."

"Oh," said Blaze. "That sounds . . . nice. What's the 'power of wings of fire'? How do I get that?"

These were all questions Glory had had about the prophecy her whole life, and yet she felt weirdly irritated to hear them coming from Blaze. As if the dragonets had all the answers!

At the same time, it occurred to her to wonder why Blister — the smartest sister — hadn't asked these questions. Perhaps she knew the answers already . . . or perhaps she wanted someone to think she did.

"We're figuring it out," Clay said.

"It's not like we chose this," Glory said. "We were sort of shoved into this whole 'destiny' thing."

"*You* weren't," Blaze said, her voice light and puzzled. "There's no RainWing in the prophecy at all. Why don't you just go home?"

In the awkward pause that followed, Glory imagined all the other dragons having the exact same thought. Why *didn't* she just go home, where she could sit safely in the rainforest and stay out of the war and sleep all day?

Maybe I should, she thought. *I mean, is it worth it, fighting for one of these three awful SandWings? Wouldn't it be easier to give in and accept that I'm meant to be a lazy RainWing?*

It was almost a relief to be distracted by a NightWing assassin landing on top of the rock pile beside them.

The others whipped around to stare at him, their tails lashing. Blaze squinted in a puzzled way.

"Oh, hello. Is he in the prophecy?" she asked. "He's cute. Cuter than this one." She waved a talon at Starflight's wounded expression.

"Why, hello, everyone," said Deathbringer. "Isn't this a coincidence? I was just talking about you all this morning." He turned to Glory and tilted his head at her purple scales. "Mystery dragon! Hmmm. There's something different about you. Did you get your claws trimmed?"

"Very funny," she said, baring her teeth at him.

"You could have told me you were one of the dragonets," Deathbringer said. "I'd have asked for your autograph. I see now that you're a RainWing, so . . . Glory, right?"

That was creepy, that he knew her name. Even if she kind of liked the sound of him saying it. But it had to confirm her theory about him; otherwise why would he have bothered to learn it?

"Right. The one you were sent here to kill," Glory said. "Somehow I think that would have started us off on the wrong talon."

"I'm not necessarily here to kill you," Deathbringer objected. "And even if I were . . . this seems like a much better opportunity to kill *her.*" He suddenly opened his front talons, revealing a pair of sharp silvery discs. Their edges gleamed like knives as he flung them, one after the other, right at Blaze.

The SandWing shrieked and stumbled back, dropping the blanket, but she didn't move fast enough. One disc embedded itself in her long neck, releasing a spurt of bright red blood that sprayed all over Sunny, who was standing next to her.

The second disc sliced through the edge of one of Tsunami's wings as she leaped in front of Blaze. It ricocheted into one of the rocks with a ringing sound. Tsunami collapsed, clutching her injured wing.

Sunny screamed, looked down at her blood-spattered scales, and screamed again.

Clay jumped forward and clapped both his talons over the cut in Blaze's neck. "Throw me the blanket!" he yelled to Starflight. The NightWing looked back at him in frozen terror.

Glory grabbed the blanket and flung it to Clay, who started to wrap it around Blaze's neck.

But then Deathbringer was there, landing on Blaze's back and tossing Clay aside as if the hefty MudWing weighed no more than a salamander. Two more silver discs appeared in Deathbringer's talons.

Glory leaped at the assassin and knocked him backward off Blaze. They rolled on the frozen ground, his black wings tangling with hers. He was very strong and astonishingly fast. A black pouch around his neck thumped against her chest and she realized that must be where he kept his weapons. She seized it between her claws just as he pinned her down, his talons on her wings.

"Killing Blaze was your assignment?" she said.

"No, but I like to work outside the box," he answered. "And if I kill her, I figure it'll get me out of the trouble I'll be in for not killing you."

"You can *try* to kill me," she growled. "But I doubt it'll be as easy as you think." She ripped open the pouch and caught a few of the silver discs as they spilled into her talons. Several others clattered to the ground around her, but one was all she needed. She pressed it to Deathbringer's neck before he could jump away.

"You missed the biggest artery on Blaze's neck," she said. "If I remember my dragon anatomy correctly, it's right here." She applied a little more pressure and Deathbringer flinched as the silver edge left a thin trail of blood on his scales. He lifted his talons from her shoulders and carefully backed off her.

Glory stood up, keeping the disc poised at his neck, and glanced over Deathbringer's shoulder. Clay had the blanket tied firmly around Blaze's neck, but blood was already seeping through the camel-hair fabric. The SandWing queen leaned against him, looking faint. Tsunami had also climbed to her feet and was examining the cut on her own wing with a scowl. Starflight hadn't moved; Sunny was still staring at the blood all over her talons and wings.

"I did mention the part about how I don't actually want to kill you, right?" Deathbringer said, eyeing Glory and the discs she held with a faintly amused expression. "I'm pretty sure I snuck that in there."

"Oh, all right," Glory said. "I'll just trust you then, shall I?"

"If you let me kill her, I can let you all go," he said. "That should give you a fair head start before they send someone else after you, especially since no one knows where you'll go next."

"All of us?" Glory said. "You're here to kill all of us?"

"No," he said, still smiling. "Just a couple of you."

"Well, that makes me feel better," she said. "Stop looking so pleased with yourself." She poked his neck and he tried — and failed — to look serious.

"Which couple of us?" Sunny asked.

"Who's they?" Tsunami demanded at the same time. "Who sent you?"

"The NightWings," Starflight said bleakly. "That's it, isn't it? Because of what happened in the Kingdom of the Sea. Because we didn't choose Blister."

"The *NightWings* wanted us to choose Blister?" Glory said as Tsunami whirled to stare at Starflight. "Why would they *care*?"

"I don't know," Starflight said. "That's all Morrowseer told me. That we had to pick Blister, and I should convince you all to agree to it."

"That's so mean!" Blaze interjected, opening her eyes and looking a bit more alive. "Why should the NightWings get to decide? They've never even met me! I'm awesome!"

"Oh, *that's* why you were acting so weird around Blister," Clay said to Starflight.

Deathbringer suddenly lunged forward, faster than a striking snake, and seized Glory's front talons. She thwacked his head as hard as she could with her wings and kicked at his underscales with her back claws.

"Ow! Stop!" he cried. "It's like you *want* me to kill you!"

Just then the sound of wingbeats reached their ears. Glory and Deathbringer both froze and looked up at the sky.

"Queen Glacier," Blaze breathed with a relieved sigh. "I knew she would save me."

The glitter of diamond wings approaching from the north was unmistakable. The IceWings were on their way.

—— CHAPTER 17 ——

Given a choice between the IceWing queen and a NightWing assassin, Glory wasn't sure she'd actually prefer the IceWing queen. Imprisonment in the Sky Kingdom and in Queen Coral's Summer Palace had been bad enough — if they wound up in Glacier's dungeon, they'd probably all freeze to death by the end of the day.

"Let me go *right now*," she said to Deathbringer.

To her immense surprise, he did. He stepped back, his talons raised to look harmless, and actually dared to smile at her.

"Time to go," Tsunami ordered. "They'll be here in about two minutes."

"Oh, no, wait," Blaze said. She spread her wings and waved at the incoming ice dragons. "You should meet Glacier. You'll like her."

"We can't leave Blaze here with him," Clay said, pointing to Deathbringer.

"That's true," Glory said. She narrowed her eyes at the assassin. "You have ten seconds to take off, or we'll knock you out and leave you for the IceWings to deal with."

"Shouldn't we do that anyway?" Blaze asked. "I mean, he *did* try to kill me. Queen Glacier will be *so* mad. This one time, a SkyWing flew all the way here and nearly got me while I was getting some sun and Glacier literally ripped off his wings before she killed him. It was really gross but also kind of sweet, you know, like she really cares about me."

Or she really cares about all the land she'll get if you become queen, Glory thought.

Sunny looked faintly sick. "Guess what I don't want to see," she said. "One dragon ripping the wings off another dragon. Not ever, thanks."

"All right, I'm convinced," Deathbringer said, backing away. "But you really should have let me kill her." He paused with his wings spread and gave Glory a cheeky grin. "So when can I see you again?"

"Get out of here," Glory said, glad that Jambu wasn't there to loudly interpret the colors that were trying to shift through her scales.

Deathbringer bolted into the sky. Blaze followed him with her eyes for a moment, then seemed to lose interest. She turned to Clay and Tsunami with a winning smile.

"Please don't go," Blaze said. "Queen Glacier will be so grateful to you for saving my life. Now we can have that party I mentioned!"

"Sorry," Tsunami said. "We are not sticking around to become captives again."

"We'll, uh — we'll be in touch," Clay said. "Keep applying pressure to this until a healer can look at it."

Blaze rallied herself to stand upright and give them all a little nod. "It was delightful to meet you," she said. "Even if you are missing a SkyWing. And some of you are a little funny-looking. I promise you'll be pleased if you choose me." She waved a wing weakly in the direction of the desert. "I can offer you whatever land you want. You could each have land enough for a palace of your own!"

"Quit giving away your territory," Glory snapped. "I know the Kingdom of Sand is big, but life in the desert is tough, and your subjects need every oasis. And if you do become queen, you'll need to rebuild your treasury somehow, so remember that, too."

"Queenly advice from a RainWing." Blaze giggled as if the pain in her neck was making her loopy. "Now I have heard everything."

Glory frowned at her, but the SandWing didn't seem to notice.

"Come on," Clay said gently to Sunny, urging her up.

Sunny held her bloodstained talons out, and Starflight jumped forward to take them between his. "You'll feel better once we're in the desert," he said.

"Don't let them follow us," Tsunami said to Blaze as the others took off.

"They'll be too busy rescuing me," Blaze said, lying down in a graceful, melodramatic pose.

Glory and Tsunami exchanged eye rolls and lifted into the air. The IceWings were almost upon them; they had to fly as fast as they could.

Tsunami faltered for a moment as she went aloft.

"Does it hurt?" Glory asked, flying close to her. "Will you make it to the passage?"

"I'll be fine," Tsunami said through gritted teeth. "It's just a cut." After a moment, she added, "But yes, it hurts."

Glory stayed alongside her as they flew through the cold, pale blue sky. She glanced back several times, but saw no sign of IceWings in pursuit. No sign of a NightWing trailing them either.

"Glory," Tsunami said after a bit. "Can I ask you something? Why didn't you use your venom on that assassin?"

Glory felt a tinge of embarrassed pink creeping along her scales and fought it back until she matched the sky.

"That wasn't an invitation to disappear," Tsunami said.

"I just didn't feel like killing him," Glory answered. "I don't want to kill any more than I have to."

"But he is literally on a mission to kill *you*," Tsunami said. "Killing him first is kind of the definition of self-defense."

"Maybe," Glory said. "I just — it didn't feel like he was trying to kill me."

Tsunami shook her head. "All right, but so you know, from where I was standing, it certainly *looked* like it."

"Whatever," Glory said. "We'll probably never see him again. The real question is why the NightWings are getting so involved. First they try to get us to choose Blister — and then they send an assassin to kill us? Don't they want their prophecy to come true?"

"Maybe, like everyone else, they only want it to come true *their* way," Tsunami grumbled.

"What's their way?" Glory wondered. "What difference does it make to them who the queen of the SandWings is?"

"I have no idea," Tsunami admitted.

"Well, if they have something to say about this war," Glory said, "they can come on out and fight it instead of hiding and making vague predictions every few years."

"And sending assassins," Tsunami added. "Cowards."

It wasn't often that Tsunami and Glory agreed about something. Glory couldn't remember the last time they'd had a conversation this long without arguing. It wasn't that she disliked Tsunami — she didn't even really mind her bossiness. But she did feel like *someone* needed to talk back whenever Tsunami started acting like the boss of everyone, just to make sure Tsunami's head didn't get too big for the rest of her.

On the other talon, Tsunami had been much better since their escape from the Kingdom of the Sea. Glory could see that she was trying to include the others more, instead of just telling them all what to do. And Tsunami never talked about her future as a queen anymore, when it used to be her favorite topic of conversation. Maybe she'd meant it when she said she didn't belong in the Kingdom of the Sea. Maybe she'd really given up on ruling her tribe one day.

It was dark by the time they spotted Burn's stronghold in the distance and the semicircle of cacti they were looking for. Glory and Tsunami spiraled down to the ground and found Starflight frantically digging in the sand.

"The hole is gone!" he cried. "It's disappeared!"

A bolt of green panic shot through Glory's scales. Trapped between the IceWings and Burn, with an assassin out hunting them, was not how she wanted to spend the night.

"It's not gone," Clay said firmly. "Let me dig." He muscled Starflight aside, looked up at the cacti, and started to dig in a slightly different spot.

"What are you doing?" Tsunami called to Sunny, who looked like she was trying to tango with a cactus up the hill.

"You heard what Blaze said," Sunny panted. "If we take this back, maybe we can heal Webs. Ouch!" She flinched back from the thorns, shaking her front talons.

"We don't need the whole cactus," Tsunami said, amused. "Break off one of those arm things and bring that instead."

"That is what I'm *trying* to do," Sunny said irately. Tsunami floundered up the sandy rise to help her. Glory noticed that Sunny had used sand to rub off some of the bloodstains, but there was still dark dried blood caught between her scales and talons.

"There," Clay said. "Found it." He swiped some more sand away from the entrance to the tunnel.

Starflight let out his breath. "Oh," he said. "That must be why no one's spotted it before. The wind covers it with new sand every day." He edged toward the tunnel. "So . . . we can go?"

Glory checked the sky again as Sunny and Tsunami slid back toward them with a chunk of cactus. No dragons anywhere that she could see. She nodded at the tunnel and Starflight darted gratefully inside. The others followed, one by one. Glory went last, piling up as much sand behind her as she could.

As she came out of the tunnel into the dark forest, a ball of fur exploded from the tree above her and landed on her neck. The sloth wrapped her arms and legs around Glory's neck and began warbling and chirruping furiously.

"I think I'm being scolded," Glory said to Clay. She reached up and smoothed Silver's fur.

"WRRRRB," the sloth said sternly, snuggling in closer.

Sunny dove into the stream above the waterfall, washing Blaze's blood off her scales. Glory realized that Jambu was gone, but Mangrove was sitting beside the stream. His wings drooped as he stared into the water.

"I assume you didn't see any sign of the missing RainWings there," Glory said to him.

He shook his head. "Nothing anywhere in that fort. I slipped in when a patrol of SandWings came out. I searched the whole place." He kicked a clump of reeds. "Useless waste of time."

"Probably," Glory said, "but at least now we know."

"How are we going to find Orchid?" he asked.

Glory stared at the hole in the boulder. In the dark, with only a sliver of moonlight slipping through the trees, it looked like a mouth, jaws wide open to swallow dragons whole.

"We heard something here a couple of nights ago," she said. "Maybe if we lie in wait we'll catch it again." She turned and looked at Tsunami. "All we need is someone who can see in the dark."

CHAPTER 18

Glory shifted on her branch and sighed. The night clung to her wings like hot, sticky cobwebs. A vine of moon-colored flowers nearby filled the air with a smell like muskrats rolled in lemons. It was not pleasant.

"You didn't have to stay," Tsunami whispered.

"Yes, I did," Glory said. "I know you. No matter what you see, you'll leap out of this tree and attack it if you're here by yourself."

"I —" Tsunami paused. "Well. I still might do that."

"Then at least I'll be here to help," Glory said, grinning in the dark.

They crouched like that for a while, listening to the creaking, chirping sounds of the rainforest at night. Some kind of insect was desperately announcing the end of the world in a shrill whine from the top of their tree. If Glory had been able to see it, she would have eaten it in a heartbeat, just to shut it up.

They'd spent the rest of last night and today in the RainWing village, recovering from their long flight. Sunny had squeezed the cactus juice into Webs's wound and reported jubilantly that she thought it was working.

The others had stayed there for tonight; Glory thought it was unlikely that they'd catch the mystery monster on their first night watching, and they looked pretty exhausted. She'd also made Mangrove promise not to follow them again, and she'd left Silver with Sunny, because the only thing they knew for sure was that the monster ate sloths.

"What did you think of Blaze?" Tsunami asked in a whisper. "Should we choose her?"

"I don't know," Glory whispered back. "I didn't really like her. Did you?"

"She really needed to shut up about SkyWings," Tsunami said. Glory couldn't agree more, but she was glad Tsunami had said it instead of her.

"She seemed much less sinister than Burn or Blister," Glory said. "But also completely incompetent. Is it fair to give the SandWings a totally useless queen like that? And she's certainly not going to win the war just by us saying she should."

"That's true," Tsunami said. "She'd never survive in actual combat, especially against one of her sisters."

"Anyway," Glory said. "It's not up to me. You guys decide whatever you want. I mean, since I'm not in the prophecy anyhow, so I shouldn't get a say."

"Stop talking like that or I will *thump* you," Tsunami said in a loud hiss. Glory could feel her glaring even in the dark, and she felt obscurely pleased.

"Shhh," Glory said, flicking her tail at Tsunami's wings. "What was that?"

Snap.

Both dragons froze with their heads lifted. Glory's ears twitched.

Snap. Sliiiiiiiiiiiiiiiither.

"That's it," Glory whispered. Her heart was pounding again. She tried to squint through the darkness at the boulder, but she couldn't see anything moving. The sounds of something large rustled through the undergrowth. It was breathing heavily, snuffling in and out like a congested rhinoceros.

"It didn't come out of the hole," Tsunami whispered. "It's on the other side of the creek, near the other tree. But I can't — I'm not sure —" She leaned forward, trying to see under the branches.

Suddenly another noise reached them, as if from a long way away.

It sounded like . . . *whistling.*

Glory leaned forward, listening intently. It was the dragonets song — the one she'd last heard when the prisoners were singing it in the SkyWing arena.

"The dragonets are coming . . .

They're coming to save the day . . .

They're coming to fight . . . for they know what's right . . .

The dragonets . . ."

Someone was whistling their song.

"That *is* coming from the hole," Tsunami whispered. She crouched to peer through the leaves.

A dark shape appeared at the opening of the boulder. At the same time, the dragons heard thumping and crackling as the mystery creature fled back into the forest.

Glory cursed under her breath and leaped to her feet. "Should we go after it?"

But Tsunami had already launched herself out of the tree and flung herself at the boulder. She collided with the shape there and they both yelped with pain, rolling and grappling on the ground.

Glory sprang after her and seized the new dragon's tail. The three of them wrestled until Glory and Tsunami had him pinned down and Glory could sit on his chest.

She was not particularly surprised to discover it was Deathbringer. The NightWing had sand between his claws and an unrepentant expression on his face, from what she could see in the ripples of moonlight that made it through the leaves overhead.

"What kind of assassin stalks his prey and *whistles* at the same time?" Glory asked him.

"We should kill him right now," Tsunami hissed.

"You scared our monster away," Glory said, poking his snout. "So now we're extra-mad at you."

"Yes, that, plus the trying to kill us," Tsunami said.

"What monster?" Deathbringer said, a little too innocently. Glory peered at him with growing suspicion. Did he know something?

"Did you follow us through the tunnel?" she asked. "Or did you already know it was there?"

"How would I know it was there?" he asked.

"That's what I'd like to know," she said.

"Let's take him back to the village and interrogate him," Tsunami said.

"I don't think that's safe," Glory said. "I mean, for the RainWings. Or for the others. We should keep him as far away from everyone as possible."

Tsunami wrinkled her snout, thinking. "Or," she said, "we go back to plan A. Kill him right now."

"Tsunami, I don't think you want to do that any more than I do," Glory said.

That shut her up. Glory had noticed Tsunami getting queasier about killing other dragons after her experiences in the SkyWing arena. Self-defense was one thing, but they had Deathbringer trapped under their talons.

"All right," Tsunami said finally, after a long pause. "You're right. I don't want to. But I was hoping *he'd* think we wanted to, so good job backing me up on that."

"Sorry I couldn't read your mind like a stupid NightWing," Glory said. "Speaking of which, are you the mind-reading kind of NightWing?" She narrowed her eyes at Deathbringer. "What am I thinking right now?"

"That I'm much too charming, clever, and good-looking to kill?" he guessed.

That was actually a little closer to accurate than Glory liked. She flared her ruff and poked his snout again. "Wrong," she said. "I'm thinking that you're starting to be an awful lot of trouble. Have you decided to kill me after all?"

The rakish grin faded from Deathbringer's face. He studied her as though he were seriously considering the question.

"Not sure I like the length of this pause," Glory said.

"I've been wondering if there's an alternative," said Deathbringer. "But that's not usually my call."

"Whose is it?" Tsunami demanded. "The NightWing queen?"

Deathbringer made a peculiar expression which Glory couldn't interpret. "I can't say."

"I don't understand why any NightWings would want me dead," Glory said.

"That has become ever more mystifying to me as well," Deathbringer said, in a manner that managed to sound both gallant and truthful.

"So you're mystified," Glory said. "But you'll still probably do it."

"I wouldn't say *probably*," Deathbringer offered. "I'd say *maybe*."

"I wouldn't call that *reassuring*," Glory shot back. "I'd call that *the opposite of reassuring*."

He grinned at her again. He really needed to quit doing that. It was very distracting.

"So what do we do with him?" Tsunami asked her. "We can't let him go. And we can't take him back to the RainWing village."

"We could tie him up, leave him in the forest, and hope the monster eats him," Glory said. She squinted at Deathbringer's face. He didn't look even a little bit worried. "Did we mention the monster?" she asked him. "It's been abducting or possibly eating RainWings around here. I bet it'll be pretty excited to find you all tied up."

"Oh, no," Deathbringer said. "Please don't leave me alone where a monster could get me."

Glory opened her mouth and then closed it. She'd just had a possibly brilliant and perfectly terrible idea. One she'd have to think about for a minute. She poked him in the snout again.

"Was that *sarcasm*?" she asked. "Tsunami, did that sound weirdly sarcastic to you?"

"Like he doesn't believe in monsters," Tsunami said. "Which I'm not sure I do either, just for the record."

Or he's in cahoots with it, Glory thought. *Or at least he knows what it is and isn't afraid of it.* She decided not to say this out loud. Tsunami's enthusiasm for interrogation might spring up again, and Glory was fairly sure it would be a waste of time. They weren't going to get anything useful out of Deathbringer by looking fierce and demanding answers.

Besides, now that a plan was forming in her mind, she wanted to try it out. Which meant she had to get rid of Tsunami.

"Let's drag him away from the tunnel and tie him up," she said. "Then you go tell the others, and we can take turns watching him until he decides to tell us who wants us dead and why."

"And which of us," Tsunami suggested. "He said he was sent to kill a few of us, not just you."

"And also, you know, how to avoid it," said Glory.

"You'll have to wait awhile," Deathbringer said. "I'm not allowed to tell you anything."

Tsunami and Glory ignored this. They ripped vines down from the trees and wrapped the strongest ones around his wings. Tsunami tied his talons together so he couldn't run, slid a rope around his neck, and prodded him ahead of them into the forest. After a short walk, they found a tree that Tsunami approved of and tied him to it with the tightest knots they could muster.

"He'll burn through these vines the moment we walk away," Tsunami pointed out.

"So we don't walk away," Glory said. "You go tell the others. I'll sit here with my extremely deadly secret weapon pointed at him."

"What's that?" asked Deathbringer. "Wait, let me guess. Your rapier wit."

"Try to escape and find out the dead way," Glory offered.

He leaned back against the tree, looking perfectly comfortable and thoroughly uninterested in escaping. *Peculiar dragon*, Glory thought.

"Send back Clay first," Glory suggested to Tsunami. "He can take the next watch."

"I hope you hear how bossy you're being," Tsunami said. "I'm letting it slide for now, but I'll remember this."

"Oh, go away." Glory flapped her wings at her until the SeaWing lifted off into the darkness.

As her wingbeats faded, the night sounds of the rainforest settled over them. An orchestra of insects warbled and chirped away as the trees rustled, night birds called, and frogs muttered in the background like a disgruntled audience.

"It's so noisy here," Deathbringer said after a moment. "So alive."

"Is it not like that where you come from?" Glory asked.

"It's a lot quieter in the Ice Kingdom," he pointed out. "And the Kingdom of Sand." He didn't say anything about the NightWing home, but she didn't really expect him to.

She stared into the trees, thinking hard. Once Clay arrived to take her place, she could slip away. No one would notice she was missing for a while. She could go out and look for the monster by herself, which was the best way to do anything, if you asked her.

"Don't do it," said Deathbringer suddenly.

"You better not be reading my mind," she snapped.

"I don't have to," he said. "You have 'I'm about to do something stupid' written all over your face."

"It's not stupid," she said. "It's quite clever. And it might be the only way to catch the monster."

"Maybe you should leave the monster alone," he said. "Forget about it. Get back to the prophecy-fulfilling business."

That stopped her for a moment. The prophecy — putting an end to the war — was important. Finding a few RainWings hardly compared. But she'd made a promise.

"I'm not even in the stupid prophecy," she said.

"I know," he said. "But I bet you'd still be remarkably good at making it come true."

"That doesn't make any sense," she said. "And the RainWings are my tribe. They need my help." She felt a burst of certainty in her chest. "And I have to do this on my own."

"Wait," said Deathbringer, with a gratifying note of alarm in his voice. "Why? You have friends. Let them help you."

Glory shook her head. "They can't help me with this. The monster, or whatever is out there, isn't going to approach a group of dragonets. It attacks RainWings who are out in the forest alone."

"So you're —"

Glory smiled at Deathbringer. "I'm going to use myself as bait."

CHAPTER 19

"Watch him carefully," Glory instructed Clay. "Don't let him talk."

"MMMMMFF," Deathbringer complained through the vines she'd tied around his snout. She didn't want him spilling the beans to Clay before she could get away into the forest. Also, she'd gotten sick of listening to him yammer all night long trying to derail her plan. This way she'd been able to watch the sunrise in relative peace and quiet, shortly after which Clay had shown up.

"No worries," Clay said. "I'll just sit here and be my usual intimidating self." He threw back his shoulders and tried to scowl.

"Absolutely terrifying," Glory assured him.

Deathbringer managed to look skeptical despite the vines obscuring most of his face.

"I'll send someone else soon to take the next watch," she said, backing away.

But first I'm going to catch a monster.

It wasn't *that* stupid a plan, no matter what Deathbringer said. A lone RainWing was exactly the kind of target the monster would go after. And she couldn't risk enlisting another RainWing as bait — they were all too dopey to be any use, even Mangrove.

Besides, as far as she could tell, she was the only RainWing willing to use her venom on other living things. It wasn't her *favorite* thing to do, but it was still a weapon — a powerful one that few dragons knew about — and she was sure she could use it to escape any situation if she had to.

She headed back to the tunnel first. She was still certain that it was connected to the missing RainWings, although she couldn't figure out how.

It started with the question: Who had put the tunnel in place? And then: What was their plan — to steal a RainWing here and there? Why?

Glory nosed around the forest near the tunnel opening until she found a clearing where she could sit and think for a moment.

Burn seemed like an obvious suspect, since her stronghold was not far from the tunnel. But Glory had seen the look on Burn's face as Glory's venom sizzled on Queen Scarlet's scales. It was pure shocked terror. The SandWing queen had clearly never seen anything like Glory's venom before. If she were the one abducting RainWings for the past year, surely she'd have heard about their training sessions and she'd know all about it.

Glory stopped at a small bush and sprayed it with her venom. Black goop spattered over the leaves, and almost immediately the whole bush wilted, shriveled up, and died. Glory tilted her head at it, feeling weirdly guilty.

Maybe she could practice her aim while she waited for the monster to attack her. She chose another bush with long dragon-tail leaves and tried to hit just one of them.

Half the bush went *fzzzzzrrrt* and melted into the grass.

"Hmmm," Glory said aloud. "Not awesome."

She tried again. And again. The clearing was starting to look a bit worse for wear.

Glory stopped and smacked herself with her tail.

Try using your brain for half a moment, Glory.

If *she* made a mess like this with her venom practice, then surely the other training dragonets would have, too. So even though Bromeliad wouldn't show her where Kinkajou had disappeared, there was a chance Glory could find it on her own.

She started at the waterfall and circled out from there, walking so she could study the bushes as she went past them. Fat spiny frogs stared at her, making *worgle-WORG* noises in their throats. A pair of red and gold birds with large beaks followed her for a while, gossiping loudly in what sounded like garbled dragon language.

But she found nothing — no signs of venom anywhere. Maybe the training sessions had been in a whole different part of the forest; maybe the secret tunnel really had nothing to do with the abductions.

Glory stubbornly kept searching. What other reason could there be for the tunnel? Who would need to get quickly between the desert and the rainforest? No one . . . no one came to the rainforest at all, and the RainWings certainly never left.

But the war is closer than they think, she thought. *It's right on their doorstep, ready to fall through into their peaceful world.* She glared up at the treetops as an image of Queen Magnificent flashed through her head. *And what is that useless queen going to do about it?*

Blaze is no better than Magnificent. If we pick her, we leave the SandWings as weak and vulnerable as the RainWings.

She looked up at the trees again. Was it getting darker? The sun had been up for only a couple of hours.

A fat raindrop splattered against her snout. The leaves above her whooshed like dragon wings as the wind rushed through them, and more rain came pattering down in scatters and sprays. Glory drew her wings close to her.

Rain probably washed away any trace of venom training days ago, she realized. But she kept going, sodden undergrowth squelching below her talons.

She found herself in a small circle where the trees above bent together to form a kind of umbrella canopy, keeping the ground below relatively dry. She stopped there, stretching and shaking her wings. *This is stupid*, she told herself. *I'm not going to find anything, and I'm not going to get caught by anything in this weather either. What kind of creature would be out hunting in the rain?* She might as well head back to the village and dry off.

But as she turned to fly away, she spotted a dark patch

on the bush of pink flowers beside her. Glory paused, then edged closer and peered at it.

Several of the leaves were withered and dead, looking sickly, black, and twisted. A glossy pattern of dark droplets had hardened on the ground under the bush.

Someone *was training here*, Glory thought. *Maybe Kinkajou. Maybe one of the other missing dragons.* She poked the piles of leaves that covered the ground and found half a talon print in the dirt — a small one, even smaller than Sunny's. She leaned down to sniff at it.

And that was when something bashed her on the back of her head.

Glory started awake to the feeling of movement and something uncomfortable pressing against her wings. She kept still for a moment with her eyes closed, trying to figure out what was happening.

It felt like she was being dragged along the ground. Her left side was unpleasantly damp and slimy, as if she were wrapped in something that instantly soaked up the mud and clung to her scales. Rain still splattered around her, the sound muffled now by whatever she was in . . . a giant sack of some kind, she guessed.

Her wings were bound to her sides, and thick cloth was wrapped around her claws. More disturbingly, some kind of vine or rope was tied around her snout, binding her mouth shut.

Which meant using her venom was out of the question.

It also meant that whatever had caught her wasn't just a mindless mystery beast. It was smart enough to tie her up. It probably knew about her venom — or it might just be wary of her teeth.

Her tail thwacked against something solid and she winced. She cracked open her eyes and saw only darkness. No, wait — not total darkness. Faint green light filtered through the thick canvas around her. The sack pressed close to her snout; it smelled like dead animals and rotten eggs and fire, overwhelming the damp leafy scent of the rainforest outside.

Glory tried to listen for clues, but all she could hear was wet slithering, which might be just the sack sliding over the forest floor. Then a shiver ran down her spine like sharp claws scrabbling to escape. She recognized the weird prickle under her scales — it was the feeling she got from the hole that led to the Kingdom of Sand.

I was right, she thought. *They're taking me to the tunnel.*

Somehow, without her venom, she didn't feel quite as triumphant about being right as she'd hoped.

She heard splashing and a moment later water soaked through the sack as she was dragged through the stream. A couple of grunts followed, and Glory felt herself lifted up into the air, then dropped onto cold stone.

Something shoved at her tail, and she started to slide, down and down as if it were slick ice below her.

Wait, she thought with a sickening lurch. *The tunnel to the desert doesn't go down. Where am I?* She smacked into a wall and slid around a corner, picking up speed again. *This isn't the hole to the Kingdom of Sand. But it feels like that hole. So is this the same kind of passageway, ripped into the world where it shouldn't be? And where does this one end?*

She tumbled suddenly into open space and slammed into a pile of thin furs, which did not do much to blunt the impact of the rocks underneath them.

Glory lay there for a moment, trying not to groan. Every bone in her body ached; every scale felt as though it had been scraped raw. She was pretty sure she'd bitten her tongue when she landed. She could taste blood in her mouth.

The smell of death and smoke was stronger now, and it was no longer raining, but there was hardly any light coming through the sack. This was definitely not the desert; it was chilly instead of blazingly warm, although the sound of a fire crackled somewhere nearby. Glory could hear a distant rumble like faraway thunderclouds, except that it felt like it was coming from below the rocks instead of up in the sky.

Heavy feet thudded down beside her, and something snuffled loudly around the sack. Its breathing sounded the same as whatever had eaten the dead sloth in the night. Glory clenched her talons. Was it planning to eat her? Because it was in for quite a surprise if it —

"Another one?" said a disapproving voice.

The snuffling hitched for a second, as if startled, and then a hoarse voice beside Glory's head said, "Yeah. Easy catch. She was all alone in the forest. Stupid like all RainWings."

Dragons, Glory thought. Relief warred with fury. *They're just dragons. Nothing mysterious and creepy. Apart from the basic mysterious creepiness of kidnapping other dragons, that is.*

Well, I can handle a couple of creepy dragons. Just as soon as they take this sack off me. She flexed her claws, wondering if she could rip through the cloth around them.

"Didn't you get the message?" said the first dragon.

"Yeah," said the one with the garbled breathing. "But I like the prey in the rainforest. And I was hungry. And then this dragon was just asking to get caught. Besides, I thought his message was stupid."

"It's not stupid if it keeps us safe." The first dragon sighed. "Throw her in with the others. But from now on, do as you're told."

"Yeah, yeah," grumbled the second dragon. "All right, I got it. No more hunting or grabbing dragons in the rainforest until Deathbringer says it's all clear."

CHAPTER 20

Glory had never been so glad that her scales were hidden. There was no way she could stop the colors flooding through them; she couldn't even guess what they were turning to right now.

Deathbringer *did* know who was taking the missing RainWings. He was connected to them. And somehow he had told them to stop . . . until "it's all clear"; what did that mean? Until he'd finished killing the dragonets? Or until Glory and her friends stopped snooping around the tunnel?

And *how* did he get a message to these dragons? Glory had left him in the Ice Kingdom and then caught him coming out of the desert tunnel into the rainforest. He'd said he followed the dragonets to the hole in the sand, but maybe he'd known about it before. Maybe he'd gotten there first, gone through to this place, warned these dragons, and then gone back to the desert tunnel after the dragonets were back in the rainforest . . . but . . .

Glory remembered that Deathbringer had conveniently appeared just in time to stop them from catching the creature in the dark.

He did that on purpose.

He was warning off the other dragon — this one with the weird breathing.

Deathbringer knew we would catch him. Maybe he wanted us to catch him.

Her tail curled. *And my friends are alone with Deathbringer. I have to get back to them. I have to get back right now.*

She flung open her wings and lashed her tail, clawing at the sack frantically.

"Whoa!" yelled the hoarse voice. "A little help here!"

Glory's heart sank at the sound of footsteps and wing-beats. There were a lot more than two dragons out there. She kicked out blindly, fighting as hard as she could, but talons grabbed her from all sides, pinning her to the ground.

"You'll never get her there like this," gasped one of the dragons. "You'll have to knock her out again."

"My pleasure," said the hoarse voice.

And once again, something slammed into Glory's head, and then all was darkness.

"Hey!"

Something nosed Glory in the ribs, and she woke up with a small yelp of pain.

"Are you awake?" Tiny claws lifted Glory's eyelids, and something blurry came way too close to her snout to peer at her.

"Mmmmf!" Glory said through the gag around her mouth. She tried to push the something away, but her talons felt heavy and she missed.

"Ha ha, don't even try," said the little voice. "I've spent my whole life waking up dragons who'd rather be sleeping instead of training me. I'm excellent at dodging when they get all mad about it." The tiny claws poked at her ruff. "How come I don't know you?"

"Mmmmf," Glory said again. Her head hurt. She rested it back on the ground and blinked until the world came into focus.

A small diamond-shaped snout hovered only a few inches from hers. Gigantic dark eyes peered out of gold and orange scales. The little dragonet couldn't have been more than three years old. She poked Glory's ruff again.

"Don't worry, I know you can't talk. I'm the only one without a gag. They decided my venom wasn't strong enough or I couldn't shoot it far enough to be dangerous, or something, I guess, which is a little unfair because if somebody would just *train* me *properly*, I think I'd be super-great at it and then these horrible dragons would be super-sorry for putting *me* in a cage." A ripple of scarlet fury moved through her wings.

Glory reluctantly sat up so she could look around. The pain in her head flared viciously, and she had to close her eyes until it receded into a dull throb.

When she opened them again, she realized that the blurriness around her wasn't just her eyes. The air was hazy with smoke. Pulsing heat wafted over her scales, although she couldn't see any sign of a fire. She glanced up and saw jagged stone walls pressing close overhead. It seemed like the heat was coming from the rocks themselves.

Back in a cave, she thought. *Awesome.*

The sack was gone, but the bindings around her wings and claws were still in place. Her mouth was still bound as well, but it felt different from before — whatever clamped her snout shut now was much heavier than the earlier vines. She crossed her eyes trying to get a look at it.

"It's a metal band," the little dragonet explained, tilting her head sympathetically. "Like this one around my neck. It's to keep you from using your venom, but it's also so we can't camouflage ourselves and disappear; they'll always be able to see the metal band." She pointed to a thick brassy clamp around her own neck. "Smart but annoying, right?" She paused. "Kind of like me! Ha ha! My name's Kinkajou, by the way, in case you were wondering."

So there's one of the missing RainWings, Glory thought. *Where are the others?* The small cave held only herself and the dragonet. A half-moon of light glowed at the cave opening, not far away. Glory took a tentative step toward it, then another when nothing happened. Nothing fell from the roof; nothing attacked her; no alarms went off. What sort of prison was this?

Kinkajou followed her, still chattering. "I know what you're thinking," she said. "I'm super-good at that, especially nowadays when I'm the only one who can talk and so I have to imagine the other side of every conversation I have. Maybe telepathy is contagious or something. But anyway, you're thinking you can walk out of this cave, and trust me, you can't, but you'll have to go see for yourself because everybody does, I guess, instead of listening to me."

Glory reached the entrance and stopped.

Kinkajou was right. There was no walking out this way.

A wide, sluggish river of molten lava flowed past just outside the cave. It glowed gold and orange-bright, the only splash of color in a barren black landscape. With her wings bound, Glory would never make it across.

She leaned out to see where the lava river started. A hulking dark mountain filled the sky, half-hidden by the smoke pouring out the top. Smaller rivulets of lava dappled the slope and a red glow came from a few holes in the rocks. It was hard to tell whether it was night or day; the light was so strange, and the sky was swathed in dark clouds. Glory guessed that she'd been knocked out for a few hours, at least. The rotten-eggs smell was thick in the air.

"Sinister, right?" Kinkajou said in her ear, and Glory jumped. "Who would actually want to live here? I don't get it."

Who does *live here?* Glory wondered. *The Talons of Peace? Is this where they hide?*

And then she realized that parts of the landscape were moving, and they weren't rocks after all . . . they were dragons.

Black dragons, with silver scales glittering under their wings. She could see at least a hundred of them scattered across the mountain and several more flying above it.

She inhaled sharply and regretted it as sulfur filled her nose.

I know where we are.

This is the secret home of the NightWings.

— CHAPTER 21 —

Glory turned to the dragonet and waved her bound claws at the gag around her mouth.

"Oh my gosh," said Kinkajou, staring at Glory's scales as they changed color. "You're excited about something. I wonder what! Ooooo, and curious. Sure, of course you are. You must have lots of questions. I sure had lots of questions when I got here. Hey, now you're . . . frustrated! Super-frustrated! And getting mad! Wow, what are you so —"

Exasperated, Glory shoved her aside and marched back into the cave.

"Oh, you're mad at *me*," said Kinkajou, trotting along behind her. "I'm used to that."

The cave was not very big, ending abruptly at a steep drop-off at the back. Glory stared down into a pitch-black abyss. With no fire and no ability to see in the dark, no RainWing would get very close to that. Even if her wings were free, Glory wouldn't go near it.

"That's how I visit the other prisoners," Kinkajou said. "All their caves, and the one I'm supposed to stay in, open out onto this."

Glory looked at the dragonet with new respect. Kinkajou's wings weren't bound, but they were tiny; most three-year-old dragons couldn't fly for long without needing a rest. She couldn't have known how long she'd have to fly when she first jumped into the darkness, looking for other prisoners. That was a special kind of brave. And crazy.

Kinkajou tilted her head at Glory. "I have no idea what that color means," she said. "Wow, you really are different." She reached up and tugged on the ropes around Glory's wings. "But this is the same." She sighed. "I can't get any of them off. I'm sorry. It's some kind of super-impossible knot."

Glory held up her claws. Thick canvas covered them, tied together with another rope around each forearm.

"Here, too," Kinkajou said, pointing to the knot. "See how tight that is?" Glory squinted at it. She didn't know much about knots. She nodded to Kinkajou's talons, and the little dragonet shook her head. "They're not sharp enough to cut through the rope. I've tried." Kinkajou sliced one tiny claw across the rope, but it didn't even look frayed.

Glory lashed her tail.

"It *is* frustrating," Kinkajou agreed. "Stupid NightWings. But if we tried to escape, they'd read our minds or foresee it and stop us anyway, right?"

Glory discovered that she could still growl.

"Does that mean you want to try?" Kinkajou asked, perking up. Her ruff flared around her face. "Because nobody else wants to try escaping but I *so* do, because oh my gosh you haven't even seen how awful the food is here. They keep bringing us horrible *dead* things. I mean, things that have been dead for *weeks*, I think. It is *mega*-gross and makes us totally sick when we eat it. There's no fruit at all. Tapir finally just let himself starve to death, it's so awful. I try to eat as little as I can."

How am I supposed to make an escape plan with a dragonet who won't shut up? Glory wondered. *When I can't even ask her any questions?*

Such as: What did the NightWings want with the RainWings anyway?

Why were they kidnapping them and holding them prisoner?

What did Deathbringer have to do with this plan? And why had he told them to stop?

"Confused!" Kinkajou guessed, pointing at Glory's scales. "And . . . frustrated again!"

I need a color for STOP THAT, Glory thought.

Something flapped outside the cave entrance. Kinkajou turned toward the sound, then winced and closed her eyes.

Glory pushed past her and peered out.

Three NightWings flew over the lava river and disappeared into another cave not far from Glory's. A few moments later, they reappeared, dragging a limp RainWing behind them.

The RainWing's scales were a heavy gray, like rain clouds; it was a color of sadness Glory hadn't seen on any other RainWing. He was conscious but neither struggled nor helped the NightWings. He just hung between them like he'd given up completely. Glory thought of Jambu's vibrantly joyful scales and felt a stab of anger — at the NightWings, for ripping innocent dragons from their homes, and at the other RainWings, for letting this happen to their friends without even noticing or caring that they were gone.

The black dragons lifted the RainWing over the river and carried him up the slope of the mountain, letting his tail bump across the rocks. Glory watched until they all vanished into a sort of fortress halfway up the mountain. It looked like a jumbled pile of rocks, so she hadn't realized it was a building before.

"Poor Gibbon," Kinkajou said. "They take him all the time. I guess his venom is *way* more interesting than mine or something."

Glory whirled to stare at her.

"Oh, yeah," Kinkajou said. "When they take you up there, try pretending your venom doesn't work right or something. That's all they want us to do — melt things. It's so weird! Like, can't they melt their own things? So far I've melted an orange and a pile of leaves. They told me to melt this metal claw-thing, too, but of course that's stupid; our venom doesn't work on nonliving stuff. And then they had me spit some venom into a bowl and who knows what they want with that. I don't get it."

They're studying us, Glory realized. *Or, at least, they're studying our venom.* She turned and began pacing the length of the cave. *Are they hoping to use it themselves? As a weapon?*

But the NightWings don't fight. They stay out of the war. So who do they need weapons for?

Are they planning to join the war soon?

On whose side?

Blister's, of course, she thought immediately, smacking herself in the head with her tail. *That's why they wanted us to choose her for the prophecy.*

But why join the war now? And why torture RainWings for their venom when NightWings have their own ever-so-special powers they never shut up about?

"That must be what thinking hard looks like," Kinkajou said, hopping onto a boulder and watching Glory with great interest. "Your scales are all kinds of colors right now. I've never seen another RainWing do that. Oh, I wish you could talk to me!"

Me too, Glory thought.

"Maybe we could escape together, and then you could be my teacher," Kinkajou said. "I swear I'm not as awful as everyone says. But we'd have to get you across the lava, and then we'd have to find the tunnel back to the rainforest, and then we'd have to get past the guards there, and then we'd have to get all your bindings off, or maybe we'd have to do that first; actually, that would make more sense, because then you could fly and fight and stuff, but I have no idea how to do any of that."

She stopped, her wings drooping, and suddenly looked very young. Glory had been wondering why Kinkajou didn't escape on her own. But if she didn't know where the tunnel was, and there were guards to fight along the way . . . it was a tall order for a little dragon. Especially when failure would surely mean she'd end up bound and gagged like the other RainWings.

"Maybe I could find something sharp enough to cut the ropes," Kinkajou said, brightening again. "Like a really sharp rock. Or — well, there's not much around here except rocks. Oh! Or I could check one of the really disgusting dead things for sharp bones when our dinner comes. That would be pretty gross, though. Maybe you should do that."

Glory thumped her tail on the ground to get Kinkajou's attention. She pointed to her mouth, then her stomach, then her mouth again, and tried to turn her scales the color of curiosity.

"You're asking me a question!" Kinkajou said with great delight. "Wait, let me guess. You're . . . hungry?"

Glory frowned and tapped the rope around her mouth, pointed to the cave opening, flapped her arms like wings, pointed to her stomach, and pointed to the rope again.

Kinkajou furrowed her brow. "Something about the NightWings and food — oh! Oh, I know! You want to know if they take off the metal band when they feed us. Am I right? Am I right?" She turned toward the cave entrance as Glory nodded. "I guess you're about to find out."

The little dragonet darted over the drop and vanished into one of the gaps in the far wall. Glory could see her eyes shining in the dark, still watching.

Four NightWings ducked into the cave, one after the other, crowding the narrow space. Glory held her ground and glared at them. At least there was no sign of Morrowseer. She was safer as an ordinary RainWing prisoner than she would be if they found out she was the dragonet messing up their prophecy — the one they'd already tried to kill more than once.

The last dragon who came in had a disturbing scar twisted across his snout. Strange bubbles of deformed skin protruded from his jawline, and one of his nostrils was sealed shut, so he breathed in a loud, snuffly way.

When he spoke, Glory recognized the hoarse voice of the dragon who'd captured her.

He was the one in the forest, she realized, listening to his peculiar breathing. *The creature in the dark — the one who ate the dead sloth.*

"Looks normal to me," he said gruffly.

One of the others gave him a scathing look. "On the contrary," she said. "There's clearly something wrong with this one."

"What do you mean?" said a third dragon.

"Observe her scales. Every other RainWing we've picked up turned instantly green — the color that seems to indicate fear. But this one — I don't know what it indicates, but I'm seeing shades of red and orange, perhaps a little black here and here." The NightWing used a thin stick to point to spots on Glory's wings with clinical detachment. She could have been describing a moderately interesting beetle for all the emotion in her voice.

"So she's matching her environment," said the third dragon. "That's something they do, too, isn't it?"

Glory narrowed her eyes at them and turned a deliberate, violent shade of purple.

"Oh, my," said the unemotional dragon. "We should take her to the lab immediately for closer study. I strongly recommend not feeding her and not touching that gag until we know more about her."

"Bosh," said the scarred NightWing. "All RainWings are the same. Rotten and useless."

"Besides, Queen Battlewinner doesn't like to have her orders questioned," the fourth dragon spoke up. He stepped forward with something furry and horrible-smelling in his talons. "It's feeding time now. You can go ask her if this one should go to the lab afterward."

"I will," she said, stepping back. "I've registered my concern here. You do what you like." The NightWing slid out of the cave and flew off.

Leaving only three for me to fight, Glory thought. *You may have studied the venom of pacifist, well-trained, frightened RainWings, but you've never studied me.*

The scarred dragon produced a long spear from a sheath on his back. The sharp end had three twisted clawlike points and glinted evilly in the reddish light. He hefted it in his talons and flicked his black tongue at Glory as if he were hoping she'd give him an excuse to hurt her.

He hates us, she thought, meeting his eyes. *It's personal for him*. Her gaze shifted to his scar. *Ah. That looks like it could have been caused by a venom strike. I wonder which RainWing was bold enough to do that*.

With a shiver, she realized he was the first dragon she'd seen who'd survived a venom attack. Which meant it was *possible* to survive a venom attack. Which meant Queen Scarlet really might still be alive.

The dead pile of fur landed by her feet, and the other two guards pulled out long spears of their own. Glory stared down at the meal they were offering. Kinkajou wasn't exaggerating. It did smell horrible and long-dead. She could barely tell what it had once been — a muskrat, perhaps. A nasty bite on its side looked a lot like the one on the sloth by the river, black and infected.

One of the guards leaned forward and jabbed his spear toward her face. Glory leaped back with a muffled snarl.

"Hold still if you want to eat," growled the scarred dragon. "Or else starve. We're fine with that, too."

Glory clenched her talons and eyed the spear as it bobbed closer. It was hard to see exactly what the guard did, but she felt the spear points hook into some kind of latch on the metal band, then twist and pull. The clamp slipped open and off, and the NightWings all jumped back with their spears up.

But not fast enough.

CHAPTER 22

Glory lunged forward with her fangs bared and seized the closest spear in her talons. She yanked it toward her, throwing the guard off-balance, and shot a jet of venom that missed his face but sprayed across his wings and back.

He let go of the spear and stumbled toward the cave entrance with a shriek of pain.

The scarred dragon dropped his spear. He shot out of the cave, shoving aside his injured tribemate as he went by.

Glory whipped toward the last guard and tried to turn the spear on him, but her wrapped talons were clumsy and she fumbled the weapon. He darted toward her, stabbing for her neck. Glory hissed a spray of venom at him, but to her surprise he dodged and rolled under it. A moment later he knocked her over and pinned her facedown. He shoved her snout into the rocky floor and pressed the points of the spear into her neck.

"Nice try, RainWing," he snarled. "But it's not that easy to fool a YYEEEOOOOOWW!" His weight suddenly disappeared from her back as his howls echoed around the cave.

Glory leaped to her feet and found Kinkajou beside her, with her front talons pressed over her snout.

"I can't believe I did that!" Kinkajou yelped. "Oh my gosh, look at him!"

The NightWing staggered into the wall, clawing at his neck. Kinkajou had hit him with only a few droplets of venom, but those were smoking and bubbling on his scales. He turned back to the two RainWings with pain-crazed rage in his eyes.

"I'm sorry!" Kinkajou cried. "Oh, that looks like it hurts so much!"

Glory yanked the spear out of the guard's claws and shoved him over the drop-off at the back of the cave. She could hear him flapping and blundering around in the dark, still yowling.

"But —" Kinkajou said.

"He'll be fine once he remembers he has fire," Glory said. "We should be gone by then."

"I didn't realize you meant escape *now*," Kinkajou said. "I mean, like, *right now*. That is *so crazy*. You're *crazy*." Her voice was edgy and manic, but her scales were bright yellow with excitement.

"Tone it down a bit, can you?" Glory said, nodding at the little dragonet's wings. "We don't need to alert the whole mountain as we escape. Try looking like them." She turned her own scales the same gleaming black as the NightWings outside. "And I'm Glory, by the way."

"Got it," Kinkajou said, flipping her tail. Inky black spread across her scales as if someone was pouring the night sky onto her. "But how do we get you over the lava river?"

Whoops. Glory had forgotten about that. Or rather, she hadn't thought that far ahead; she'd seen an opportunity to use her venom and took it without thinking. *Who am I, Tsunami?* she scolded herself.

Worse yet, she knew the scarred NightWing would be back any moment with reinforcements.

She clamped her teeth down on the canvas that covered her talons. With a violent shake of her head, she ripped at the cloth until it tore loose. As soon as her claws were free, she seized a spear and turned it on the ropes wrapped around her body.

"The guards are coming," Kinkajou said anxiously.

"Pretend you're a NightWing dragonet and stall them," Glory said. She jabbed the spear point awkwardly at one of the ropes and stabbed herself in the underbelly. With a hiss, she hefted the weapon and tried again.

"Yes. All right. Stall them. No problem," Kinkajou said. She darted toward the cave entrance. The first NightWing Glory had attacked was lying halfway across the opening, moaning softly and writhing as if he were trying to wriggle out of his own skin.

Kinkajou blinked at him for a moment, then lifted one of his wings so it draped across her shoulders and back, covering the brass band around her neck. She leaned a little way out of the cave and looked up.

"Quick!" she shouted suddenly, making Glory jump. "She attacked us! And escaped! We saw her go that way!" She pointed down the mountain. "Hurry! Don't stop! She was flying super-fast! No, no, I'll take care of him! Go after her! She's getting away!"

The whoosh of wings shot by overhead, sending a blast of hot air back into the cave. At the same time, Glory finally hooked the spear into the knot of the rope. With a twist, she managed to saw the sharp points across the fibers until they split — but as that rope slid off, she realized there were four more separately knotted around her.

I'll never get these all off before they realize it was a trick and come back, she thought. There had to be another way across the river. Maybe there was something they could use as a stepping stone.

She hurried to the opening and stared out, looking for large boulders. Kinkajou watched her trustingly. A squadron of five NightWings was flapping away down the mountain, toward a black-sand beach and an expanse of gray, stormy water.

Only five NightWings to stop me? Glory thought. She glanced up the mountain, but there was no sign of an alarm or extra forces mobilizing.

"I guess they're not really that worried about me escaping," she said uneasily.

"*I'm* getting pretty worried about it, though," Kinkajou offered.

"Hey," Glory said, poking the wounded guard. "You can still fly, can't you?"

He flinched away from her. "I can't," he moaned. "Everything hurts."

It didn't even look that bad. He'd avoided the worst of the spray, and most of the damage was along one side of his back.

"You're going to hurt a lot more unless you carry me over this lava," Glory said. "Or cut these ropes off for me." She bared her fangs at him, and he threw his wings over his head, scuttling backward into the cave.

"Actually," said a new voice, "I have a better offer."

Glory whirled around as a black dragon descended from the sky and gave her a cheeky grin.

"Hello, Glory," said Deathbringer.

CHAPTER 23

"Don't give me that smug face," Glory snapped.

"This isn't my smug face, it's my heroic face," Deathbringer said. "And how funny is this? First I was your prisoner, now you're mine?"

"Perhaps you haven't heard what I do to dragons who try to keep me prisoner," Glory said with a hiss.

"All right, stop it, you two." Clay flapped up behind Deathbringer and landed beside Glory.

"Clay!" Glory cried. "What are you doing here?"

"We came to rescue you," he said, nudging her wing with his. "Aren't you pleased?"

"I'm right in the middle of rescuing myself," Glory said. She was having a hard time keeping her scales black when the sight of Clay made her feel as pink as her ridiculous brother. "Maybe some other time."

"Don't listen to her!" Kinkajou cried. "We definitely need rescuing! Please rescue us!"

"How did you even get here?" Glory asked. "I mean, how did you know to look for me here?"

Clay nodded at Deathbringer, who flicked his tail and managed to look even *more* smug. "He talked me into it. When you didn't come back, he told me he knew where you'd gone and that he'd help me find you if I set him free."

"Sounds like a trick," Glory said, eyeing Deathbringer suspiciously. Why would he work against his fellow NightWings? Was this a way to get Clay into their clutches as well?

"Let's escape first and ask skeptical questions later," said Kinkajou. She jumped into the air, wings flapping.

"Sensible dragonet," said Deathbringer. He gave Glory an unreadable look — teasing but worried, and self-satisfied but sweet all at once. "You can express your undying gratitude to me later. I'll wait."

"Go ahead and hold your breath," Glory suggested.

"Up you go," Clay said. He spread his wings so Glory could climb onto his back.

She hesitated for a moment. Part of her said, *You can do this yourself. You don't need help. Just get your wings free and save your own scales.*

But there wasn't time, and although she couldn't trust Deathbringer, there was no one more trustworthy than Clay. She clambered onto his back, still holding the spear and awkwardly adjusting her balance without her wings.

He was in the air almost before she could get her talons around his neck. She slipped sideways and nearly knocked him into the lava. Clay's tail brushed the bubbling, red-hot river below and he lurched upward with a hiss of pain.

"It's all right," he said quickly. "It'll heal fast, don't worry."

Fire-resistant scales like Clay's would definitely have come in handy here, Glory thought, glancing down as he flew higher. She saw several other caves overlooking the lava river, but no snouts sticking out.

"We have to get the other RainWings," she shouted in Clay's ear. "We have to set them all free."

"Now?" he asked. "We'll be lucky if *we* make it out without getting caught."

"I can't just leave them here," she cried. "I promised Mangrove I'd find Orchid."

"And you did," he said. "Now you know where she is, we can come back and get her. With backup." He glanced over his shoulder and put on a burst of speed. "Lots and lots of backup."

Glory looked behind them as well and saw a cluster of NightWings standing on a high rocky ledge. Three of them were pointing at Clay and shouting to the others. Black-scaled heads were turning toward the sky all across the volcano.

She also saw Kinkajou flapping madly to keep up with them. What she didn't see was a certain dangerous know-it-all assassin.

"Deathbringer's not with us!" she called.

"Of course not," Clay called back. He swooped down between two curved stone columns and banked right. "His tribe can't know he helped us."

Glory thought uneasily of the dragon she'd wounded, back in the prison cave. Surely he had seen Deathbringer and overheard their conversation. But really that was Deathbringer's problem. "What happened to his mission? The one about killing us? Remember?"

"Maybe he doesn't want to anymore," Clay said with a shrug.

Suspicious, Glory thought. *Or as Kinkajou would say, mega-suspicious.*

And yet she also felt a weird loss, like she wished she'd had a chance to say good-bye. She twisted to look back again, but he really wasn't there. *Ah, well. Maybe the next time he shows up to kill me.*

She realized that Clay was winging rapidly toward the black-sand beach that ringed the island at the base of the volcano. Twisted, leafless trees grew on the volcano's slopes, like bones sticking out of the dirt. Beyond the beach, the ocean roared and churned, gray and unfriendly and speckled with foam.

"Um, Clay?" Glory said. "We're not flying back to the rainforest across that ocean, are we?"

"No way," Clay said. "I don't even know which way the rest of Pyrrhia is, or how far. Do you?"

"Nope," Glory said. "But it makes sense to me that the NightWings live on an island — one that's not on any maps. I would have thought they'd pick a nicer one, though. This place is ghastly." She coughed, wondering if the smell of rotten eggs would ever clear out of her snout.

Clay dove toward a cave halfway up a small rocky cliff at one end of the beach.

"The passage to the rainforest is in there," he called. "Get ready to fight."

"Always. Ready," panted Kinkajou beside them. Glory opened her mouth and tasted the smoky air. She couldn't see any guards on the beach below.

"Didn't you have to fight them on your way out of the tunnel?" she asked.

"No — Deathbringer went ahead of me and distracted them. But they'll be back by now."

"Also," Kinkajou gasped. "Company. Behind."

Glory didn't have to look back; she'd already heard the wingbeats, and she didn't really want to know exactly how many NightWings were on their tails. She gripped the spear in her claws, imagining Morrowseer on the pointy end of it.

The cave yawned wide in front of them. Clay didn't slow down as he shot between the rocky walls. Glory blinked, her eyes adjusting to the darkness, and then she saw the light of a fire glowing up ahead.

Four NightWings were gathered around the fire, each of them carrying one of the wicked-looking spears. The *wrongness* feeling emanated from a perfectly circular hole in the rock wall behind them. And they were clearly not planning on letting anyone get to it.

We have to get past them fast, Glory thought. *Or else we'll have all the ones behind us to deal with as well.*

The first guard saw them coming, jumped up, and slammed into Clay. Glory catapulted over his head, dropping the spear and just missing the fire as she crashed into one of the other dragons. Talons seized her tail and wings and more talons fumbled for her snout. *Not happening*, Glory thought. No one would muzzle her weapon again.

Her jaw sprang open and she swung her neck around, spraying venom at the guard who was trying to hold her down. Black droplets spattered across his chest. Screaming, he leaped back and stumbled into the fire, then fled toward the beach with smoke rising from his scales.

The other two guards pounced on Glory from behind, wrestling her back down again. They were both huge, the size of Morrowseer, with metal armor buckled over their underbellies and strange helmets protecting their snouts. Glory's face was pressed into the ground. She lashed her tail furiously, trying to smack them the way Tsunami would have, but one of the guards stepped on it and pinned it down.

Glory struggled against the weight of the two dragons. Above her, Clay was battling the first NightWing. Their claws clashed and bouts of fire blasted through the air.

Kinkajou, Glory thought. Where had she gone? Had she made it into the tunnel?

The tiny dragonet suddenly popped up behind the guards, holding the spear Glory had dropped. She swung it hard and smacked one of the NightWings on the head with the blunt end. He tottered sideways with a yell, then whipped around with a murderous gleam in his eyes.

"Kinkajou!" Glory shouted. "Use your venom!"

"But —" Kinkajou said, dodging a swipe of the NightWing's claws. "I don't —"

"Or the spear! The pointy end this time!"

Kinkajou looked down at the spear with a surprised expression. She hefted it and jabbed it at the guard as he came at her again. He knocked it aside and thrust his own spear at her. Kinkajou yelped and Glory saw a streak of blood slashed across her neck.

Glory clenched her talons with rage. How *dare* he. Kinkajou was just a tiny dragonet. Not only that, she was a RainWing, which meant she'd never been trained to fight.

There was just one guard holding Glory down at the moment. She thought of Sunny's tricks from battle training and stopped struggling. On top of her, the guard let out a pleased hiss.

Glory let her scales ripple into the color of the rocks below her.

"Foolish RainWing," hissed the guard. "I can still feel you. I can still see your wing bindings."

Glory knew that, but she was hoping the strangeness of holding something he couldn't see would make him slower. Taking a deep breath, she suddenly twisted herself into a tight spiral. The NightWing's talons slipped on her scales, and she was able to get her tail free for a moment — long enough to swing it around and jab him sharply in the middle of his back.

Sunny loved this move, and at first none of them had understood why. If she'd had a poisonous barb on her tail like other SandWings, it would have been terrifying — but with a harmless tail, what was the point?

Then they'd each experienced it and discovered there was something freaky and unsettling about it. It felt like being hit by lightning at just the wrong spot. It was as if their scales knew they *could* have been badly injured — if there had been poison at the tip of that tail, it would have paralyzed their spines instantly and killed them a few moments later. So it was weirdly chilling, and an effective distraction in the middle of a fight.

Glory had no idea if this would work when a RainWing did it to a NightWing, but it was worth a try.

The guard stiffened as if he'd just been shocked by one of the electric eels in Queen Coral's prison. It was only for a moment, but in that moment Glory was able to throw him off her and free her snout. She went straight for Kinkajou's attacker, shooting venom at all the exposed scales she could see.

He screamed and slammed back into the rocks. Glory saw another gash along Kinkajou's side. The little dragonet was shaking, and her scales were ripples of pale green and white.

Claws seized Glory's tail before she could get to Kinkajou.

"Get out of here!" Glory shouted, pointing at the hole. "Go!"

Kinkajou hesitated, looking beyond Glory at the NightWing guard. For a moment, Glory was certain that she'd disobey and stay to help fight. But then, without arguing, Kinkajou darted for the tunnel and vanished into the darkness.

Well, good, Glory thought as a spear viciously clocked her in the head. *Someone being sensible for once. Unlike my friends.* She tried to turn around, but the NightWing threw her into the wall. Stars spun dizzily in Glory's vision. *Don't pass out. Don't pass out.* If the NightWings recaptured her, she'd never get another chance to use her venom and escape. They'd probably let her starve to death instead.

Blurrily she saw Clay suddenly drop out of the air, and her heart leaped into her throat. Was he hurt? She staggered a step toward him, but a sharp pain in her back leg stopped her. The guard had stabbed her with his spear.

Glory hissed angrily and lunged for the spear as the guard pulled it back. He stabbed it at her again, violent and fast, and she felt it scratch her underbelly like a sharp line of bee stings.

At the same time, Clay landed right in the middle of the fire. Flames licked at his underbelly and wings, and a scorched smell filled the cave. Glory's scales hurt just looking at him. Even if he healed fast, she knew his skin was burning right now.

Clenching his jaw, Clay crouched and picked up smoldering coals from the fire in his talons. The NightWing in the air above him didn't have time to figure out what was coming.

Clay flung the coals right in the guard's face and started grabbing and throwing more as the guard frantically clawed at his snout.

"Clay!" Glory yelled as her own opponent flung her off-balance. Glory fell backward and the NightWing was on her in an instant, wrapping his strong talons around her snout to force it shut.

Red-hot coals came flying through the air. Most bounced off the dragon's armor, and one ricocheted painfully against Glory's bound wings, but a few found the gaps in the armor and slid inside. The guard let go of Glory and started clawing at his armor, howling with pain.

Glory had just made it to her feet again when someone grabbed her shoulders. She whipped around with a hiss and barely managed to stop herself from shooting venom in Clay's face.

"Quick!" he cried, shoving her onto his back. She grabbed his neck again as he bunched his legs and flung himself over the guards at the hole. One of the injured NightWings lunged for Clay's tail, but when he saw Glory opening her mouth, he flinched away.

Clay dove into the tunnel, which spiraled up and around. Glory held on tight, burying her head in his scales as they flew.

She could hear rain falling up ahead.

Almost there, she thought. *Almost safe. For now.*

CHAPTER 24

They emerged into a sun shower. Rain dripped down through the leaves, but shafts of sunlight still dappled the trees, reflecting flashes of light off the droplets and catching rainbows in the spider webs and waterfalls.

Clay tipped Glory off onto the ground and flopped into the nearest mud puddle, breathing heavily.

She sat up, shaking herself, and looked up at the tunnel to the NightWing island. There was no sound of pursuit; no thumping wingbeats, no black snouts crawling out to continue the battle.

It took her a moment to realize how close they were to the other passage, the one that went to the desert. The first tunnel was in a boulder; this one went straight into the second dark tree, on the other side of the stream.

She wouldn't have noticed the hole in the tree trunk if she hadn't been looking for it. It was above her eye level, carved into the tree at a height where most dragons would have to look up to see it. It was as dark as the tree itself, disappearing into the wood, and it pulsed with such a feeling of not-supposed-to-be-there that she wanted to look away the moment her eyes came anywhere near it.

"A second tunnel," she said to Clay. "That is so weird. Do you think there are more?"

"Wake me when you figure it out," Clay said. "No, hang on. Never wake me up again. I'm going to sleep for a few hundred years." He scooped up two talonfuls of mud and poured it onto his head, closing his eyes with a sigh.

Kinkajou shot out of the treetops and cannoned into Glory. "I'm so glad you're all right!" she yelped. "I didn't want to leave you there, but I was so scared —"

"You did the right thing," Glory said, ducking to avoid the spear Kinkajou was still swinging around. "Here, give me that. And go look in that hole to see if anyone's following us."

Kinkajou's eyes went wide. "But what if they are? Then what do I do?"

"Scare them back to their hideous island," Glory said, poking the spear at her bindings. "I'll come help you as soon as I get my wings free. And if I can figure it out, I'll use this thing to get your neck band off, too." She nodded at the metal ring on Kinkajou.

The little dragonet shuffled her feet. "But — um — listen, I — I'm not sure I want to use my venom on any more dragons. It made me feel really, really awful."

"Then just pretend you're going to," Glory said. She nudged the dragonet toward the tree. "Sit in the tunnel entrance with your mouth open and try to look sinister, all right?"

Kinkajou perked up. "Sure, I bet I can look sinister! Super-sinister! Just watch me!" She flapped up to the hole, curled her tail around her talons, opened her mouth, and squinted fiercely down the tunnel. She looked more like a decorative doorstop than a guard, but it would have to do for now.

Glory kept one eye on her as she worked to free her wings. It was a little unsettling that no one had chased them through the tunnel. Maybe the NightWings thought there'd be more dragons waiting on this end to fight them off.

How long had she been gone? She squinted at the angle of the sunbeams and realized it must be morning. It felt like she'd been trapped in the Night Kingdom for a month, but it had been only a day.

She had one rope left to untie when she heard voices approaching through the forest.

"This is a terrible idea! Can't we discuss it like sensible dragons?"

"There's no time! Clay and Glory have been kidnapped by that NightWing assassin! I have to save them!"

"But we don't *know* that he took them and we don't know that he went through the tunnel or where they might be in the Kingdom of Sand and —"

"We're over here!" Glory called.

There was a pause, followed by some vigorous flapping. Starflight and Tsunami burst out of the trees and soared down over the stream to land beside Clay. A few moments later, Sunny caught up to them. Glory's sloth was sitting on her head, clutching Sunny's horns with a startled expression.

"Oh, I knew you were all right," Sunny said brightly. She hesitated, squinting at Clay and the mud dripping over his snout. Her eyes took in the wounds slashed along Glory's scales. "Um — *are* you all right?"

"Of course," Clay said, squishing himself farther down into the mud puddle.

Silver leaped from Sunny onto Glory's neck and started tugging on Glory's ears, warbling a furry complaint. Glory caught her between her claws and stroked her head. "Sorry," she whispered. "But it wouldn't have been safe for you."

"HRRRF," the sloth objected.

"Where were you?" Tsunami cried. "Deathbringer's escaped! He could be anywhere! He could jump out and try to kill you at any time!"

"Actually, he's in there," Glory said, pointing up at the tree. Her friends all craned their necks to peer at the hole.

"Another tunnel?" Sunny said. She glanced across the stream and shivered. "I mean, I noticed the weird feeling, but I thought it was still coming from that one."

"Where does this one go?" Starflight asked.

Glory tilted her head at him. "It goes to the Night Kingdom," she said.

Starflight inhaled softly and stared up at the tree. She saw the anxiety and curiosity tingling through him as clearly as if his scales could change color, too. His tribe was through there, and his original home. She wondered what he would think of the island — the smell, the scorched air and unfriendly rocks, the horrible smoky cloud that hung over everything, and the fact that his fellow NightWings were kidnapping RainWings for their venom. All things considered, she thought she'd rather have her own tribe of lazy but *not* evil dragons.

"Listen," she said. "You may want to sit down for this."

They decided to leave Tsunami and Clay guarding the tunnel.

"Don't let *anyone* come through there," Glory said fiercely. "If you even see a hint of a snout poke out, you jab it with this thing as hard as you can." She handed the spear to Tsunami.

"No problem," Tsunami said with relish. She spun the spear between her talons.

"We'll be back soon," Glory said. "With an army of RainWings."

Tsunami and Starflight exchanged glances, and Glory flared her ruff at them. "I know what you're thinking," she snapped. "So don't say it."

"It's just —" Starflight said. "I mean, is that a good idea? RainWings aren't very . . . army-like. The NightWings would crush them easily."

"Especially if any of them look into the future and see you coming," Sunny said.

"They didn't foresee me escaping," Glory pointed out. "They're not all-powerful. We can stop them and rescue the others."

"Maybe it's a misunderstanding," Starflight said, resting his front talons on the tree. "Maybe if I went through and talked to them . . ."

"Then maybe you'd end up in a lovely lava prison, too," Glory said. "Or dead. Let's not forget that you might be one of the dragons Deathbringer was sent to kill." She spread her wings, letting them shimmer into the colors of the cobweb rainbows. "But feel free to stand here worrying about it all day. I'm going back to get my tribe, with or without you." She beckoned to Kinkajou and leaped into the air.

It was a relief to use her own wings again. She stretched them wide as they soared up to the highest branches. Silver clung to her shoulders, making happy furry noises. Kinkajou took the lead with an eager flick of her tail. Glory had figured out how to get the band off with the NightWing spear; it had left a painful-looking dent in Kinkajou's neck, but the little dragon was too happy to mind. Bursts of pink and yellow spiraled through her scales, getting brighter the closer they got to the village.

"Have they been looking for me every day?" the dragonet asked, looping back to circle around Glory. "Did Bromeliad just have a heart attack when I disappeared? I can imagine her face." Kinkajou pursed her snout in a hilariously accurate impression of Bromeliad. "That dragonet got herself kidnapped on purpose! She's always been trouble!" Kinkajou giggled. "I hope she wore out her wings looking for me. Grumpy old cow. Gosh, won't everyone be excited when I finally turn up!"

"Um," Glory said, "don't be upset if there's no welcome-home party."

"There's Coconut!" Kinkajou cried, spotting a small dragon lounging in a hammock on the outskirts of the village. "Aw, look how exhausted he is. We took gliding lessons together all last year. I bet he's been helping to search for me. Coconut! It's me! I'm back!" She swooped up to the hammock and poked it vigorously with her tail until the emerald-green dragon inside sat up, blinking.

"Hmmm?" he said. "What?"

"I'm back!" Kinkajou said, wrapping her wings around him and nearly knocking him out of the hammock. "I'm all right! I made it home!"

Coconut disentangled himself politely. "Kinkajou?" He squinted at her. "You went somewhere?"

"I've been gone for almost three whole weeks," Kinkajou said. Her smile faded as the other dragon shook his head. "Didn't you miss me?"

"Erm," he said. "I've been very busy."

"I bet," Glory said disgustedly. "You, be at Magnificent's pavilion in one hour, and bring every other RainWing you can find. We're having a tribe meeting."

"A what?" Coconut said.

"And if you're not there, I will know, and I will personally come tie you into this hammock so you're stuck here forever," Glory said. "Go start telling everyone. Go!"

Coconut flailed out of the hammock and flapped away, looking confused.

Glory steered Kinkajou toward the center of the village. The dragonet's wings were drooping and speckled with blue-gray.

"Disappointing young dragons who count on them," Glory said. "Seems to be a RainWing specialty."

"Someone must have looked for me," said Kinkajou.

"Yes — I did," Glory pointed out. She saw the queen's treehouse up ahead and veered that way. Starflight and Sunny hadn't caught up yet. Maybe they were busy talking about how this plan of Glory's would fail. Or maybe they were checking on Webs again, as if that was at all important compared to saving the RainWings.

The line to see Magnificent was shorter today; only two dragons sat on the waiting platform, and neither of them looked particularly upset. Glory swooped right past them and dove through the vine curtain, skidding to a stop on the wood floor.

The RainWing queen jumped, and her sloth leaped onto her head, looking startled.

"I found them," Glory announced. She glanced at the dragons Magnificent was meeting with — a young RainWing whose blue-green scales looked like he was trying to match Tsunami's, complete with white dots to mimic her pearls, and a shrunken old dragon with a silvery tinge to his ruff. "I found the missing RainWings, Your Majesty."

"Oh, call me Maggie," said the queen. "What missing RainWings?"

"The ones you sent me to find," Glory said impatiently. "Like Orchid, and Queen Splendor — and Kinkajou here."

"Oh," said Magnificent. A shimmer of dark purple rippled through her scales. "Marvelous! I'm so pleased. Do go tell Mangrove. It'll be so nice not to have to deal with *that* headache anymore." She turned back to the other RainWings.

"No, no, listen," Glory said. "They were abducted. We have to go rescue them."

Magnificent blinked at Kinkajou.

"Except her," Glory said. "I mean, we got her out. But the others are still there. We need to get the tribe together and organize an expedition to save them."

"An expedition?" Magnificent echoed. Her eyes wandered to a lizard that was crawling slowly through the window.

"Save them from what?" asked the bluc-green RainWing.

"From the NightWings," said Glory. "They've been kidnapping RainWings and holding them prisoner." She hissed, remembering the gray dragon's tail thumping sadly along the ground as the NightWings carried him off.

"You want us to fight *other dragons*?" said the queen. "How would we do that?"

Glory clutched her head. She knew her scales were vibrating with furious sunset colors, but she needed all her energy for arguing with the queen. "With your venom," she said slowly. "With your camouflage. With your claws and teeth. With *anything* that will save your fellow tribemates."

"We're not fighters," the queen said, as if she were explaining the three moons to a very small dragonet. "RainWings aren't built for it. We're a peaceful tribe."

"So what do you· suggest?" Glory snapped. "Ask the NightWings nicely to give back the dragons they stole? Because kidnapping dragons certainly makes them seem like a pretty reasonable tribe. Open to negotiations and all that."

Queen Magnificent examined her claws for a moment, then picked up her sloth and scratched it under its chin. "Well, let's think about this sensibly. Do we really need to get them back?"

Glory felt as if she'd just been dropped in the NightWings' volcano. She stared at the queen. "You mean — you would *leave them there*?"

"Whoa," said the blue dragon, staring at Glory's scales. "I've never seen anyone turn that color red before."

"It's only a few dragons," said the queen with a wave of one talon. "Right? Five or six?"

"Fourteen," said Kinkajou. "Not counting the three who already died there."

Even Mangrove didn't realize how many were missing, Glory thought. She felt another wave of anger. *Three dead before anyone even went looking for them. Were they waiting to be rescued? Did they believe someone would come for them, or did they know there was no hope?*

"See? Only fourteen," said Magnificent. "It doesn't really make that much difference, does it? There are plenty of other dragons in the tribe."

For a moment Glory was speechless. She had never, ever, not once in a million years, imagined there could be a queen who would let her subjects die without lifting a claw to save them. If the queen didn't even care, what chance did any RainWing have?

And there was nothing Glory could do. She wasn't part of the prophecy, she wasn't a normal RainWing, and she couldn't save the RainWings on her own, no matter how much she wanted to. Without the queen, with no army, she was as useless as a sloth.

She wanted to scream a million things at the queen: What is wrong with all of you? Don't you have any loyalty? Or empathy?

Someone should care when a dragon disappears.

And then she realized exactly what she wanted to say.

She spread her wings and pointed at the larger dragon. "Queen Magnificent, I challenge you for the throne of the RainWings."

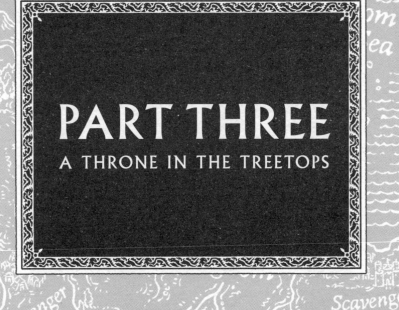

PART THREE

A THRONE IN THE TREETOPS

──── CHAPTER 25 ────

"You mean you want a turn at being queen?" said Magnificent, tilting her head in a puzzled way. "I'm sure that could be arranged, if you insist. I can talk to the others and try to fit you in between Grandeur and Exquisite next year."

"No, I need to be queen now," said Glory. She tried not to think about how much bigger than her Magnificent was, or how many years older she must be. *Then again, I'm sure she's never had any battle training or faced a SkyWing's claws every morning for six years.* "Because if you won't rescue those RainWings, I will, whatever it takes. Even if it means taking the throne from you."

"Oh, *wow*," Kinkajou breathed.

"I don't see how you could possibly do that," said Queen Magnificent. She looked down and started rearranging one of her flower necklaces.

"It's not very complicated," Glory said. "We fight. Whoever survives gets to be queen."

The other RainWings in the room all gasped.

The queen's scales shimmered white and green. She stared

at Glory. "You would kill another dragon just so you could be queen?"

"That's how it works in every other tribe," Glory pointed out.

"Not *here*," said Magnificent. "That's *barbaric*."

"What's barbaric is abandoning dragons of your tribe when you could save them," said Glory fiercely.

Queen Magnificent waved her front claws airily and addressed herself to Kinkajou and the blue-green dragon. "I'm sure no RainWing would follow a queen who got her throne by violence. Agreed?"

The blue-green dragon shrugged, but Kinkajou puffed out her chest and glared at the queen. "I'd follow Glory anywhere," she said.

"It's not the RainWing way," Magnificent protested.

"As far as I can tell, the RainWing way is to lie around and do nothing," Glory snapped. "So why don't you do that, and I'll just go ahead and be queen. After all, no one really wants the job, right?"

"Maybe I don't want *you* to have it," said the queen with a growl.

"There is an old tradition," interjected the ancient dragon suddenly. "If anyone wants to hear about it." The old RainWing chuckled as they all turned to him. "Don't look at me like that, Maggie. It's the fair thing to do, and it gives you as much chance, if not more, of keeping the throne."

"What is it?" Glory asked.

"A contest," he said. "Legend has it that dragons once vied for our throne like any other, but over time the RainWings devised a new method that did not end in death. If a challenger wished to take the throne, she had to defeat the present queen in a competition — and the queen had the right to choose the nature of the contest."

"That sounds exhausting," Magnificent said peevishly.

"It sounds fair to me," said Glory. Typical RainWing nonsense, but honestly, becoming queen without any killing would be fine by her. "What kinds of contests did they have?"

The old dragon squinted into the air. "Let me think," he said, counting on his claws. "Once there was a gliding race through the treetops. And when I was a very young dragonet, I saw a camouflage contest — one would hide while the other tried to find her, and then vice versa. The winner was the one who found the other fastest."

"A game of hide-and-seek to become queen," Glory said. "Why not." She hoped no one could tell that she was a bit shaken. She was pretty sure she'd be better at a fight to the death than she would be at tree gliding or flower picking or whatever Magnificent would come up with. But if she wanted to be queen of the RainWings, she'd have to start acting like one. Keeping her scales evenly red, she turned to Magnificent. "Go ahead and name your contest, Your Majesty."

Magnificent narrowed her eyes. "I want a day to think about it," she said.

"That is customary," agreed the old dragon.

Glory lashed her tail. The kidnapped RainWings might not *have* a day. Who knew what the NightWings would do now that they'd been found out? What if they killed all their prisoners to hide the evidence? Or what if they were gathering an army and shoring up their defenses right now? A quick, overwhelming attack, before the NightWings could prepare — that's what Glory had been planning.

Maybe I could go back tonight, by myself, she thought. *Maybe I could sneak through the tunnel and free them all and melt any NightWings who tried to stop me and bring everyone home.*

But she remembered the feeling of NightWing claws pressing her into the stone, and the cold band of metal around her jaws. If she went back alone and got caught, there wouldn't be time for anyone to come after her. The NightWings would kill her on sight. And then there would be no hope for the imprisoned RainWings at all.

No, she couldn't rescue anyone without an army, which meant she needed the power of the throne behind her, and to get that, she had to win this contest. And with a day she might at least have a chance of preparing. Maybe Jambu could teach her tree gliding, like he'd promised.

"All right," she said, meeting the queen's eyes. "Sunrise tomorrow."

"At the Arboretum," said Magnificent with a sly smile, as if she knew perfectly well that Glory had no idea where that was.

Also memorize the layout of the RainWing village, Glory noted to herself. *Just in case she chooses, like, a scavenger hunt or something.*

Magnificent nodded toward the old dragon. "What was your name again?"

"Handsome," he said. He winked at Glory. "Our names don't always end up suiting us."

"Handsome can oversee the contest, since this was his stupid suggestion," Magnificent said. "If that's all right with you, pipsqueak."

"Sounds perfect," Glory said. "Enjoy your last day as queen."

She ducked out through the vine curtain and stood on the bridge for a moment, breathing deeply. The full impact of what she'd just done was finally starting to hit her.

Am I crazy?

Do I even WANT to be queen of the RainWings? And be stuck here forever? Trying to organize these hopeless dragons?

She could just *imagine* what her friends were going to say about this.

She looked up and saw about twenty-five RainWings all crowded onto the waiting platform, staring at her. One of them was Coconut. Apparently this was the best he could muster when asked to gather the whole village.

But judging from their expressions, they'd heard Glory's conversation with Magnificent. And from what she knew about RainWings, this was the kind of news that would spread quickly — mainly because it meant they'd have some entertainment at sunrise tomorrow.

Kinkajou bounced out of the treehouse behind her and saw the dragons as well. "Coconut!" she cried. "Did you hear that?"

The other dragonet scuffed one talon across the wooden platform. "Sure," he said.

"We're going to have a proper queen for once," Kinkajou said proudly.

A few of the RainWings exchanged glances, turning an odd shade of light purplish-orange. Glory guessed it meant puzzled or confused; it wasn't a color she wore — or let herself wear — very often.

"A proper queen?" echoed another of the RainWings. "Is, uh . . . is that something we need?"

"What's wrong with the ones we've got?" asked another.

"Why don't you ask Gibbon that question?" Kinkajou shot back. "Or Orchid? Or Splendor, or Tualang or Loris?"

All of the dragons were frowning now; several of them glanced around at the trees as if they expected Orchid and Splendor to come sauntering out to be interviewed.

"Hmmm, that's right," Kinkajou said. "Haven't seen them in a while, have you? That's because they've been kidnapped, like I was. And they're still trapped there — except for Tapir and Bright and Orangutan, who died awful deaths, alone and far away from everything and everyone they loved. And the only dragon who's willing to do anything about it is Glory. That's why she should be our queen."

Glory did not enjoy the awkward pause that followed. A number of the RainWings wrinkled up their snouts as if they were trying to figure out who this "Glory" character was.

"Don't listen to her." Bromeliad shouldered her way through the other dragons and glared at Kinkajou. Her tongue flicked in and out of her mouth. "This dragonet is trouble. She's been hiding in the forest for three weeks to spite me, and now she's made up a ridiculous tale just for the attention."

Violent orange shot through Kinkajou's wings, and she bared her fangs at Bromeliad with a hiss.

"Put a sheep in it, Bromeliad," Glory said, pulling Kinkajou back behind her. "It's all true. I was there, too." She turned her attention to the other dragons on the platform — and the ones who were starting to gather in the trees as well. "Listen to me. Your friends are suffering. They're tortured and trapped in caves in a horrible place that smells of smoke and death. There's no fruit. There's no sun time."

Horrified murmurs swept through the branches overhead. "No *sun* time?" somebody squeaked.

Glory took a step along the bridge and several of the RainWings quailed back. "This could have happened — could *still* happen — to any of you. If you won't go rescue them, who will? They'll be lost there forever." Glory lashed her tail. "I know you'd rather sleep than deal with problems, but these dragons are from your tribe, and they need you."

She glanced back at the treehouse behind her and raised her voice. "That's why I'm going to take the throne tomorrow. It's not because I want the biggest pieces of fruit or the highest sun platform. I'm doing this for the missing RainWings — and for you, so that you don't have to spend the rest of your lives looking over your shoulders and thinking, *Our friends are still lost . . . and we could have saved them.*"

CHAPTER 26

Glory took a deep breath and studied her audience.

Most of the dragons looked confused, but a few had dark purple stripes rippling over their scales — guilt and shame, living right next to pride on the color spectrum.

Hmmm, Glory thought. *That's about all the noble speechifying I've got in me.* Somehow it had always seemed more believable and less awkward in the scrolls she read. The stirring speech was always where chapters ended — but right now a host of dragons were just staring at her, and she couldn't remember anything from the stories about what you did at the end of a noble speech or how to slink away gracefully afterward.

"So there," said Kinkajou, sticking out her tongue at Bromeliad.

Glory was pretty sure *that* wasn't it.

"What do we do now?" Kinkajou asked Glory brightly. The blue-gray was gone from her scales and all her energy had returned. "Never mind, I know exactly what we're doing first. Finding something decent to eat!"

Glory turned her back on her wide-eyed audience and focused on Kinkajou. "You go ahead. I have to tell my friends what just happened. And also find someone to teach me everything about RainWing skills in the next day."

"I can do that!" Kinkajou said. "After I eat. I'm going to eat every piece of fruit in the rainforest. Where should I meet you?"

"Try the healers' hut," Glory said with a sigh. "Bring Mangrove, too."

Kinkajou shot off into the trees. Glory swiveled her head around and checked that Silver was still asleep on her shoulder. Ignoring the crowd, she spread her wings and flew away. If she remembered Magnificent's directions correctly, the healers' treehouse was not far.

She spotted the red berries growing on the balcony and swooped down to a treehouse whose leafy roof was dotted with skylight holes. Inside, only two of the beds were taken: one by Webs, and the other by a sleeping RainWing with a bandage on his snout, as if he had bumped into a tree while flying around. Three RainWings in shades of white and soothing blue were gathered in a corner, eating bananas and talking in low voices.

Sure enough, Sunny and Starflight were crouched beside Webs, watching him anxiously. Well, Sunny was watching Webs. As usual, Starflight was watching Sunny.

Webs was sprawled across a nest of spider-shaped leaves in the sunlight. He was asleep, breathing peacefully for the first time since Blister had attacked him. Sunny was right; the cactus juice clearly *was* working. The scratch on his tail wasn't completely healed, but the edges looked much less raw and the black had faded instead of spreading further.

"I guess you saved him," Glory remarked, sliding up beside them.

"I hope so," Sunny said. "But he's still really sad. He keeps mumbling in his sleep about how it's his fault the SkyWings found and destroyed the Summer Palace."

"Well. It is," Glory said.

"Oh, very sympathetic," Starflight said. "Come on. Webs didn't know Crocodile was following him."

Crocodile — the last dragon Glory had used her venom on before the Night Kingdom. She saw a flash of the MudWing's terrified face and shoved the thought away. That was self-defense. It was always self-defense. The kind of self-defense her fellow RainWings really needed to learn.

Sunny brushed Glory's shoulder with her wing, and Glory flinched back. "You should put something on your scratches," Sunny said.

"This isn't a scratch," Glory informed her, pointing to the bleeding slash on her back leg, which had started to throb in a fiercely painful way. "It's a battle wound."

"Yes, you're very tough and scary," Sunny said. She beckoned to the white and blue RainWings while Glory wondered if that was sarcasm. Sarcasm from Sunny? It didn't seem likely. She twisted to watch as the RainWings dabbed some kind of paste on her injuries.

"Watch it," she hissed, but after a moment the stinging faded, and all she could feel was cool numbness. Glory studied the wounds and sniffed the paste, which smelled a bit like mint. "Hmmm," she said finally. "A dragonet named Kinkajou is on her way here. She needs some of that, too." She caught Sunny's significant look and gave the healers a nod. "Thanks."

"Where's your army?" Starflight asked Glory, only a little snidely.

"They're . . . a work in progress," said Glory. Sunny leaned over Webs, adjusting the dressing on his injury. "So, by the way," Glory went on, "I've decided to be queen of the RainWings."

Sunny tripped, and Webs let out an "oof" as she landed on him, but he didn't wake up. Starflight turned to stare at Glory incredulously.

"But why? You've never wanted to be a queen," he said.

"You don't know that," said Glory. She was aware of the healers hovering just within earshot, trying to look busy but obviously eavesdropping. "It just didn't come up because we were too busy hearing about how much Tsunami wanted to be queen. Anyway, I have to if I want to lead them into battle against the NightWings."

"Battle?" Starflight said anxiously.

"I think you'll be a great queen," said Sunny with a flutter of her golden wings.

"RRRBBL," agreed the sloth, waking up and leaning around Glory's neck.

"Maybe we don't have to fight the NightWings," Starflight said in a plaintive voice. "Let me talk to them. Maybe I can find out why they've been taking RainWings in the first place."

"They still need rescuing," Glory snapped.

"Maybe the NightWings will let them go," Starflight said. "Maybe if I explain to them —"

"That keeping dragons tied up in caves is wrong?" Glory said. "Sure, that's probably never occurred to them. Or that they should have asked politely before stealing RainWing venom?"

"And don't forget the MudWings," Sunny added. "Why did they kill those two soldiers?"

Glory *had* forgotten about the dead MudWings. If that had been the NightWings, too — then what on Pyrrhia were they up to?

"Listen," she said to Starflight, "I know you don't want to meet your tribe for the first time on the opposite side of a battlefield. But they can't be trusted. It's not even safe for you; we have no idea whether Deathbringer was supposed to kill you as well."

"They would never kill me!" Starflight protested. "I'm one of them!"

"Barely," said Glory. "Anyway, I'd rather find out the truth with a whole lot of venom as backup, wouldn't you?"

Starflight twisted his talons together. Glory glanced out the nearest window and saw a pair of dragons shift quickly to camouflage on the branch outside. She squinted and thought she could see shimmers of movement on several other branches as well. Apparently her tribe was finally interested in her.

"Wait," said Sunny, sitting up and flaring her wings. "If you want to be queen, don't you have to kill Magnificent?"

"They have this whole no-killing way of taking the throne," Glory said. "They're RainWings, of course they do."

"They *do*? That's *fantastic*," Sunny said with unexpected intensity. "That's how all the tribes should do it. Maybe after we stop the war we can teach everyone the RainWing way of changing queens."

Glory gave her a quizzical look. That was a lot of enthusiasm for a RainWing way of doing things. She was pretty sure most dragons wouldn't feel that way.

"Why don't we take our revolution one step at a time," she said, flicking her tail at Sunny. "The other tribes have been doing things their way for hundreds of years."

"So?" Sunny said. "Things can change."

"If queens didn't kill their challengers," Starflight interjected, "what would stop the challengers from trying again the next day, and the next? Or if the challenger won, the queen could just come try to take it back. Instead of ruling her kingdom, a queen would have to spend all her time simply trying to keep her throne."

"Then we make new rules," Sunny said stubbornly. "Like she can only be challenged at certain times of the year, or each challenger can try twice before giving up, or something like that. We're dragons, not caterpillars. We can do things differently if we choose to."

"Dragons are dragons, Sunny," Glory said. "Fighting is part of our nature."

"Not for the RainWings," Sunny said, "and they're dragons, too."

"But —" *But there's something wrong with them*, Glory thought. She didn't want to say that out loud with the healers listening — and however many dragons were just outside the window — but she knew Starflight must be thinking it, too.

"Maybe RainWings are more evolved than the rest of us," Sunny said. "Maybe all dragons should try to be more like them. They're happy, aren't they?"

True, Glory thought. *But maybe I could have been happy as Queen Scarlet's prisoner, as long as I got to lie in the sun and eat pineapple all day. And then where would my friends be?*

"I don't think it's enough to just be happy," Glory said slowly. "I think you have to care about something, too. Like other dragons who need you, for instance. And you still have to be ready to fight, just in case some creepy 'less evolved' dragons decide to invade your territory and kidnap a bunch of you."

"*I* don't believe anyone can be truly happy without scrolls," Starflight said wistfully. "I haven't seen a scroll in weeks and I'm perfectly miserable."

"Poor Starflight," Sunny said with genuine sympathy, brushing his wings with hers. "Well, when Glory is queen she can fix all that. Starflight can teach everyone to read, and Tsunami can teach them to defend themselves."

"And we'll make a list of all the eggs and all the dragons in the tribe so no one will ever get lost again, plus save the missing RainWings and choose a SandWing queen and stop the war," Glory said. "No problem. Give me a week."

Sunny beamed as if this sounded like a perfectly reasonable plan to her.

When I'm queen, Glory thought. *I like the sound of that.*

Through one of the windows, Glory saw Kinkajou and Mangrove approaching. A few more curious dragons were tailing them through the trees, and Glory spotted more eyes watching from the leaves.

Mangrove was an unexpected dappled mixture of bright yellow and lime green. *Excited and terrified*, she thought, *but more complicated*. With the return of Kinkajou, now he knew that Orchid was alive — but he also knew what an awful place she was in and how hard it would be to get her back. Glory hoped Clay and Tsunami were ready to stop him if he tried to dash through the tunnel and do any rescuing by himself.

"Well, before we change the fundamental essence of dragons and revamp the RainWing tribe, first I have to win," she said. "So right now I have to go train for this contest thing tomorrow. If anyone wants to come watch while the others guard the tunnel, it's in the Arboretum at sunrise."

"I'll be there," Sunny said. "It'll be nice to know a queen we actually like."

"*If* you win," Starflight added gloomily.

"I will win," Glory said, glancing again at Mangrove's scales. She thought of Orchid and the other rainforest dragons, chained and muzzled and fed rotting prey, imprisoned away from the sun and their own tribe. "I have to."

CHAPTER 27

"Papaya," Glory said. "Star fruit, tangelo, clawmentine, kumbu, dragonberry, mango, fire pear, and that one's a trick that only looks like a fruit, but is actually a poorly designed snail." She poked the purple snail shell with one claw and its nervous antennae vanished again.

The sun was high above them, and the morning rain had stopped, although the leaves kept showering the dragons every time someone bounced through and shook the trees. All the toucans and parrots and lorikeets that had disappeared during the rainfall were back, perched on the highest branches and hollering joyfully at the sun as if they'd never expected to see it again.

And now Glory could identify all the birds in sight, after studying with Mangrove and Kinkajou all morning. Birds, insects, flowers, fruit — anything Magnificent might test her on, she would memorize. Whenever she felt her brain getting tired, she'd think of the smoky air choking the caves of the RainWings, and that would snap her back into focus.

"Wow," said Kinkajou. She blinked large dark eyes at Glory. "How did you learn all of that so fast?"

"You've really never had any of these before?" Mangrove asked, surveying the forty or so fruits arranged around the platform.

"One or two, maybe," said Glory. "I should taste them all, too, right? Just in case she chooses a blind taste test?"

"I don't think anyone's ever thought of that before," said Mangrove. "But you never know." He peeled the banana with a few swipes of his claws and tossed it to her.

"Clay would dominate a blind taste test," Sunny offered from her perch in the trees above them. Sunlight danced on her golden scales. A small orange monkey with a black face was playing with her tail, but Sunny either didn't notice or didn't mind.

"I would," Clay said wistfully. "Are you going to eat that whole thing?"

Glory took another bite and then lobbed the rest of it at him. Clay fumbled to catch it and ended up with banana smeared all over his talons. He licked it off with a contented expression.

"You can practice your camouflage at the same time," Mangrove said. "See if you can match this mango." He rolled it to her with his nose.

Glory studied the outside of the mango and let her scales slowly turn a dull green with black speckles, shading to warm red around her wings and tail.

"So cool," said Sunny.

"Are you going to eat *that* whole thing?" Clay asked.

Glory laughed. "Clay, let me at least try it." She tried slicing it open as neatly as Mangrove had opened the banana and made a terrific mess. Cheerful orange-yellow pulp squirted all over her scales, and Silver scrambled down Glory's arm to lick it up.

Stop wasting time, she scolded herself as she helped the sloth balance. *The day's half gone and you still need to practice venom targeting and tree gliding and camouflage.*

"I'm not sure this is the right time to tell you this," Sunny said, "but you're being watched."

Glory and Mangrove looked up sharply. She'd asked him to choose a spot where they could practice without attracting too much attention. It was unsettling to keep finding RainWing eyes on her every time she turned around. The whole tribe must know she wasn't a normal RainWing, but they didn't need to see all of her mistakes the day before she tried to become their queen.

But Sunny was right. Even though they were in a secluded corner of the village, Glory could see dragon heads peering around tree trunks and poking out of hammocks, staring her way. As she whipped her head around to look at them, most of them quickly changed color and disappeared. But if she'd spotted those few, she could imagine how many more might be out there, camouflaged and curious about the challenger for the throne.

Well, take me or leave me, Glory thought. *I'm not a typical RainWing, but maybe that's what you need for a queen.*

"All right, what can we do next?" she asked, popping berries in her mouth. *Raspberries are sharper than cloudberries. Figs taste like desert winds. Guavas are the ones I could eat every day for the rest of time.* "Venom practice?"

"Next is sun time," Kinkajou said, and Mangrove nodded with a glance at the sky.

"Are you crazy?" Glory said. She seized a papaya and accidently crushed it between her front talons. "I have one day to prepare for this. I'm not going to spend it snoozing like a slug."

"Sun time isn't about *snoozing*," Mangrove said sternly. "It's about recharging."

"Hrrrble frrrble," agreed Glory's sloth, climbing up to tug on Glory's ears.

"I'd rather study," Glory said. She saw Kinkajou's crestfallen face and added, "You two can go ahead. I'll practice on my own."

"You will not," said Mangrove. "You need this energy to win. You will sleep if we all have to sit on you to make it happen."

"I volunteer," Clay said. "I'm a world champion at sitting on my friends."

"Clay!" Glory said over Sunny's giggling. "This isn't a joke! I don't have time to be lazy!"

"Glory has some issues with the word 'lazy,'" Sunny announced. "Our guardians used to call her that all the time, so she feels like she needs to prove something by showing she doesn't need to sleep."

Glory flared her ruff and glared at Sunny. "Excuse me. Are you *explaining* me?"

Sunny shifted her wings in a friendly shrug. "Well, that's what Starflight said," she offered. "But it makes sense to me."

"Sleeping when you need to is not lazy," said Mangrove. "That is a crazy dragon's way of thinking. Sleeping is as important as breathing. You wouldn't skip *that* because there's no time for it."

"Or food," Clay agreed. "You can't skip sleeping or food." The MudWing dragonet hopped off his branch and thudded down next to her, squashing a mango under his big claws. He crouched so his brown eyes were directly even with Glory's. Silver leaned over Glory's head and tried to poke at his horns.

"Glory," he said. "Stop panicking for one moment and think about how you feel right now. And I don't mean mad; I mean, physically."

"I'm not panicking," Glory said, ruffled. "I am pretty close to mad, though."

"And?" he prompted.

"And getting closer," she shot back. He gave her a patient look.

And . . . *exhausted*, Glory realized, as she took a deep breath. She hadn't really slept in a . . . well, in a really long time, not properly. She thought about the brush of sunlight on her scales.

"Fine," she snapped. "But wake me up in *one hour*, understand?"

"We'll see," Clay said.

"Rrrrrrrlleee!" cheered the sloth.

"Come on," Kinkajou said excitedly. "I know the best spot!"

As Glory, Kinkajou, and Mangrove took off, there was a flurry of wingbeats throughout the trees around them as camouflaged RainWings none-too-subtly followed them. Kinkajou led the way to a platform that was built right above the treetops, with no leaves between it and the blue arc of the sky. The surface dipped in the center and was lined with cloud-soft pink blossoms, growing along the vines that were woven around the wood.

"You take this spot," Kinkajou said, pointing to the hollow in the middle. Glory reluctantly curled up in the vines and immediately felt warmth soaking into her bones. Silver flopped happily into her spot on Glory's shoulder and snuggled in. Glory jumped as Kinkajou nestled on one side of her and Mangrove settled on the other. That answered that question — other RainWings didn't mind touching one another, so it was just her who had a problem with it.

"Um —" she started to say, but the two RainWings were already breathing deeply.

Glory closed her eyes, certain she'd never fall asleep like this.

A moment later she opened them and found herself looking into the amber eyes of Queen Scarlet.

——— CHAPTER 28 ———

Glory leaped back with a hiss and opened her mouth.

"Don't you dare," snarled the queen. "Haven't you done enough already?"

Glory paused, studying the SkyWing's face.

It was perfect — as perfect as it had ever been, a shimmering orange like the orchids growing from the moss behind her, with the small rubies above her eyes glittering in the bright sunlight.

And then Scarlet's whole body . . . *flickered* somehow, and under the perfect scales Glory saw something dark and melted, a horrible smeared mess where a face used to be. Behind Scarlet she caught a glimpse of a dim room with glass jars hanging from the ceiling, some of them glowing strangely.

"Oh. You're not really here," Glory said as the rainforest reappeared and Scarlet's scales smoothed back to perfect. The queen was perched on the edge of Glory's sleeping platform, but now that Glory looked closely, she could see that the SkyWing's claws didn't sink into the leaves below her.

Glory sat down and curled her tail around her talons. Kinkajou and Mangrove were fast asleep on either side of her, the sloth was snoring on her shoulder, and the sun had climbed higher in the sky.

"Am I even awake?" Glory asked.

"No," said Scarlet. "I've been trying to catch you asleep for days." She held up a small star-shaped sapphire that glowed an eerie blue light through her claws. "Once I realized what this was."

"A dreamvisitor," Glory said, recognizing the shape from her scrolls. "I read about those. An animus dragon made three of them hundreds of years ago, right? I thought the last one in existence was lost with the SandWing treasure, when the scavenger killed Queen Oasis and stole it all."

"Apparently not," Scarlet said, opening her claws to glance down at it.

"So you're really alive," Glory said.

"You don't sound as disappointed as I thought you would be," Scarlet said.

Glory flicked her tail. "It's not that I want you dead. I just want you not trying to kill us."

"I never tried to kill *you*," Scarlet pointed out. "I quite liked you. We could have had a thrilling time together." She stood up and paced toward Glory until their snouts were almost nose-to-nose. "Which reminds me. I wanted to try something."

Abruptly she lashed out with her free talon, slashing at Glory's face. Her claws sliced right through Glory's scales like raindrops splashing icy water over her. It was cold, but it didn't hurt. Scarlet's claws weren't really there. Glory fixed that thought in her head as Scarlet lunged again. She closed her eyes and sat perfectly still. There was nothing the SkyWing queen could do to her right now. She was no more dangerous than any dream.

After a few moments, Glory opened her eyes again, and Scarlet stepped back, hissing. Smoke rose up from her nose, winding around her horns, and the dark misshapen snout underneath flickered through again for a moment, along with the room beyond.

"Where are you?" Glory asked.

"If I tell you, will you find me and free me?" Scarlet asked.

"Not likely," Glory said. "Wait, let me think. Absolutely, *definitely* not."

"But you *owe* me," Scarlet said, stamping one foot.

Glory tilted her head sideways. "How, exactly, do you figure that?"

"For what you did to me," Scarlet seethed. "I was beautiful before. I had everything."

"Including a pretty rainbow dragon on a tree," Glory said. "I remember."

"If you *don't* free me," Scarlet said, "I will find a way out of here myself, and then when I find you, I will kill you."

"You know, something tells me that's on your agenda either way," Glory said.

Scarlet hissed deep in her throat and then shot a blast of flame at Glory's face. *Calm and blue*, Glory thought. *Stay calm and blue.*

"Is someone keeping you prisoner?" Glory asked. A thought occurred to her. "Is it the NightWings?"

"If you're not going to help me," Scarlet growled, "I'll find someone else who will."

And suddenly she was gone, leaving only a curl of smoke in the air.

So there's my answer. Scarlet is alive. Glory noticed that the leaves below her were shaking. *Oh, wait. That's me.*

Kinkajou stirred as if she felt Glory shaking, too. She nestled closer and Glory felt sun-drenched warmth along her scales.

Slowly she closed her eyes, breathing deeply, and drifted out of the dream.

When she woke up, she knew right away it had been longer than an hour. Silver was crouched in front of her, stroking Glory's nose with a worried expression. The other two were awake and stretching contentedly.

"Don't you feel better?" Kinkajou asked.

"Yes," Glory admitted. *And no.*

"Then let's do tree gliding next!" Kinkajou said cheerfully.

"Fine by me," said Mangrove, and Glory nodded. She was too shaken to argue.

She wondered what Scarlet would think of Glory becoming queen of the RainWings. She wondered if being a queen would make her any safer.

Sunny and Clay waved from their branch down below. *Should I tell them? I should tell them. I will tell them, but not yet.* Glory wanted to talk to Starflight first, to see what he could remember about dreamvisitors and if he could guess anything about the room she'd seen behind Scarlet. His giant brain was what she needed for a puzzle like this.

As Glory lifted into the sky, setting off a commotion of hidden wings, she wondered where the SkyWing queen was . . . and when she would see her again.

~ CHAPTER 29 ~

The Arboretum, it turned out, was the heart of the RainWing village. Vines and branches were woven tightly together to form a wide field high above the ground, open to the sky and surrounded by treehouses, walkways, and hammocks. Several of the treehouses around the edge appeared to be set up for trading fruits and flower garlands. Brilliant blue and coppery orange birds darted through the leaves, chattering and calling to one another like an audience gathering for a performance.

There seemed to be room for the entire village to gather around the edges of the circle — and it looked like the entire village had shown up. The rumble of dragon voices mixed with the chirruping of sloths and sent shivers through the wooden walkway where Glory stood, studying the green stadium in front of her.

Glory was reminded, uncomfortably, of the SkyWing arena where her friends had battled for Queen Scarlet's amusement. From the way Tsunami's tail was twitching, Glory guessed she felt the same way.

"This is unfair," Tsunami grumbled. "If you win —"

"You'll have to call me 'Your Majesty,'" Glory said, grinning. "I know. Won't that be hilarious?"

"Arrrgh, and your face will look like that *all the time*," Tsunami said. "It's going to be so hard not to bite you."

"But if you do, my guards will throw you in my dungeons," Glory said with an imperious wave of her talons.

"RainWings don't have dungeons," Kinkajou pointed out.

"There's a surprise. Well, I'll make one just for Tsunami," Glory said.

"Maybe I should have let Starflight come to this instead," Tsunami said. "Postpone my agony a little bit."

Starflight and Clay were taking a shift watching the NightWing tunnel. They'd seen nothing come out of it yet — not so much as a puff of smoke. Glory found that both alarming and reassuring. Maybe the NightWings were afraid to fight RainWings. That would make attacking them a bit easier.

She hadn't had a chance to talk to Starflight yet; he'd stayed out by the tunnel all night. *I'll talk to him right after the contest*, she thought. *Telling him about Queen Scarlet ought to distract him from fretting about fighting NightWings.*

And I cannot think about Queen Scarlet right now.

"*I* could have watched the tunnel," Sunny said. "I don't understand why no one will let me take a turn on guard."

"Well, for one thing, I need you here to cheer me on," Glory said. "Who could do that better than you?"

"I think I'm being patronized," Sunny said. She poked at the wooden platform below them with the harmless point of her tail. "But I'll cheer for you anyway. You're definitely going to win. I'm not worried."

Glory was a little worried. For one thing, her opponent had apparently multiplied overnight.

Queen Magnificent was waiting in the center of the canopy. Her scales were resplendently purple with scalloped gold edging on each individual scale, which was a color trick Glory had never tried. She had taken off most of her flower necklaces, replacing them with one small wreath of lilies on her ruff, which had the effect of looking like a lacy white crown.

Arrayed behind her were four more RainWings — all quite large, quite beautiful, and quite outraged, judging from their expressions and coloring.

"Who are they?" Glory asked Kinkajou.

"The other queens," Kinkajou whispered. "I mean — you know, the ones who take turns being queen. I guess they don't particularly want you to take their job either."

"Are any of them better than Magnificent?" Glory asked. Maybe there was another option. It didn't have to be her, as long as the RainWings had a queen who would take care of them.

But Kinkajou was shaking her head. "They're all pretty much the same," she said. She pointed to one of the queens, who looked like she'd eaten a few too many avocados and papayas during her reign. "That one's Dazzling. She'll grant anyone anything they ask if they bring her enough tribute.

She has the throne before Magnificent; after Magnificent, it passes to Grandeur."

Grandeur was a stately older dragon with half-asleep eyes and a sour expression. Her ruff was indignantly pale orange at the moment, but the rest of her scales were pale lavender and seemed to glitter with tiny dewdrops.

"During her reign," Kinkajou said, "she'll only see petitioners once a week, for an hour. First come, first served, and if you don't get in during that hour, you have to wait until the next week. The lines practically stretch around the jungle. And then she says no to pretty much everything. She's really, really old. She's been one of the queens for as long as anyone can remember."

Kinkajou pointed to the next dragon, who had two sloths flopped on her back and one more perched in the curve of her tail. This queen had scales the same silvery color as the sloths, with a soft shimmer to them that looked like wind brushing through fur.

"That's Exquisite," said Kinkajou. "Obsessed with sloths. She has about twenty more at home. Talks about them constantly, feeds them the best fruits, grooms them with her own claws, and whenever she's queen, she has everyone build tiny hammocks for the sloths to sleep in and weave them tiny flower necklaces. No dragon is as important to her as those sloths."

"Dazzling, Grandeur, Exquisite," Glory muttered, adding those to the list of things she'd memorized in the last day.

"And the last one? Let me guess — Splendiferous? Astonishing? Too Beautiful for Dragon Eyes to Bear?"

"That's Fruit Bat," said Kinkajou.

"All right," said Glory. "Didn't see that coming. Who picks the names for newly hatched dragonets, if no one has any parents here?"

"There's a list we cycle through," Kinkajou said. "Usually the ones with shiny names are more likely to want to be queen. Fruit Bat is an exception. She's working on this experiment to see if she can take the scents out of flowers and make herself smell like them all the time."

Glory wrinkled her nose. "Weird. But interesting, at least. What in the world does that have to do with being queen?"

Kinkajou shrugged. "It's not going very well. She's been working on it for something like thirty years. She started taking a turn as queen so that she could have access to the royal gardens, and by the end of her month, the gardens are always a wreck. My friend Tamarin is one of the flower caretakers and it drives her crazy."

"Sounds like Magnificent might be the best of all of them," Glory said, twisting one claw through a hole in the wood.

"Magnificent's main problem is that she's forgetful," Kinkajou pointed out. "She can never remember what she's agreed to do or what's going on in the tribe or who asked her for what, and she doesn't really care. We're all pretty used to it by now." She turned her dark shining eyes to Glory. "But if we had *you* as our queen instead — then everything would be different!"

I hope so, Glory thought. *I hope different in a good way. But what if I'm no better than they are?*

She glanced across at Fruit Bat, who had her nose buried in a massive orchid necklace hung around her neck.

All right, I'm pretty sure I'll be better than some of them.

The old dragon who had been in the queen's treehouse slithered out to stand next to Magnificent. He squinted around and beckoned to Glory.

"Wish me luck," Glory muttered, handing her sloth to Sunny. Silver burbled something anxious-sounding and clambered immediately up onto Sunny's head for the best view.

Magnificent flattened her ruff and looked down her nose as Glory landed in front of her. The other four queens lashed their tails.

"So what's the plan?" Glory said, shaking out her wings. "I have to defeat all five of you?" She'd chosen a summery gold color for her scales that matched the dragonflies darting through the treetops. She was determined to stay that color throughout the contest, no matter what Magnificent threw at her. Glory's first goal: *Don't let anyone see that you're upset, or angry, or worst of all, scared.*

"No," Handsome interjected before Magnificent could answer. "That is not the tradition. The challenger competes only against the current queen."

"But my fellow royalty didn't want to be left out," said Magnificent. "So I worked them into the competition." She smiled in a way that made Glory want to strangle her with a hammock. "Which means you're going to need a team as well."

"I don't have a team," Glory started, and then stopped herself. *Well . . . I kind of do.* She turned and glanced back at Sunny and Tsunami, who were watching with round eyes from the platform.

I don't need to drag the others into this. Surely I can defeat the queens myself. What can five RainWings do that I can't? And wouldn't everyone be impressed if I beat all of them, all by myself, with no help whatsoever?

She flexed her wings, which were still sore from the ropes that had bound them tightly just one day earlier.

This line of thinking felt familiar. It was how she had convinced herself to go out alone as bait.

And I made it back, didn't I? I could have handled that situation fine on my own.

But she knew it wasn't true. Without Kinkajou, Clay, and Deathbringer, she'd still be stuck in a NightWing prison . . . or perhaps even dead, if the NightWings had had time to figure out who she was.

So don't be an idiot. Winning the throne with help won't make you any less of a queen.

"You get to choose your dragons," said Magnificent. "Any four you wish."

That makes it easy for me, Glory thought. She had exactly four friends in the world, after all. She could ask Mangrove to go guard the tunnel and send back Starflight and Clay.

She opened her mouth to call him and hesitated.

Maybe a little too easy. She studied Dazzling, Grandeur, Exquisite, and Fruit Bat. They looked ready, alert, and eager to compete. Not a look she'd seen on many RainWings before.

They're convinced they're going to win.

"Go ahead," said the queen. "Call them out here. Anyone you like."

Glory tilted her head at Magnificent. *This is a trick. She wants* me *to pick my friends.*

And then the contest will involve camouflage or venom or something that only RainWings can do.

Not only that, but my future subjects will think I trust outsiders more than I trust them.

Which, frankly, I do, because most RainWings are hopelessly incompetent.

But right now I need their help.

"I choose . . . Kinkajou," Glory said. She heard a loud squeak of surprise behind her, and a murmur ran through the watching dragons.

"A three-year-old dragonet?" said Magnificent archly. "This should be funny."

"And I choose Mangrove," Glory went on, ignoring her. Mangrove stepped out of the crowd opposite her and gave her a small bow. Orchid was still out there. He'd do anything to save her; Glory could count on that.

Now it got a little harder.

Glory closed her eyes and sighed. "I choose Jambu."

"YES!" her brother shouted, leaping into the air. "That's *me*!" He bounced across the vines toward her, grinning all over his goofy pink face.

Who else? Glory ran through the dragons she'd met in the rainforest. *Liana. Bromeliad. Coconut.* Not a promising set. She didn't know much about any of them, but none of them had impressed her as team players.

Kinkajou came up beside her, fidgeting excitedly and spilling deep purple-blue bubbles through her green scales. Glory remembered someone the little dragonet had mentioned when she was describing the queens. It was a risk, choosing a dragon she'd never met, but she couldn't be worse than any other RainWing.

"And I choose Tamarin," she said. All Glory knew about her was that she was friends with Kinkajou, she cared about her work with the flowers, and she wasn't the biggest fan of Fruit Bat. Which sounded like three good features to Glory.

The crowd murmured again, sounding like waves rushing in from the ocean, and Queen Magnificent barked a startled laugh.

"Tamarin!" Kinkajou cried. "But — are you sure?"

"Too late," said Magnificent. "That's who she chose. Someone give Tamarin a shove in the right direction."

A small dragon popped out of the crowd and stumbled forward a few steps, then stopped. She stood very still, with waves of pale green rippling across her scales. Her eyes were an odd light shade of blue and stared blankly past Glory at the trees.

"What is it?" Glory asked, glancing at Kinkajou. "Why shouldn't I pick her?"

"You can," said Kinkajou. "It's just that . . . Tamarin is blind."

CHAPTER 30

Kinkajou hurried forward and whispered in her friend's ear, then led Tamarin over to Glory. The blind RainWing moved confidently across the unsteady vine surface as if she knew where every leaf and every gap would be. She kept her wings up and out like an insect's antennae.

"This is Glory," Kinkajou said. "Our next queen." She held out Tamarin's front talons to feel Glory's face and wings.

"Why would you pick *me*?" Tamarin blurted. She wore only one garland of flowers around her shoulders. The shades of red and pink and purple didn't match at all, but they smelled amazing. It made Glory think of coconuts and honey without making her hungry.

"I told her about you," said Kinkajou. Her voice faltered a little, giving away that she hadn't quite mentioned everything.

"I had no idea there were any blind dragons, except in old scroll stories," Glory said. She fluttered a wing in front of Tamarin's eyes, but the RainWing didn't blink. "How do you fly between the trees? How do you land? Don't you accidentally walk off platforms and fall out of hammocks all the time?"

"Not anymore," Tamarin answered. The green was starting to fade from her scales as she relaxed. "The first year, yes. All the time."

She lifted her wings higher to reveal an old scar twisting across her underbelly. Glory spotted a few others on Tamarin's wings and neck. These weren't like the battle scars the war had given to so many dragons. These told the story of a tiny dragonet crashing into trees, plummeting off walkways, and impaling herself on stray branches as she tried to learn to fly in total darkness.

"But everyone took care of me," Tamarin said. "There was always a dragon watching me, helping me and teaching me." Glory glanced at the watching tribe. She would have guessed that no one would take responsibility for a little blind dragonet. Instead, everyone had, which gave her hope. "And now I have the village memorized, so I know all the distances and obstacles." Tamarin's ruff folded down and then opened again, as if she was sensing the shifting wind currents.

Queen Magnificent unfurled her purple wings and stood up on her back talons. "Let's begin!" she called. "Unless you've changed your mind?"

"We're ready," Glory said.

"No inspiring speech?" Jambu said, sounding disappointed.

Kinkajou and Mangrove tilted their snouts toward her expectantly. Tamarin's ears twitched.

"I gave one yesterday," Glory protested.

"So now do one just for us," Kinkajou said. Her scales kept shifting to match the dark green leaves below them, as if she was trying to hide whatever she was really feeling. Mangrove, on the other hand, was a resigned sky-blue.

"Um. All right. Do your best," Glory said. "And thanks and stuff."

Kinkajou stifled a laugh.

"Wow," said Mangrove. "I feel so moved."

Queen Magnificent beckoned imperiously and two portly RainWings flew up beside her, carrying a low table carved from a single log of mahogany. Arranged neatly on top were five nuts, each polished brown and about the size of a dragon eye.

"This contest has five parts, each related to the special talents of our tribe," said Queen Magnificent. "You assign one team member per part, and whichever team wins three out of the five contests, wins the crown." She pointed a sharp claw at the first nut. "Venom targeting." She pointed to the second. "A flower hunt." The third: "Treetop race." The fourth: "Fruit gathering."

The last nut she picked up and turned over in her front talons. "And naturally there must be a camouflage competition. We are RainWings, after all." She set it down again with a toothy smile. "Let's start with fruit gathering, so the competitors can work on it while we finish the other contests."

"Certainly," said Handsome. "Quite logical. It's a very straightforward contest. Each dragon has an hour to collect as many different types of fruit as he or she can find. The one who comes back with the most variety wins."

"Dazzling will compete for our side," Magnificent said, sweeping one wing toward the portly queen. "And for yours?"

Glory studied her own dragons, beating back the anxiety that threatened to climb up her scales. The contests all featured RainWing skills, so on the one talon, she had outwitted Magnificent by choosing RainWings instead of her friends. But on the other talon, she barely knew her teammates. She had no idea what they were good at.

"All right," Glory said to them, keeping her voice low. "Who should do what? Jambu, you teach tree gliding — are you fast? Can you do the treetop race?"

"Of course!" her brother said, glowing with bright pink enthusiasm.

"Give me the flower one," said Tamarin. "If it's about flowers, I can do it."

Glory hesitated. "She said flower *hunt*, though."

"I know flowers," Tamarin insisted.

Give her a chance, said a voice in Glory's head. *It's what a good queen would do.* "All right." Glory glanced at the row of nuts on the table, thinking through the other contests. Her day of training hadn't exactly left her feeling confident about most of these.

"I guess I should do the camouflage contest," she said. "I have no idea where to find fruits in the rainforest, and I'm not exactly a venom expert." She thought of the mess she'd made of everything they'd put in front of her yesterday. "Mangrove, I know you're a fruit gatherer. But Kinkajou . . . sorry, but I got the impression from Bromeliad that venom practice wasn't going well with you."

"That's because Bromeliad is a slow old baboon," Kinkajou said hotly. "I'm super-great at venom shooting! I swear! Plus Mangrove can carry more fruit than I can."

Glory rubbed her forehead. She only had to win three of the five contests, after all. "All right," she said, turning back to the waiting queens. "Mangrove will do the fruit gathering for us."

Mangrove spread his wings and bowed to Dazzling. At a signal from Handsome, they both flew off into the trees, heading in opposite directions and sending up tornadoes of tiny crimson butterflies as they went.

"Now," said Handsome. He glanced up at the sky and turned in a slow circle so that all the watching dragons could hear him. "Next! The treetop race, a test of speed and agility!"

Magnificent spun one of the nuts on the table. "Exquisite, that means you."

"And me!" Jambu said delightedly.

Handsome grinned. "I'll never forget the last treetop race I saw. Weren't you in that?" he asked Grandeur. "Who was your challenger?"

"No one worth mentioning," Grandeur said frostily. "Naturally I won."

"But you're too old for racing now," Magnificent said

dismissively. Grandeur gave her a wholehearted glare that Magnificent completely missed.

The sloth on Exquisite's tail clambered up to her neck as the silver queen stepped forward. She dipped her wings so the other two sloths could slide off onto the vines.

Strong shoulders, Glory noticed. *Big wings. I bet she's fast.* Jambu looked like a bright pink monkey next to the sleek silver dragoness.

Handsome pointed up at the treetops surrounding the Arboretum. A small platform, about three dragons wide, was set in the high branches. Peach-colored flowers studded the dark wood planks, tied in bunches with strands of silver sloth fur.

"That is the start and end of the race," he said. "You will fly three times around the Arboretum, staying outside the ring of trees. If you fly inside the ring, you will be disqualified. If you touch your opponent, you will be disqualified. As long as you stay outside the ring, you may take any path around, but you must touch down on the platform as you complete each circuit. Understood?"

"Got it," Jambu said, flexing his wings.

Exquisite didn't answer. She had her front talons curled around her two sloths and was cooing at them as they clambered over her claws.

"Your Majesty?" said Handsome, and then caught himself. "That is — I mean, Exquisite? Do you understand the rules?"

"Of course," she said, disentangling her pets. She set the third one down next to them and stroked their heads. "I'll be back in a moment, darlings. I just have to win this race for Auntie Maggie."

"Stop calling me that," Magnificent said crossly. "I'm nobody's *auntie*. Certainly not a bunch of sloths. And this isn't just for me, you big furhead. It's your throne, too."

"There, there," Exquisite said to the sloths, who had curled up into a sleepy pile of fur. "Auntie Maggie isn't mad at you. She's just in a bad temper because she has to actually do something today." In a loud whisper that absolutely everyone could hear, she added, "Besides, she's jealous that you all are so much prettier than *her* sloth."

Magnificent snarled in a very unqueenly way and shot a dark look at the three sloths, as if she might throw them off the Arboretum while Exquisite was racing.

"Good luck," Glory said to Jambu. "Please win."

"That's the plan," he said cheerfully. He followed Handsome and Exquisite up to the platform, then leaned over the edge and waved at the crowd of dragons around the edges of the Arboretum. Sunny and several other dragons waved back. It occurred to Glory to wonder who everyone was rooting for. Did anyone *want* her to win? Did they know what that would mean, or about all the things she wanted to change about their world?

Her gaze swept across the RainWings — the tribe that might soon be *hers*. She tried to read their scales, but as far as she could tell, today most of them had chosen their colors for their looks, as though they were showing off at a party. The only emotions she spotted were bright yellow bursts of excitement in their scales here and there. And she had a feeling they'd be like that about anything new that happened.

Handsome stepped onto a branch shaped like a coiling dragon tail and spread his wings.

"Start when you hear the toucan call," he said to Jambu and Exquisite. "Don't forget the rules. Ready? And — *CAW*!"

Glory was so startled by the sound that came out of his throat that she missed the beginning of the race. Handsome had perfectly imitated the noises she'd been hearing from the big-beaked birds. If that was another RainWing talent, it was one she'd never even thought of trying before.

Exquisite shot ahead of Jambu, swinging smoothly from branch to vine to branch. Her tail was longer than Jambu's, giving her a wider swing and farther reach. But his narrower wings helped him dive between some tangles of branches that she had to maneuver around, and by the time they got back to the platform for the first time, his snout was almost brushing her tail.

"Go Jambu!" Sunny yelled from her spot on the walkway. "You're going to win! You're the fastest dragon in the forest! Woo hoo!" Kinkajou nudged Tamarin, and they both started hooting and shouting as well.

Personally Glory thought that much noise would have been an annoying distraction, but it seemed to add wind to Jambu's wings. He banked around a trunk, dodged a loop of hibiscus-covered vines, and shot past Exquisite on the outside.

Well, if it works, Glory thought. "Yay!" she hollered. "Jambu is the best! Uh — you're an awesome glider! Good, uh . . . flying! Yaayyy!"

She caught Tsunami giving her an amused look and stuck out her tongue at the SeaWing.

Jambu brushed the platform a second time with his claws and took off again. A few moments later, Exquisite thudded down in the same spot and gave chase. Her wings pumped and her brow was furrowed angrily.

Glory's heart pounded as she watched them swerve through the trees. One more circuit — if Jambu could stay ahead just a bit longer, he'd win. *Hang in there.* She dug her claws into the vines below her, wishing she could be up there, giving him her speed somehow.

Jambu ricocheted off a tree and dipped through a hole in the branches. He veered around the last curve and suddenly flung his wings up to stop his momentum. He thrashed in place for a moment, and Glory saw a vine wound around his neck. He twisted backward, gasping for air, and flailed to the side.

With a horrible lurch in her stomach, Glory watched Jambu tip over, crossing into the ring of trees. At the same time, Exquisite whisked past him and landed neatly on the platform. She lifted her wings and turned in a triumphant circle as deep blue-purple waves whooshed through her scales.

But Glory had seen something else, too.

That vine hadn't appeared out of nowhere. Something was scurrying away from the spot where Jambu had nearly strangled himself.

Several somethings, in fact, with shaggy silver fur.

CHAPTER 31

"How dare you accuse us of cheating?" Magnificent demanded.

"The better question is, how dare you *cheat*?" Glory demanded right back.

"My teammate's sloths were right here in front of us the whole time," said the queen.

"These three were," said Glory, pointing to the furballs that were clambering up to Exquisite's shoulders. "We know Exquisite has several others who could have been planted out there in the trees, just waiting to get in the way if it looked like she wasn't going to win."

"Hmmm," said Grandeur, narrowing her eyes. She'd been sitting in the same position, looking bored and regal, throughout the race.

"Ridiculous," scoffed Exquisite.

"Her sloths aren't nearly smart enough for that," said Magnificent.

"They most certainly are!" Exquisite snapped, flaring her ruff. She glanced at Glory and carefully settled it again. "But they would never do such a thing."

"They'd do anything you told them to," Kinkajou cried as a surge of orange outrage rippled down her tail. She snapped her teeth at the nearest sloth and it chirped fiercely at her.

"Enough," said Handsome. "Jambu, what did you see?"

Glory barely recognized her brother with his scales this dismal blue-gray color. He lifted his shoulders despondently. "I don't know. It all happened so fast. One moment I was flying, and the next I was choking. I saw sloths in the trees, but —"

"But you can't be sure they were Exquisite's, or that they had anything to do with the vine in your way," Magnificent finished.

Jambu gave Glory a mournful look.

"It's all right, Jambu," she said. "I know you would have won in a fair race." She made sure her voice was loud enough to carry to the crowd of watching RainWings. Magnificent hissed softly and snatched up the treetop-race nut from the low table. Lashing her tail, she dropped it in a hollowed-out coconut on her side of the Arboretum.

"Let's move on," Handsome said, clearing his throat. "Perhaps the flower hunt next?"

Tamarin stepped forward. Her wings trembled, and her scales were rippling with pale green again. Glory wondered whether she could tell that her emotions were on display.

Another question occurred to her. "Can you use camouflage?" she asked Tamarin. "I mean, since you can't see what you're trying to match?"

"Yes — it works anyway," Tamarin said. "Don't ask me exactly how." She took a few deep breaths, closing her eyes. Dark green, dappled with sunlight and shadows, spread across her whole body until she matched the vines below her.

"I can't choose what color I am," Tamarin explained. "So if you asked me to make my scales red, for instance, I couldn't do that. But if I relax, they automatically switch to whatever's around me."

"Fascinating," Glory said. More important, Tamarin didn't look quite so terrified anymore.

Fruit Bat shuffled forward, swinging her bulky orchid necklace around so most of it hung down her back. An odd smell wafted forward with her, of decaying leaves underneath something sickly sweet. It wasn't as bad as the smell in the NightWing kingdom, but it wasn't pleasant either.

"So how does this contest work?" Glory asked. "And how can we be sure there's no cheating this time?"

She was gratified to see that Magnificent couldn't keep her scales from turning red. Making other dragons angry was one skill Glory already knew she was good at. She glanced over her shoulder at Tsunami, who had her fierce face on. She looked ready to charge into the Arboretum and take on all five queens herself.

"Ahem," Handsome said hastily, clearing his throat a few times. "Yes. The contest. For this member of the team, the queen has requested a flower hunt. Therefore, early this morning I hid a particular flower somewhere in this

Arboretum: the rare, majestic cinnamon orchid — not the more common yellow variant, but the elusive red variety."

"Ooooo," went all the watching RainWings.

"Whoever finds it first, naturally, will win," said Handsome.

One flower? Glory thought. *In this whole giant place? It could be anywhere. And she can't see. How can Tamarin even begin to look for it? Even if she could feel the difference between flowers, how will she know whether it's red or yellow?*

For the first time Glory thought maybe she was going to lose this contest after all. Maybe she wouldn't be queen. She narrowed her eyes at Magnificent and lashed her tail. *Fine. I'll think of another way to rescue the RainWings from the Night Kingdom if I have to.*

Handsome spread his wings. "You may begin!"

Fruit Bat leaped into action. Faster than Glory would have expected from looking at her, Fruit Bat started dashing around the circle, poking her nose into every crevice and pocket. She scrabbled up drifted piles of leaves and lifted bundles of vines. She nudged aside dragon tails that were draping over the edge of the platforms. She pounced on every glimmer of orangey-red, startling quite a number of innocent birds and beetles.

Meanwhile, Tamarin stood very still, right where she was. Her nostrils twitched. Her wings went up and down as she breathed deeply.

After a few moments of this, Glory said, "Um . . ."

"Shhh," Kinkajou said. "She's busy."

"Could she be busy in a more . . . busy-*looking* way?" Glory asked.

Tamarin inhaled again and lifted her snout. Small feathers of flame flickered along her ruff, shaped like the flower she was looking for.

"She can smell it?" Glory whispered to Kinkajou. "Is that what she's trying to do?"

"She *will* do it," Kinkajou promised fiercely. "Her nose is amazing."

"I believe you," Glory said, "but there have to be a million flowers within smelling distance right now, not to mention all these dragons and monkeys and other things that smell much stronger than any one flower. There's no way she'll find it."

"You don't know Tamarin's nose," Kinkajou said. "Now shhh."

Glory sat back and curled her tail around her talons. There wasn't anything she could do now anyway. She badly wanted to start tearing up the Arboretum the way Fruit Bat was doing, but she wasn't allowed to help.

Is this what being queen would be like? Issuing orders and then sitting around waiting for dragons to carry them out?

She thought of the other queens she'd met. Queen Scarlet and Queen Coral preferred to have their minions do their dirty work, but Burn and Blister both seemed rather claws-on. Perhaps because they weren't really queens yet . . . or because they'd learned, after years of war, that the only dragon you could really trust was yourself.

Glory glanced at Sunny and Tsunami again. She did trust the other dragonets, a little, in different ways. She trusted Sunny to at least *try* to do whatever was brave and right, even if she was too small to do it effectively. Starflight had neither courage nor fighting skills, but if Glory ever needed to figure out something, she'd trust Starflight's brain in a second. That's why she wanted to talk to him about Scarlet before anyone else.

She could trust Tsunami to fight tooth and claw — really in almost any situation, including several where it would be quite inappropriate — and, of course, there was Clay, who would do anything to save his friends.

She wished they were her team, instead of these RainWings she barely knew. As much as she liked Kinkajou, it was agonizing to feel this powerless over her own destiny. *I'm the one who wants to be queen. I should be the only one who has to fight for it.*

Magnificent's eyes darted back and forth between Tamarin and Fruit Bat. When Tamarin finally took a step forward, the queen let out a hiss, and Fruit Bat whirled around to see what her competitor was doing.

"Tamarin," Glory said quietly. "If you know where it is, move fast, because Fruit Bat is watching and I think she'll try to beat you to it."

The blind RainWing took another deep breath, crouched, and launched herself into the air. She nearly overshot the platform she was aiming for, but her tail brushed it and she swung back to land on it in a graceful motion. It was the start-and-finish racing platform used by Jambu and Exquisite — the one littered with bouquets of peach-colored, star-shaped blossoms.

Fruit Bat bolted after her. Tamarin quickly bowed her head and sniffed the bouquets. Just as Fruit Bat landed heavily beside her, Tamarin snatched up one of the bundles and pulled off the sloth fur ribbon that bound it together.

The pale pink flowers fell away, revealing a flower hidden inside. It was shaped like a cluster of dragon claws, each glowing like a tongue of fire.

Magnificent and Fruit Bat let out matching cries of rage.

"That sounds promising," Tamarin said with a smile.

"You did it!" Kinkajou shouted. "You found it!" She poked Glory with her tail, beaming. "Told you she could do it."

If RainWings had fire, Glory was pretty sure Magnificent would have had smoke coming out of her ears and nose.

"Nicely done," Glory said as Tamarin landed beside them again, clutching the flower in her claws. "I'm really impressed."

Glory sauntered over to the table and took the flower-hunt nut. With an arch look at Magnificent, she dropped it in her own coconut bowl. One to one. Three more contests to go.

And then she'd be queen.

"What should we do next?" Glory asked Magnificent. She was feeling a lot more confident now. "How about the camouflage one?"

Magnificent bared her teeth. "Sounds perfect."

"Have you ever been in a camouflage contest before?" Handsome asked Glory.

"Not precisely," Glory said. "But I have had to use my camouflage to avoid dragons who want to kill me, so if you're asking whether I can handle the pressure, I'm going to go with yes."

"Actually, I was wondering if you knew the rules," Handsome said, hiding a smile. "But they're not complicated. One of you hides first, somewhere within eyesight of this spot. Then the other will search for you, and then you'll switch roles. I will judge who finds the other fastest. If it is too close to tell, we will try again."

"Got it," Glory said.

"Do you remember —" Handsome began, turning to Grandeur. Glory wondered which of them was older; they both seemed as ancient as the Claws of the Clouds Mountains.

"Of course I remember," Grandeur snapped. She drew herself up and hissed at the gathered crowd until they were all quiet, listening. "I remember everything. I remember when we actually *needed* our camouflage, to protect ourselves from invading dragons. It wasn't a game back then. It was what we had to do to survive."

"Enough boring stories," Magnificent commanded, earning herself another glare. "Grandeur, hush up until it's your contest. I'll hide first."

Handsome tied a long, fat leaf around Glory's eyes. As darkness settled around her, she thought that this must be what it was like for Tamarin all the time. She could remember only one story about a blind dragon in the scrolls, and it was from long ago, before the Scorching.

A moment later, the blindfold was lifted away. The curious faces of hundreds of RainWings filled her vision.

"You may begin," said the old dragon with a nod.

Glory blinked and turned in a circle, searching for clues.

Magnificent had vanished very thoroughly. Her small crown of white flowers lay abandoned on the vines. There was no sign of her gold-tipped purple scales, and none of the hammocks around the arena had a sudden unusual bulge in them.

Where could she be?

Where would I hide if I were a particularly forgetful, spectacularly lazy RainWing?

She didn't think Magnificent was the type to climb trees or hang by her tail if there was somewhere she could lie down comfortably instead. And most of the platforms and walkways were too crowded with dragons for her to squeeze in there easily.

Which gave Glory an idea. She turned to study the watching RainWings. Some of them might have seen where Magnificent hid. And all of them had been playing this kind of hide-and-seek their whole lives. They must be scanning the area, too, trying to find her first.

She noticed that Exquisite and Fruit Bat were staring straight up at a nearby tree swathed in fuzzy moss. They were staring at it a little *too* hard, as if they were hoping Glory would notice that they were. Fruit Bat nudged Grandeur, and the stately old dragon gave her a look of disgust.

Then Glory caught a couple of RainWings glancing in the direction of a fruit stand on the far side of the arena. They narrowed their eyes at it, then leaned in to whisper to each other.

Worth a look, Glory thought.

She flew across the arena to the fruit stand. It was a wooden platform with low walls that were built to also be tables, most of them covered with mangos, pineapples, the red sticky spheres, and the star-shaped green fruits. Crowded bunches of bananas hung from the branches overhead.

She swept her tail across the floor of the platform, then studied the tables, but she couldn't see any sign of a dragon hiding anywhere. She looked up and poked the dangling banana bunches. Finally she jumped over one of the walls and flew up above the bananas. There was something a little odd about the way some of them were hanging — as if something heavy were lying on top of them.

It was eerie. All she could see were shadows and light, green leaves and bright yellow bananas. But when she reached out, her claws brushed against dragon scales, and the indignant hiss that came from them told her she'd found what she was looking for.

"Your Majesty," Glory said with a polite bow. "Very impressive camouflage," she added honestly.

"Let's see what you can do," Magnificent grumbled, her scales shifting back to purple.

They returned to the center of the arena as the RainWings all applauded. It took Glory a moment to realize they were applauding for her. She hoped that meant she had found the queen fairly quickly. Now she just had to hide even better than Magnificent had.

Handsome stepped up to tie the blindfold around Magnificent's eyes.

Glory let her scales shift into the greens of the vines below her. She didn't want anyone to see where she went, especially the other queens.

Her first idea had been to go straight up and blend into the sky overhead, but to stay aloft she would have had to keep her wings moving, and she was worried that Magnificent might feel the breeze.

So instead she headed for the tree Exquisite and Fruit Bat had been staring at. She swarmed up the side of it, feeling the shaggy moss squish below her talons. Her scales had changed instantly to the dark brown and yellowish-green of the moss-covered tree. Once she thought she was high enough, she twisted around so she could see everything below her. Then she flattened herself against the trunk and concentrated, adding the shape of a tiny blue tree frog on her back for extra camouflage, which was a trick Mangrove had taught her.

Down below, she heard Handsome tell Magnificent that she could start looking. The queen's eyes popped open and she turned immediately to the other queens. Exquisite and Fruit Bat lifted their wings in befuddlement. Grandeur yawned coldly.

Magnificent spun in a circle, peering at everything. She let out a small hiss of frustration, then gathered her wings.

Suddenly she bared her fangs and charged toward the edge of the circle where Sunny was standing.

She wouldn't dare hurt my friends! But Glory felt herself flinch as Sunny jumped back. At the same moment, Silver leaped off Sunny's back with a yelp of alarm and bolted toward the tree where Glory was hiding.

Magnificent saw where the sloth was going, shot past her, and slammed into the tree trunk, nearly jarring Glory loose. The queen scrambled up the tree so fast she stepped on Glory's wings before realizing she'd found her. With a triumphant yell, she backed up and poked Glory in the snout.

"Found you!" Magnificent crowed.

Silver caught up and flung herself into Glory's arms, shivering. Glory swung onto a branch so she could hold the sloth to her chest and stroke its fur.

"Did you think that was funny?" Glory asked Magnificent. "Scaring a harmless sloth like that?" From the murmurs and shocked expressions on the faces below them, she guessed this wasn't a very popular way to treat one of the RainWing pets.

"She'll survive," Magnificent said. "And here's the important part. *I won.*"

Glory looked down at Handsome with a sinking feeling. He spread his talons in a "What can I do?" gesture.

"The queen is correct," he said. "Magnificent wins this round."

CHAPTER 32

"Oh, look," Magnificent said cheerfully, pointing to the glint of sunlight on wings flapping through the trees. "The fruit gatherers are coming back." She flew back to the center of the Arboretum and snatched one of the nuts off the mahogany table.

Two to one.

"Wasn't that cheating?" Sunny called as Glory glided back down to her team. Kinkajou had furious red stripes marching along her scales, and Jambu was back to blue-gray again. Glory wondered if her brother had more than two moods.

"That was *totally* cheating!" Tsunami shouted. "You can't let her get away with that! Boo! Hiss!"

"Silence them," Magnificent said to Handsome with a frown. He spread his wings and cleared his throat.

"Nothing in the rules forbids what the queen did," he announced. "She is the winner. Officially. If not in spirit."

Magnificent glared at him while Mangrove and Dazzling swooped down from the trees.

Glory was too dazed to chime in. The others might call it cheating, but as far as she was concerned, Magnificent had only found a trick to reveal Glory's hiding place, the same way Glory had used the RainWing audience for clues.

So Glory had really lost. She'd *lost*.

She couldn't pay attention to the sorting and counting going on as Mangrove and Dazzling spilled fruits of all shapes and sizes across the greenery. Handsome picked each one up, muttered over it for a moment, and set it in a pile.

If I were competing alone, it would be over by now, Glory realized. She would have lost the throne in a direct contest with Magnificent. If she won it now, it would be only because the other RainWings made it happen. Tamarin, who didn't know her at all, Mangrove, and Kinkajou. If they could do it.

Kinkajou's eyes were fixed on Mangrove's fruit pile. She fidgeted with her tail and counted along under her breath.

Handsome examined the last fruit, a dark blue prickled ball that oozed bright green juice when he poked it. He nodded and placed it on Mangrove's pile. Kinkajou shot Glory a delighted look.

"Seventeen to sixteen," said Handsome. "The winner is Mangrove."

"What?" shrilled Magnificent. She whipped around to glare at Dazzling, who had yellow speckles around her mouth and a trail of green splatters down her chest. "You *ate* some of them! I know there were nineteen there when I —" She stopped abruptly.

"Sorry," Dazzling muttered. "I thought sixteen would be enough."

"Well, you thought wrong." Magnificent growled.

"Excuse me," said Handsome. "Did you say, 'There were nineteen there'?"

There was an awkward pause as the two queens glared at each other. Magnificent flicked her tail and looked down her nose at Handsome.

"Are you accusing me of something?" she asked coldly.

"*I* am!" Kinkajou blurted. "You collected fruits and stashed them somewhere ahead of time!"

"Ludicrous," said the queen. The red flickers along her wings vanished abruptly. "And impossible to prove."

It occurred to Glory that Magnificent might have chosen to be purple today so that no one would spot any shimmers of guilt in her scales. *Clever*, she thought, glancing down at her own. The yellow had faded a little, and small gray clouds were gathering around her shoulder blades and wing tips.

"Doesn't matter anyway," Dazzling pointed out to Kinkajou. "You won."

Kinkajou jabbed Glory with her tail, and Glory snapped back into focus. There was still a chance. Now they were tied, and there was one contest left.

"It matters if you're planning to cheat again," she said sharply.

"That won't be necessary." Wind rustled through the leaves as Grandeur slid majestically between Glory and Magnificent. Her bones creaked like ancient forests and the silver cast of her scales made her look as if she were reflecting moonlight instead of sunlight. She wasn't like the other queens. In fact, she wasn't like any other dragon in the village. Glory thought Grandeur might be the only RainWing who actually looked, moved, and sounded like a real queen.

She arched her neck and peered down at Kinkajou. "I can crush this little creature easily on my own."

"We'll see," Kinkajou said bravely, but anxious streaks of green flickered in her ruff. *This is asking too much of her,* Glory worried. Kinkajou was barely half Grandeur's size, with hardly any training. The NightWings had been so underwhelmed by her venom that they hadn't even bothered binding her mouth. How could she possibly win?

Handsome beckoned the two dragons into the center of the Arboretum. "Standard venom practice rules apply," he said. "Take the utmost caution to hit no living creature. We'll be testing distance and targeting. Who'd like to go first?"

"I," said Grandeur. She eyed Handsome and his two helpers as they rolled a long, polished plank of wood across the vines. It was as wide as five talon prints and four times as long, with small measurement marks all the way along it.

One end stopped at Grandeur's front talons. She stretched her neck and jaw while the RainWings scurried out of the way, leaving the plank laid out in front of her like a welcoming carpet.

"Whenever you're —" Handsome started.

Grandeur's mouth snapped open and a spray of black venom shot out. The droplets spattered on the wood near the far end of the plank, sizzling and burning small holes where they fell. The watching dragons all ooooohed admiringly.

"I'm guessing that's pretty impressive," Glory said to Mangrove.

His sigh answered her question.

Grandeur stepped aside with a polite gesture at Kinkajou. The little dragonet stepped up nervously, opened her mouth as wide as she could, and shot a tiny jet of venom at the plank.

It landed barely a quarter of the way between her claws and Grandeur's drops.

Glory's heart sank. Mangrove dropped his head into his front talons with a groan. Kinkajou turned to Glory with a heartbroken expression.

"There's still the targeting part," Jambu said hopefully. He patted the little dragonet on the back. The helpers were already dragging out a kind of easel painted with three yellow and white circles.

"What if I fail?" Kinkajou said to Glory. "All those dragons — it'll be my fault if we never see them again. It'll be my fault that you're not queen."

"Stop that," Glory said, placing one talon over Kinkajou's. "I lost my own contest, remember? It's my fault more than anyone's. But I *will* be queen one day. And in the meanwhile —" She caught Mangrove's eye to make sure he was listening. "We'll get Orchid and the other RainWings back no matter what it takes. Maybe I won't have an army, but we'll make a rescue mission out of my friends and anyone else who's willing to go.

"So don't think about that right now. All I can ask is that you try your best — and I know I don't even have to ask, because you're the kind of dragon who always does."

"That's true," Kinkajou said. "I *am* that kind of dragon." She squared her shoulders. "I will. That's what I'm going to do."

Glory glanced up and realized that Grandeur had been listening, too. The old queen turned around and casually shot a spray of her venom at the painted board. It landed precisely in the center of the first circle.

Magnificent gave Glory a triumphant smile. *It would have been really nice to wipe that smile off her face. And one day I will. I* will *be queen of this tribe. That's what I'm meant for. I'm sure of it.*

Kinkajou stepped up beside Grandeur, opened her mouth, and sprayed her venom at the circles. The drops splashed right on top of Grandeur's, and a hissing sound came from the board as the wood melted a little more.

The older RainWing made a sound of approval and patted Kinkajou's head. Then she tilted her head just a little and shot a black jet directly into the center of the second circle.

Kinkajou took a deep breath and did the same. More sizzling and smoking came from the wood.

Don't get excited, Glory told herself, although she couldn't help feeling impressed with Kinkajou. She knew for a fact that she wouldn't have been able to aim that precisely. But if the two dragons tied on this part of the challenge, Grandeur would still win because of the distance part. *Practice a gracious-in-defeat face. And then get ready to study like life depends on it so I can try this again. I wonder how long I have to wait between challenges.*

Grandeur opened her mouth.

And then a sloth tumbled out of the trees, landing in front of the board.

Kinkajou leaped to shove it out of the way.

And time seemed to slow down, so Glory could watch each drop of venom sail in an unhurried arc to land, *splash, splash, splash,* right on Kinkajou's wing.

——— CHAPTER 33 ———

All around the Arboretum, RainWings started screaming.

Kinkajou collapsed in a ball of scales that went instantly white with pain, except for the three spots where black venom was eating through her wing.

Glory rushed to her side and found Grandeur opposite her, grabbing Kinkajou's talons. Grandeur's face was horrified.

"Help her!" Glory yelled. She remembered what Jambu had told her about how a relative's venom would counteract your own. "Who's related to you? Get them over here!"

"I don't know," Grandeur said hopelessly. "I haven't had any eggs in decades. I haven't tried matching venom with anyone in so long. I don't think there's anyone related to me anymore."

"That's insane!" Glory shouted. "Why can't you dragons keep track of these things? You must have had dragonets at some point, and they must have had dragonets, too . . ."

"Maybe, but no one has —"

Kinkajou shrieked, a high wailing sound of agony.

"Start trying," Glory cried. "Try everyone. Try me." She grabbed the easel and spat a messy puddle of venom on the corner. The wood hissed and melted as if it were burning from the inside.

Grandeur didn't hesitate. She sprayed her venom right on top of Glory's.

And the melting stopped.

Glory didn't have time for the shocked expression on Grandeur's face. She couldn't risk trying to aim neatly for the same three spots where Grandeur's venom had hit Kinkajou; she might end up causing far more damage. Quickly she ripped three leaves off the vine below her, dipped them in the puddle of her own venom, and stuck them to Kinkajou's wounds.

The sizzling sound faded and the black acid stopped spreading.

"You're all right. You're going to be all right," Glory said to Kinkajou, lifting the dragonet's head in her talons. She realized the little dragon had fainted.

Also, Grandeur was staring at her as if sloths were parading out of Glory's ears.

"What?" Glory said. "So I'm your granddaughter or great-grandniece or something. It's not like anyone around here really cares, right?"

"I do," said Grandeur, "because it means that you are descended from the original line of RainWing queens, and so I am not the last one worthy of the throne after all."

Glory blinked at her. "I didn't think anyone cared about royal blood here."

"Nobody but me," said Grandeur. "We used to keep track

of the royal eggs, but my daughters were useless, so we merged our eggs with the tribe's, hoping to find successors who were queens in spirit, if not blood. There were a few who might have been great if they'd ever tried for the throne, but the truth is, I've never found a dragonet who both *wanted* to be queen and deserved to be. Until now."

She stood up and faced Magnificent like an enormous storm cloud. "I forfeit. Kinkajou wins."

"What?" Magnificent shrieked.

"Did you hear that?" Glory said to Kinkajou. "You won."

The dragonet's eyes fluttered open and she managed a smile. "That is . . . *super-cool*," she whispered. Tamarin came up behind them and slid her wing under Kinkajou's head so Glory could stand up next to Grandeur. She felt dizzy with disbelief.

"It's my throne anyway," Grandeur said to Magnificent. "I have merely tolerated all of you on it because I thought experience might transform you into worthy queens." She shot a disgusted look at Dazzling, Exquisite, and Fruit Bat. "That theory turned out to be quite wrong."

"You don't know anything about this dragon," Magnificent complained, pointing at Glory.

"I know she'll be a better queen than you," said Grandeur. She turned to the assembled tribe with a sweeping gesture. "Behold! Your new queen! Queen Glory of the RainWings!"

And they *cheered*.

Glory stepped back, dazzled, as what looked like the whole tribe rose into the air, beating their wings and singing out joyfully. The rainbow of different colors was swept away on a tide of sunflower-gold excitement, and Glory thought to herself, *Wow.*

I'm a queen. Queen Glory of the RainWings. That'll be my name in the history scrolls — not Glory the mistake, or Glory the lazy RainWing, or Glory who could never be as good as some nameless SkyWing who died six years ago.

I'm responsible for all these dragons now. We can rescue the missing RainWings and make sure no more dragonets ever get lost again. Starflight can help me teach them all how to read and write. I'll protect them. I'll lead them. I'll make them — us — a tribe we can be proud of.

Glory, the queen who chose her own destiny, saved her subjects, and turned her tribe into the greatest dragons in all of Pyrrhia.

"Speech!" Jambu demanded, barreling into her. His scales were a pink so vibrant it almost hurt her eyes to look at him.

"Don't you start. Luckily no one would hear me over all this noise," Glory said with a wave at her jubilant subjects. She gave her brother an affectionate shove and he wound his tail around hers for a moment, and she didn't even mind.

As he bounded off to assault someone else's eyes, she felt movement at her wing and turned, thinking it was Kinkajou, but it was Sunny. Sunbeams danced on her gold scales as the little SandWing beamed at her.

"You did it," she said.

"Not by myself," said Glory. "I needed these dragons to make it happen." She spread her wings to encompass Jambu and Mangrove, but they were bouncing around in excitement.

Tamarin was hugging Kinkajou, and even the wounded dragonet was pale pink with joy.

"This is so unfair," Tsunami said, landing beside them. She sighed dramatically. "This was supposed to be *my* story. Stupid SeaWings, already having a decent queen."

"Maybe you'll still be the SeaWing queen one day," Glory said. "And then I can give you tips on how to be majestic and brilliant."

They grinned at each other.

"This just proves what I've always said," Tsunami observed. "Who needs a prophecy to tell you how to make an awesome destiny?"

"True," Glory said. "Take that, prophecy. You're not about me? Well, I'm not all about you either."

Sunny fluttered her wings like a settling butterfly. "We still need you, though," she said. "You're still one of us, and no one will ever convince me otherwise."

Glory brushed Sunny's wing with hers, feeling a warmth that wasn't coming from the SandWing's scales. "The first thing we have to do is rescue the RainWings from the Night Kingdom," she said. "Which means turning these dragons into an army as fast as possible — Tsunami can help with that."

"Yes, I can," Tsunami said, flexing her claws.

"Well, actually," Sunny said. "I was thinking maybe there's another —"

The sound of branches thrashing overhead made Glory spin around. Clay came barreling through the trees, trailing broken twigs and wrestling loops of vines out of his way. He stared around wildly at the rejoicing RainWings, spotted Glory, and crashed down in front of her.

"Clay!" Sunny cried. "What is it? What's wrong?"

Horrible images popped into Glory's head — of her friends hurt, of a NightWing army marching through the tunnel to invade the rainforest. . . .

"It's Starflight," Clay said. "He's disappeared." He shot an anxious look at Glory, and she remembered the argument she'd had with Starflight the last time she'd seen him. Surely he hadn't —

"Glory, I'm sorry," said Clay. "But I think he's gone to warn the NightWings."

EPILOGUE

"I hate this place," Flame said, glowering at the dark rock dust caught between his claws. "Hate, hate, hate it."

"I hate it more," Squid moaned. He coughed gloomily. "My scales feel so dry. My talons hurt. And I'm hungry."

"I hate that big old stupid horrible NightWing," Viper hissed.

"I can't believe my dad let him take me." Squid edged to the mouth of the cave and stared at the smoky sky as if hoping Nautilus would appear suddenly, winging to his rescue.

"Oh, stop," Fatespeaker said, flicking her tail. "It's not that bad."

Actually, it really was that bad, but she certainly wasn't going to admit it to these four. She had never ever imagined that the Night Kingdom — *her* kingdom — would be so dark and smelly and that all the dragons here would be *so incredibly cranky*. It was as if being the most awesome dragons in the world didn't even make them happy at all.

But hey, she was home, and Morrowseer said she was part of a prophecy, which was even more awesome than being a NightWing. So what was there to complain about, really?

"I want to die," Ochre groaned. The MudWing dragonet had been lying on the floor of the cave for practically the entire day since they'd been dumped here by Morrowseer.

"I want you to die, too," Flame volunteered.

"You smell ghastly," Viper agreed.

"I don't think I should have eaten that dead thing," Ochre mumbled. He paused, then added, "Or all of your dead things."

"Well, *I* wasn't going to eat it," Squid said snootily. "We are on an island. I think *someone* should be able to bring me a fresh fish, considering who my father is and the fact that I'm a dragonet of destiny. I mean, really."

Fatespeaker shifted on her talons uncomfortably. She hadn't really liked the look of what the grumpy NightWings had brought them to eat either. Why was everything so decayed and horrible-smelling?

Have a vision, she told herself. *That'll make you feel better.*

She closed her eyes and scrunched up her forehead and concentrated as hard as she could.

"I foresee —" she said in a portentous tone.

"No!" shouted Viper.

"Spare us," Squid cried.

"Aaaaaarrrrrrgh," Ochre moaned.

"Now I want you *both* to die," said Flame.

"Oh, shush," Fatespeaker said with her eyes still closed. "I'm using my *POWERS*. Behold! I foresee a . . . walrus! A walrus in our future! An entire walrus for us to eat!"

"Why are you torturing me?" Ochre wailed.

"We hardly ever had walrus even when we lived next to the sea," Squid pointed out.

"Despite the fact that you predicted we would just about every week," Viper added sourly.

"My visions are not always *precise*," Fatespeaker said breezily. "It does not say *when* this walrus will arrive, only that it will, and then we shall feast. And everything will be wonderful again."

"When has it ever been wonderful before?" Flame snarled.

"Do us a favor and stop sharing your stupid powers with us," Viper snapped.

Grumpy ungrateful lizards. Fatespeaker sat down in the mouth of the cave and turned up her snout, ignoring everyone. If they couldn't appreciate the gifts she bestowed upon them, WELL THEN FINE, she would just keep her visions to herself. Until she had another great one, anyway.

The Night Kingdom volcano stretched below her, dark and craggy and swarming with black dragons. There weren't nearly as many NightWings as she'd expected. It felt more like the Talons of Peace camp than a whole kingdom. But the dragonets hadn't exactly been given a tour. They hadn't even been taken to the big fortress, which Fatespeaker assumed was where the queen lived. Nor had they been introduced to the NightWing queen. Or anyone, actually. Morrowseer had stuffed them in this high cave and stomped away again.

Fatespeaker squinted down at the black-sand beach in the distance. A cave was set into the cliff there, and earlier she'd seen several dragons swoop into it. Now they were coming out again, and they had a NightWing dragonet in their talons.

He looked about the same age as Fatespeaker, and he was unconscious. His wings drooped and his claws dragged in the sand.

Her scales began to tingle in that way that she was sure meant a sign from the universe.

There was something important about that dragonet.

"I'm having *ANOTHER VISION*," she announced.

The bones left over from Ochre's dinner splatted on the ledge beside her. She was lucky that Squid didn't have very good aim.

"I'm just letting you know that I'm *NOT TELLING YOU ABOUT IT*," she said. "Even though I'm sure it's *VERY SIGNIFICANT*."

The others ignored her, which they did way too often.

Well, it didn't matter.

She was home with her own kind now. She had a destiny to follow. And she was sure the unconscious dragonet, who was now being carried into the fortress, would be part of it.

s not
om this
nent.

The adventure continues in

WINGS OF FIRE

BOOK FOUR:
THE DARK SECRET

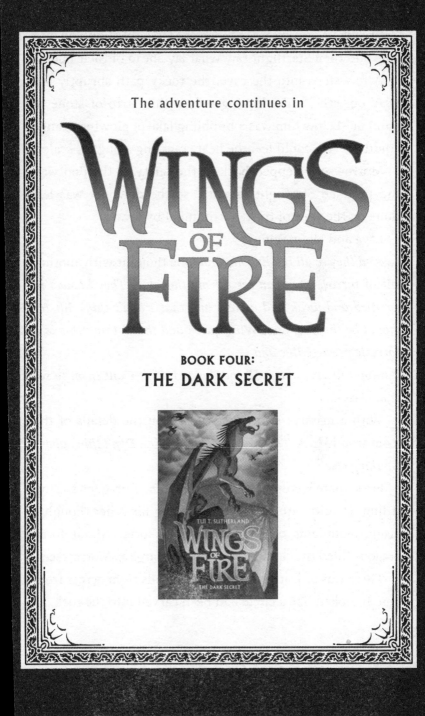

"Watch it," Morrowseer growled as Starflight stumbled into him, and then Starflight saw what lay ahead of their talons.

A few steps into the cave, the rocky path abruptly fell away on either side, leaving only a thin strip of stone to stand on. Below him was a bubbling lake of glowing orange liquid fire. He could feel the heat crackling along his scales.

Morrowseer stepped back to the safety of the doorway and prodded Starflight forward, so the dragonet was left alone on the spur of rock, surrounded by lava.

Lava and NightWings.

And they're all reading my mind, he thought with another jolt of terror. *They can see all my thoughts. They know I'm terrified and weak and useless and that I don't think Blister should be the next SandWing queen and that I think this is a horrible place to live and —*

Stop thinking about all the things I don't want them to see in my head!

With a massive effort, he focused on the details of the room around him. *Think about what you see. Don't think about anything else.*

First, there weren't actually hundreds of dragons staring at him. He did a quick estimate, hiding his other thoughts inside mountains of numbers. Maybe forty. About forty dragons filled the cave, most of them as large as Morrowseer.

There was a clear spot on the cave walls right across from him. It looked like a circle had been carved into the rock, as wide across as Starflight's wingspan, and then jabbed full of small holes, none of them bigger than a dragon's eye.

The other dragons kept glancing at this circle as if waiting for it to do something.

On a ledge beside the circle perched a dragon with a scar rippling down her chest. Her wings drooped in an odd way, as if they were weighted down with rocks, and she wore a cluster of diamonds around her neck. Another chain of smaller teardrop diamonds was wound around the horns on her head.

But that can't be the queen, Starflight thought. She didn't have authority in her bones. She didn't radiate power all the way through her wing tips like the other queens he'd met.

It took him only a moment of puzzling this out before he realized that there was someone *behind* the screen, staring through those holes at him. A chill sliced through his scales. Nobody could see her, but her presence filled the cave like heavy smoke.

The queen of the NightWings.

The scrolls always referred to her as mysterious and unknown, but Starflight hadn't imagined that she would keep herself hidden even from her own tribe.

Why?

Because it's extra-terrifying, he answered himself.

"*This* is him?" barked one of the dragons.

"Yes," Morrowseer growled. "We snatched him from the rain-forest this morning."

Wings rustled uneasily all around the cave.

"Has he told us anything?" asked another dragon. "What do they know? What are they planning?"

"How soon will they attack?" growled another.

"And how did that RainWing escape?" another one shouted as several dragons began to speak at once. "We've heard reports that there was a MudWing with her. A MudWing! How did he get here? Why didn't we kill them before they got away?"

They're talking about Glory and Clay, Starflight thought with a shudder.

"That was the RainWing I warned you about," Morrowseer snarled. "The one the Talons of Peace got to replace the SkyWing they lost." He spat into the lava. "This is exactly why I told them to kill her."

"A RainWing, of all things," said the dragon with the diamonds. "What an unfortunate mistake."

"Who knows what she saw?" cried another dragon. "If she warns the RainWings what we're planning —"

"She can't possibly know that," Morrowseer said.

"She knows about the tunnel between our kingdoms," challenged a dragon from the far wall. "And that little one escaped with her. She'll have told her everything she saw in the fortress. What if they figure it out?"

A clamor of voices filled the cave.

Figure what out? Starflight looked down at his talons and wished they weren't shaking so much. He was half-afraid that he'd tremble himself off balance and into the lava, but that wasn't even in the top twenty things he was worrying about right now. *What are they planning?*

He glanced up at the screen where the queen was hidden. She hadn't spoken at all yet. But he could feel her watching; from the way his skin prickled, he thought she hadn't taken her eyes off him since he'd entered the cave.

All at once, the dragon with the diamonds leaned toward the screen, tilting her head.

A hush fell instantly around the room. Nothing moved except the *bloop-bloop* of bubbles in the lava. Every NightWing present seemed to be holding his or her breath.

Starflight didn't hear anything — no queen's voice issuing regally from her hiding spot — but the diamond dragon nodded and straightened up again.

"Queen Battlewinner says to shut up and ask *him*." To his horror, she pointed at Starflight. "That's why he's here. Make *him* tell us what they know and what they're going to do next."

The listening dragons all swiveled their heads toward him.

Falling into the lava suddenly sounded like a pretty great option.

"Um," Starflight stammered several times. "I — I — um —"

"Speak or I kill you right now," Morrowseer growled behind him.

Starflight pressed his front talons together and took a deep breath. "Her name is Glory," he blurted.

The dragons all hissed. This was not something they cared about.

"She — she said you have RainWing prisoners." *Please tell me she's wrong. Tell me it's all a mistake.*

But no one corrected him.

Should he tell them Glory's plan? That she was trying to become queen of the RainWings so she could build an army to come rescue their lost dragons? That they shouldn't underestimate her?

Would he be betraying his friends if he said all that to the NightWings?

Or would he be betraying his tribe if he didn't?

The close, smoky air of the cave pressed down around Starflight.

What if I can fix everything?

This is the chance you wanted. You asked Glory to let you talk to the NightWings. You wanted to give them a chance to explain themselves — you wanted to find a peaceful solution, so you wouldn't have to pick sides in a war.

But now that he was here, facing their dark eyes, he couldn't find any of the brilliant words he'd meant to use.

Suddenly, one of the nearest dragons snapped, "Just tell us if they're planning an attack!"

"Yes," Starflight blurted. "I mean — I think so."

This met with such an uproar that Starflight had to sit down and cover his head with his wings. Surely he'd said the worst possible thing. He'd made everything worse for

Glory and the RainWings, and he couldn't even bring himself to speak up and try that famous "diplomacy" he'd always thought was such a good idea.

They wouldn't listen to me anyway, he told himself, but he didn't know if that was true. He wasn't brave enough to find out.